LOVE AT
ON DECK
Café

LEAH DOBRINSKA

Copyright © 2021 by Leah Dobrinska

All rights reserved.

No portion of this book may be reproduced in any form without written permission from the publisher or author, except in the case of brief quotations embodied in critical articles or reviews.

In accordance with the U.S. Copyright Act of 1976, the scanning, uploading, and electronic sharing of any part of this book without the permission of the author is unlawful piracy and theft of the author's intellectual property. Thank you for your support of the author's rights.

This book is entirely a work of fiction. Names, characters and incidents portrayed in it are either the work of the author's imagination or are used fictitiously. Any resemblance to actual persons, living or dead, businesses, companies, events or localities is entirely coincidental.

Editing: Jenn Lockwood

Cover Design: Ana Grigoriu-Voicu with Books-design

Author Photo: Beth Dunphy

Library of Congress Control Number: 2021912563

ISBN: 978-1-7374483-0-3 (paperback) | 978-1-7374483-1-0 (ebook)

In memory of Michael and in thanksgiving for my village.

Chapter 1

JULIA

JULIA DERKS STOOD BEHIND the counter at On Deck Café, but she may as well have been on top of the world. In fact, if she was offered an all-expenses paid trip to anywhere else, she would turn it down. No doubt about it. This place was her pride and joy.

Julia swept a content glance around the café as she poured a cup of coffee for Charlie Pozinski, one of her regulars. Her patrons sat on rich, caramel-colored leather benches flanking tables she had personally salvaged and restored to make one-of-a-kind booths. Mismatched chairs she'd hunted down at estate sales and local antique shops were positioned around the remaining tables in the center of the dining room, infusing the space with an unpretentious, homey vibe. Wide, crank-open windows let in streaks of the summer morning sun, and light dappled the worn wooden floor. A hum of chatter filled the air as stories were shared and laughs exchanged. Julia topped off Charlie's mug with cream and a scoop of sugar—his fixed request.

"Here you go, Charlie." Julia raised her voice to grab the attention of her hard-of-hearing customer, who also happened to be a dear family friend. She offered him a deep smile as he reached for his beverage.

"Thank you kindly." Charlie tipped his hat and walked over to a table of his buddies, the village's crew of older gentlemen, referred to with affection as the *grandpa patrol*. They were all retired and did odd jobs around Mapleton, a small, close-knit community nestled in northeast Wisconsin. The grandpas immediately started heckling Charlie over something or other, and their good-natured laughter echoed through the café, rising up and warming the room like steam from a hot drink.

Yep, there was nowhere else Julia would rather be.

A grin tugged at her lips as the brass bell over the door jingled, and a handsome man she didn't recognize strolled into the café. He looked left and right before his gaze collided with hers. Julia's pulse popped.

Snubbing the flicker of heat working its way up her back, she tossed him a practiced smile before diverting her attention to the counter. She stacked mugs and wiped down the granite work surface so she'd be ready to prepare his order while, out of the corner of her eye, she watched the stranger approach.

The man appeared to be around her age. He wore a crisp, dove-gray button-up shirt that stretched tautly across his broad shoulders. His sandy-blond hair, styled in a way that made it look like it wasn't styled, brushed his collar. A navy-blue tie finished off his business-professional ensemble, the whole thing a contrast in formality to her simple jeans and white t-shirt.

"I'm going to grab another gallon of milk from the kitchen." Amanda Wallace, Julia's best friend and coworker, scooted behind her and disappeared down the hallway as the handsome man arrived at the counter.

"Happy Friday." Julia took up Amanda's position at the register. "What can I get started for you?"

"A large coffee, black. To go, please."

"You got it." Julia entered his order and took the cash payment he fished out of his wallet. Their fingers brushed, and she ignored the shock of electricity at the contact—because, seriously? She wasn't about to let herself become some romance novel cliché in the mere presence of an attractive stranger.

She bent, clearing her throat and tugging a travel cup out from under the counter. "So, what brings you to Mapleton?"

When she rose and met the man's grassy-green eyes, his brow was arched in question.

"How do you know I'm not from Mapleton?"

Julia placed his cup on the counter and swished her hand back and forth, motioning to the crowded café. "I know everyone around here. We have our regulars and the folks who come in occasionally, but you?" She tipped her head, letting her gaze rove over his distinguished-looking face. "I've never seen you before."

The stranger's eyes twinkled, and the sides of his mouth quirked, accentuating the square angles of his jaw and exposing pinprick dimples in either cheek. "Very astute of you."

Whoever this guy was, he was too smooth for his own good—the type of man who knew how good-looking he was and had no shame in flaunting it.

Julia kept her spine straight and gave an easy shrug. "That's me. Astute." She winked, but not—she told herself—in a flirty way. She reached for her pot of coffee. "So again I'll ask, what brings you to Mapleton?"

"I'm here to develop the old paper mill site."

Julia froze mid-pour. With calculated deliberateness, she raised her head to face the man. The collective gasp reverberating through the café informed Julia she'd heard him correctly, but she needed to be sure.

"What did you say?" She gripped the handle on the coffee carafe until her knuckles turned white and waited for him to confirm or deny his business with the mill.

Confusion scampered across the man's face before he masked it with a neutral expression, squared his shoulders, and pulled himself up to his full height.

Julia had a feeling he did so as a show of power—to force her to look up to him. It irked her.

"I said I'm here to develop the mill site. I work for Gabler, Burns, and Associates, the development firm that bought the property. I'm the liaison with the crew who's handling construction."

Judging from his indifferent tone, the stranger had no idea what the mill meant to Mapleton, nor was he interested in learning. Julia stared at him for a second longer, wishing her gaze would zap him into oblivion. When that didn't happen, she broke eye contact and concentrated all of her attention on preparing his drink.

Around her, the café patrons buzzed with displeasure.

"I tell ya what, he's got some nerve!"

Julia recognized Val Marshall's midwestern twang from where she was tucked into a booth near the register with her husband, Dave, and their adult son, Ford.

"It never should have been like this." Charlie's voice, shaking with barely controlled indignation, rose above the rest of the unhappy murmuring coming from the table of grandpas.

At the sound of his raspy outburst, Julia's heart lurched. She snapped on the lid to the coffee cup, and slammed it down on the counter in front of the man. "Here."

The brown liquid sloshed out of the tiny opening, dribbling down the side of the cup and pooling beneath it.

At the same moment, Amanda returned from the kitchen, carrying the milk. She audibly inhaled at Julia's lack of hospitality...for good reason. Never before had Julia made such a scene in front of her customers. She was a professional, after all, and she didn't have a confrontational bone in her body. But this was different. This had to do with the mill.

"Um, thanks, I guess." The man reached for a stack of napkins.

Julia turned away from him, her skin prickling with irritation. She wasn't going to give him any more of her time or emotional bandwidth. He wasn't worth it. If she never saw him again, it would be too soon.

"Hey," he raised his deep voice, and even with her back to him, she could tell he was trying to recapture her attention.

Julia ground her jaw. Didn't he realize she was trying to make a statement here? Still, she couldn't just ignore a paying customer. She glanced briskly over her shoulder, her long ponytail whipping the side of her face. "What?" she snapped.

"Is there something I should know about the mill? Like you pointed out, I'm not from around here."

The smirk he shot her was a clear attempt at charm. It was as if he thought she was willingly going to spill all of Mapleton's secrets.

Julia balled up her hands at her sides. "It's nothing someone like you would understand."

Without giving him a chance to say another word, she spun on her heel, walked past an open-mouthed Amanda, and strode into the storage closet behind the bar.

A moment later, the bell over the door jingled, signaling the stranger's departure, and the conversation in the dining room reached fever pitch. Julia groaned, slumping against the closet wall and trying to reign in her galloping heart.

In a village the size of Mapleton, it would take about ten minutes for word to spread that Julia had confronted the new guy about the mill development. Most people wouldn't complain, but Julia didn't like the attention.

And if her mom caught wind of her manners, she'd be scolded as if she were seven and not twenty-seven.

Julia sighed and tugged her shoulders back. There was no use hiding. The man was gone—hopefully for good.

She made up her mind to do her best to avoid him for however long he was in Mapleton, which shouldn't be too difficult to do. He had the sort of dazzling face that attracted all the light in a room. Not that she cared about that, but she was sure he'd stick out in a crowd, and when he did, she'd walk in the opposite direction.

Julia found a fresh dishcloth on the shelf and returned to the bar, setting to work scrubbing the counter as if her life depended on it.

"Woah. Take it easy there, boss." Amanda held up her hand, giving Julia the universal *stop* sign.

"I am taking it easy." Julia bent closer to the counter and rubbed back and forth over a tiny spot.

"Right. Come on. Give me the rag before you scrub the finish right off of the stone."

"Very funny." Julia made a face but stood upright and conceded the cloth. "I'm fine. Everything's fine."

Amanda dangled the rag from her finger and cocked her head. "Okay, then." She stretched out the words, exaggerating her skepticism. "If you say so."

One of their regular customers came in and saved Julia from having to say anything more on the subject.

Amanda turned her attention to the register and smiled at the middle-aged woman who bustled forward. "Hi, Susan. Do you want your usual?"

"You better believe it." Susan Tillersand plopped her oversized purse on the counter to retrieve her payment.

Julia got to work fulfilling the order, half listening as Susan gave them the play-by-play of how she was nearly rear-ended the other night coming out of the ballpark.

Most days, Julia loved hearing about what her customers were up to. It kept the job fresh. But right now, her mind felt fuzzy, like an out-of-focus camera. Fortunately, she'd whipped up so many lattes since opening the café that at this point she could do it half asleep with one hand tied behind her back. She tried to regain her composure as she waited for the milk to steam. But her conversation with the arrogant developer continued to eat away at her until it felt like steam was escaping her ears.

Julia took a calming breath and added a shot of espresso into the to-go mug before pouring the steamed milk over the top of it. Dolloping a scoop of foam onto the drink, she sprinkled on some cinnamon and *wah-lah!*

"Here you are, Susan."

On the outside, she was as perky as could be. After all, Julia could fake it with the best of them. *Fake it 'til you make it*—that was her motto. She'd gotten this business off the ground doing just that. And it was a business that depended on her regulars.

"Thanks, Jules." The mom of three smiled. She took a sip then closed her eyes and moaned. "I'm going to need this today. Swimming lessons, then straight to baseball practice, home for lunch, then an afternoon of tot time, and a soccer game for the oldest tonight."

Julia grinned. "You should have asked for a large drink."

"No, then I'd get all jittery. Life is crazy, but I wouldn't have it any other way." With a wave of her fingers, Susan turned and left through the front door.

The crowd in the coffee shop had thinned a bit with folks leaving for work. Daniel Smith took up his usual position by the front window, laptop open and wireless headphones in. A couple years behind Julia in school, he now worked as a freelance writer, and he used the café as his office. He was a great customer—friendly, well-mannered, and a good tipper. Since they spent most of their days together, Julia considered him a friend. She caught his eye and waved.

Satisfied everything was in order, Julia decided to check on the outdoor space and give herself a chance to reset. "I'm heading out to the deck."

Amanda nodded, and Julia cut down the hallway along the west side of the building where a door opened onto the café's outdoor seating area. She caught a faint whiff of coffee beans as the door swung shut behind her, but on the deck, the smell of freshly cut grass prevailed.

In Julia's opinion, her deck was the crown jewel of On Deck Café. It overlooked Sunrise Park, a massive expanse of trees and trails that was also home to the village baseball diamonds and soccer fields. For those who weren't interested in up-close-and-personal seats to the games, the deck at On Deck Café made for a clear, though distant, viewing spot. For others, it was a comfortable and friendly place to come and rehash the game—to celebrate a victory or to drown a defeat with some caffeinated beverages.

Around the deck, blue-and-white-striped umbrellas were strategically positioned to shield the sun. Flower boxes hung from the wooden railings, stuffed with sun-loving petunias and snapdragons in a rainbow of bold colors.

Julia walked along the railings, stopping to deadhead the flowers that needed care. The morning sun warmed the back of her neck, and signs of the day ahead swirled all around her. A field maintenance worker chalked new foul ball lines in the grass of the field closest to the café. Another man ran a weed-eater around the dugouts. A couple of senior ladies pumped their arms back and forth as they power-walked on the path circling the ballfields, their windbreakers billowing in the early morning breeze and their mouths flapping in time. Mourning doves warbled in the trees, and the faint echo of the rushing Squirrel River beyond the park made it to her ears. These sights and sounds were the fabric of her day. They reminded her of all that was good in life and in her little town.

Yet, even as she stood in her favorite spot, Julia couldn't quite get rid of the sour taste in her mouth left by the stranger who'd stopped by the café.

Any mention of the old mill nettled her. It had been ten years, but the memory of the day she found out about the mill shutting down would stay with her forever.

The party line of the powers-that-be was, "It's not personal; it's business."

Julia loathed that sentiment.

Doing good business was personal. Separating the two was impossible because personal and business were two sides of the same coin. You couldn't have a business without being a decent person or without thinking about the people affected by your actions. That was why what she'd built with the café was a business that was like a beloved friend. She could be proud of that.

"Hey, girl. Can I get a hand?"

Julia turned to see Amanda motioning to her from the entrance to the shop. Her best friend stood like Rosie the Riveter, hands on her hips, curly auburn hair tied up with a cute blue bandana. Her fitted chambray shirt peeked out from under the black apron she wore as part of the café uniform.

"Of course!" Julia inhaled the summer air one more time, smoothing down her own apron before heading inside with a smile on her face.

She wouldn't let some good-for-nothing man ruin a lovely day.

Chapter 2

SAMSON

SAMSON BAKER WALKED DOWN the brightly lit corridor leading to the Mapleton village offices. The quiet but cheery space smelled of lemon and lavender floor cleaner. On the walls hung black-and-white pictures of the village's water tower, a baseball team hoisting a large trophy, and a large canvas sign that read *Welcome to Mapleton, WI!*

Straight ahead, a woman who appeared to be in her late forties sat smiling at him from behind a desk. "Good morning! What can I do for you?"

"Hi, there. I'm hoping to speak to Milo Moore. My name is Samson Baker." Samson gave her his signature grin.

"Sure thing, Mr. Baker."

"Just Samson is fine." He winked.

The woman beamed. "Okay, Samson. Let me see if Milo is in his office. Just give me one sec..." she trailed off as she propped the phone receiver up to her ear. "Milo? A gentleman by the name of Samson Baker is here to see you." She hung up the phone and nodded up at him. "He'll be right with you."

"Thanks so much for your help."

No sooner had Samson taken a seat on the bench along the front wall of the office than a man appeared from the rear of the building.

"You must be Samson."

Samson stood again. "I am."

"Milo Moore. It's a pleasure to meet you." He pumped Samson's hand. "Come on back."

Samson followed Milo down a narrow hallway to a neat office. Milo ushered him inside. "Here, take a seat."

"Thanks for seeing me on such short notice." Samson sat in the closest guest chair. "I didn't know exactly when I'd be getting to town. But now that I'm here, I'm anxious to get started."

"It's no problem at all." Milo shut the door and crossed to his desk.

Framed photos lined the sill of the window to Samson's left. As Milo walked past the picture frames, Samson did a double take. If he wasn't mistaken, in one of the images, Milo stood with his arm around the barista from the café.

Samson hadn't been able to shake her fiery attitude and evident disdain for him from his memory. Most women didn't react to him in the way she did, and he'd be lying if he said he wasn't intrigued.

"So." Milo reclined in his desk chair, drawing his attention. "What can I do for you? I assume you've seen the site?"

Samson nodded. "Just finished up hiking the grounds."

Milo rocked in his chair. "What do you think of the land?"

"It's impressive. What we have in mind for the space will be excellent for all involved."

Milo preened.

The man seemed to be the one person in town who was excited about the mill development, so Samson pressed his advantage. "My boss sent the preliminary plans the village board approved. I'll be working from those. I'd like to have the terrain gradients, the electrical and sewer maps, and the village's street and sidewalk plans, if you have them available. Having all that information up front will make it easier to finalize blueprints and coordinate with our contractors."

Milo stood. "Come this way, then." He tipped his head in the direction of the door and crossed in front of the picture frames.

Samson took the opportunity to study the photos again. It was definitely the woman from the café in the picture with Milo. Samson had a feeling he'd recognize her anywhere. She was as beautiful in the still shot as she was in real life. Her blonde hair hung in waves, and bright intelligence glistened from her eyes as they crinkled, thanks to her smile.

Samson gave the woman in the image one last look—purely out of curiosity—before he trailed Milo back down the hall and into another room.

"What you want should be over here." The Village Administrator gestured to a bank of cabinets. "We prepped all the relevant documents once we sold the land to your company." Milo peered out the door before turning back to Samson and dropping his voice. "I have to say. I'm thrilled you're here to get started on this. Between you and me, that mill site has been an eyesore in Mapleton for nearly a decade. I've wanted to do something about it since I came to the village."

"You're not from here?" Samson kept his tone casual as he tried to get a read on Milo.

"No, no. I moved here for this job. I've been in the position five years now. I'm originally from Milwaukee, went to school in Oshkosh, so still a Wisconsinite, but this is the smallest town I've ever lived in." Milo gave a dry laugh before puffing up his chest. "I was brought in to get things organized around here. The previous Village Administrator had been in the role for nearly two decades. Nice guy, but not super business-minded and certainly not thinking about the future like we need to be. We've got to remain relevant."

Milo prattled on about his desire to keep the village moving forward, and it didn't take long for Samson to determine that the guy was a total showboat. Even though Samson agreed with him about progress and development, Milo's whole demeanor turned Samson off.

"I've got a lot of ideas. The first one was getting the mill site taken care of. It took me five years to get the ball rolling there. Things don't move at lightning speed around here." Milo laughed in a buddy-buddy way and rocked on his heels. "But the villagers will come around. What you're going to do will be good for the community as a whole."

"I agree." Samson shuffled through the maps in the cabinet Milo directed him to and gathered what he needed. "So, some people weren't too keen on the idea of the development?"

Milo shrugged and rolled his eyes. "You could say that. You see, the old guard…well, they were very attached to the mill. It was the pulse of Mapleton for years and years. It was all people here had ever known. And change is hard, as I'm sure you know in your line of work."

"That I do."

Samson thought about the people who were upset over his previous contract. His company purchased farmland from a family and zoned it for commercial development. They built a new strip mall, and Samson's job was to find businesses to fill the space. It was a smashing success, but the people in the neighborhood beyond the farmland put up quite a fight.

Change was hard when it wasn't what you wanted. Still, business was business. And in the case of the mill, the past was the past, wasn't it?

He brought his focus back to Milo. "It's helpful to have a little background on Mapleton, so thank you. I stopped into a coffee shop on my way here, and when I mentioned the mill, I got the cold shoulder."

Milo shook his head, scoffing. "Doesn't surprise me, but sorry about that. I'm sure that was some of the old guard. They head to On Deck Café for their morning coffee with a side of gossip."

"Some of them were old. But the young woman behind the counter also seemed pretty put off by my being here."

"Oh, you must have met my girlfriend, Julia."

Samson raised his gaze from the map he was uncurling in time to see Milo shrug.

"She's something else, and she has her opinions, but she's harmless." With that, Milo turned to leave. "You go ahead and take what you need. I've got to jump on a call here. Melly Ratler up at the front desk can help you if you run into any technical difficulties. Otherwise, holler if I can do anything for you. I'm sure I'll be seeing you around. It's not that big of a town!" Milo laughed at his joke and walked out of the room.

Samson stood still for a moment, digesting everything the administrator had shared with him.

What had he learned?

The town was attached to its mill—or what used to be its mill.

The administrator was an aggressive one with lots of plans for growth and development. That was a bonus for Samson's company, even if Milo himself was over the top.

And finally, the woman from the café was Julia.

And she had a boyfriend—Milo—who thought she was 'harmless'.

What a terrible adjective. 'Harmless'? Samson had spent all of seven minutes in Julia's presence (not that he was counting), and, objectively speaking, he could think of about fifteen better words to describe her—starting with clever and ending with breathtaking.

But no one asked him...which was as it should be.

Samson never got involved with people in the towns he worked. Keeping them at arm's length worked best for everyone. In this case, Julia was openly antagonistic toward him and clearly didn't want anything to do with him.

But as he stood in the semi-dark room and reflected on their interaction, his heart gave an unusual stutter. She *had* offered him a warm greeting when he first walked into the café—a welcome that stirred something in the deepest part of him. Her blue eyes sparkled when they connected with his, and there was a playful ease in their conversation...at least until he brought up the mill. Even then, when her eyes flashed with indignation and a crease of anger appeared along the bridge of her nose, there was no denying she was stunning.

And taken.

It was good he found that fact out when he did.

Julia wasn't interested or available. And neither was he.

Chapter 3

JULIA

"YOU THINK EVERYTHING IS going to come together in time for the Fourth of July Festival?" Amanda asked Julia around a mouthful of turkey-and-avocado sandwich. Pieces of her curly hair flopped forward against her bandana as a gust of wind came off the water.

Julia swallowed a bite of apple. She and Amanda had traded places with the café's afternoon and evening staff—Nick Quinnly and Seth Jensen—and short-order cook—Jimmy Campbell—and were enjoying their lunch on one of the docks jutting out into the Squirrel River.

"It always does, doesn't it?" Julia put her hand over her plate to prevent her veggie crisps from blowing into the water. Her mouth curved into a smile in anticipation of the festival—one of her favorite events of the year.

Since opening On Deck Café, Julia joined the planning committee. Now, it was part of her job to carry on the traditions of the Fourth of July Festival. A byproduct of the festivities, which took place in Sunrise Park, was an uptick in business for her café.

Amanda was on the same wavelength. "We should check on our disposable coffee cup supply and make sure we have enough," she said.

Julia nodded. "You're right. We burned through way more than I expected to last year. Maybe we could come up with a signature Fourth of July drink."

"That sounds good. What are you thinking?"

Julia nibbled her lip as ideas flitted through her mind. "What about a mixed-berry Americano? People could choose their syrup flavor—strawberry, blueberry, or even raspberry. Then, we could add it in with the shots of espresso, cold water, ice, and maybe something creamy to bring the flavor to life?"

"I bet half-and-half would work." Amanda rubbed her hands together. "That sounds amazing, actually."

"Let's do it!"

Playing to the season always delighted her guests. Christmas time was easy with the rich options of gingerbread, cinnamon, and peppermint. They did a lot of mint drinks around St. Patrick's Day and, of course, everything pumpkin the second the calendar turned to fall. But she hadn't considered changing up her drink menu for the Fourth until now.

Amanda licked her lips. "I can't wait to try it. I might have to make up a sample tomorrow if we're slow. Gosh, my feet hurt thinking about how busy we are for the festival, though."

Julia laughed. "I can't complain. I'll take any business we can get. When I started out, I didn't know if we'd make it one year. Sometimes I still wonder how we're doing it." Julia and her employees had a healthy system, and any time she stopped to think about it, she was still shocked her little café had turned into anything more than a one-woman show.

Amanda furrowed her brows. "You need to start owning the fact that what you have on your hands is a strong operation. You're infected with imposter syndrome."

Julia fluttered her feet in the water, avoiding Amanda's stare. "What is that supposed to mean?"

"You always doubt your accomplishments when you should be celebrating your success and building on it!"

Julia focused on tracking the ripples she made as they swelled farther and farther into the river and eventually disappeared.

Amanda was right, but the truth was, opening up On Deck Café had maxed out Julia's risk quota. She was afraid to change anything for fear it would fail and everything she'd poured her heart into would be ripped away. She was fortunate she had the town's support of the café as it was. She drew the line at inventing fun drinks. She had no business pressing her luck with large-scale innovation.

Julia crossed her legs, sending one last spray of water out into the river before meeting Amanda's gaze. "Can you blame me for having to pinch myself with the way this all came together? I'm still learning as I go and grateful for what we've got going. I owe it all to the village and its support."

"You can take some credit too, you know. And I guess it doesn't hurt that your boyfriend is basically your landlord." Amanda nudged her shoulder.

Julia bit down on her bottom lip and looked away again. "Yeah. What are the chances Milo's first week on the job was the week I'd decide to open a coffee shop."

"I'd say that worked out pretty well for everyone. That man worships the ground you walk on. Sometimes I wonder if he gave you a deal on the rent for the property to get on your good side—even if you did put him off for literal years before agreeing to date." Amanda chuckled before swinging a questioning look in Julia's direction. "Hey, speaking of Milo, he was our most regular customer for a while. He came in every day. What's he been up to lately? Now that I think of it, I haven't seen too much of him."

"He went sugar-free six months back. And since he only liked his coffee with sugar and can't stand artificial sweeteners, he just gave it up altogether."

Amanda snorted, and they fell quiet, listening to the raw screech of the gulls mewing overhead.

Julia uncrossed her legs and leaned back on her elbows, letting the sun kiss her face while she worked up the courage to share something she'd been keeping from her friend for a month.

She blew out a breath. "I don't know. Things have grown a little stale with Milo." Julia gauged Amanda's reaction to her admission out of the corner of her eye.

"What do you mean?" Amanda futzed with her bandana, tightening the knot.

"He's a good guy. You know that. But I don't really desire his company lately. What we have in common is Mapleton and the fact that we both work here and are invested in the community. But beyond that, we're different people. I can't put my finger on what made me realize it. He's swamped with work, and so am I, so we haven't seen each other a lot lately, but it's more than that. I've started to think things have run their course with us."

Amanda dropped her hands and turned to stare at Julia, jaw hanging slightly open. "Are you going to break up with him?"

"Yeah, I think I am." Julia pressed her eyes closed and squished up her cheeks. Now it was out there. She blinked, letting her head roll to the side.

Next to her, Amanda scooted into a position that mirrored her own and gazed out over the river. "I had no idea. Are you doing okay?"

This type of question was what made Amanda a true friend. Amanda thought Milo was an excellent boyfriend. Everyone in the village did, as a matter of fact. But when Julia gave her the inside scoop on what could turn out to be the juiciest bit of gossip the small town had seen in years, Amanda focused her concern on how Julia was doing and not on what everyone else would say.

"I'm okay. It'll be weird to be single." Julia sat up, rubbing her elbow before hugging her arms to herself. "I hate the thought of hurting him, but I should talk to him sooner rather than later. I've been sitting on this for a few weeks, and that's not fair to Milo." The guilt of the impending breakup weighed heavier each day she put it off.

"Well, you had to be sure," Amanda defended. "And now that you are, it'll be good to get it over with. I'm sure the two of you will be fine."

Julia's shoulders fell forward and she sighed. "I know. Hopefully he takes it okay."

· ♥ · ♥ · ♥ · ♥ · ♥ ·

Hal's Diner was the only full-scale restaurant in Mapleton and the only place Milo wanted to meet Julia that evening. When she worked up the nerve to call him after her talk with Amanda, she hoped he'd agree to get together someplace private. Instead, he whined about an evening commitment and how busy he was but said he could squeeze in a quick, early dinner. So here Julia sat, waiting for him and trying not to cringe every time the door opened and another familiar person walked into the restaurant.

Most of the time, living in a small town was wonderful, but when you wanted to break up with your boyfriend and not have it be front-page news in *The Village Tattler*, it was less than ideal.

The bell over the door chimed, and Julia looked up, expecting to see Milo. Instead, it was Charlie. She smoothed out her grimace and replaced it with a sincere smile as he approached her table.

"Hi, Charlie!" Julia shouted her greeting. She'd gotten used to talking louder when he was around so she didn't have to repeat herself.

"Julia! What a nice surprise. Are you waiting on your folks?" Charlie scanned her empty table.

"No, actually I'm waiting for Milo." Julia winced at the way Milo's name carried throughout the diner. More than a handful of the dinner crowd turned and beamed smiles in her direction.

"Ah, of course. Young love." Charlie gave her a conspiring nod, his droopy eyes glowing with good humor. "Well, I won't keep you. Maybe you could ask that boyfriend of yours about this new guy in town. Some nerve he had showing up at your café this morning, huh? I still can't believe what they're doing with the mill."

Julia flinched at the mention of the stranger. She'd pushed him to the deepest recesses of her brain and planned to keep him there, covered in cobwebs.

As for Milo, he and Julia didn't talk much about the mill since it had been the source of some of their only arguments.

He never understood why she—and much of the town—was so sensitive about the property, so they agreed to disagree about it, and seeing as how she was planning to break up with him, now wasn't the time to bring it up.

"It'll be okay, Charlie. I'll tell Milo you said hello." She patted his arm. "See you tomorrow morning?"

"I wouldn't miss my daily cup of joe!"

Charlie shuffled to the back of the restaurant, and the bell over the door rang. This time, Milo strolled in. Julia said a silent *Hail Mary* to steady her nerves.

"Hi, darling." Milo bent and kissed her cheek before taking the seat across from her and immediately reaching for the menu. "So sorry to keep you waiting. It's been a crazy day, and it's not finished yet." He skimmed the specials, seeming to care more about the burger supreme than her.

Julia fought the urge to roll her eyes. Getting annoyed wouldn't help her carry out the breakup speech she had rehearsed on the walk to the restaurant.

"Well, I appreciate you making time to see me. I know you've been busy lately, and so have I, so we don't have to stay here long, but I did want to talk to you."

Milo made a noncommittal grunting sound and still didn't look directly at her. Instead, he returned the menu to its stand and reached for his cell phone, swiping at the screen and frowning at whatever he saw.

When had he gotten so flakey? The two had been together for almost a year. She at least merited some eye contact, didn't she? Julia pushed down her irritation.

"I'm just going to say it, Milo."

Something in her tone must've made him realize she was serious, because he placed his phone face-down on the table and looked at her. "What?"

"You're a really good person, but I don't see a future between the two of us. I think it's best if we went our separate ways."

There. Direct. Honest. To the point.

Julia waited for Milo to say something, but he just stared at her.

A chilly silence settled between them that seemed to stretch on for longer than a Wisconsin winter.

Finally, Milo cleared his throat. "Wow. That is not what I was expecting out of a dinner date. What's going on, Jules? This is out of left field."

Julia shifted in her seat. She was afraid he'd react like this. She had hoped he'd understand and even agree that their time together had run its course. Evidently it wasn't going to be so easy.

"I know, I know." She traced her finger up and down the side of her water glass. The cool condensation felt good on her hand as she, too, started to sweat. "That's because there is nothing wrong with our relationship, but there's nothing that's super right, either. I see us drifting apart, and I don't think prolonging the inevitable is good for either of us."

"What do you mean by 'inevitable'?" Milo screwed up his face in an unbecoming scowl.

"A breakup, Milo." Julia heard the strain in her tone, but she tried to keep her voice down so the rest of the patrons at the restaurant wouldn't overhear. Heads were already swiveling in their direction. "You can't honestly tell me you've been particularly fulfilled with the way our relationship has gone these past few months."

Milo sat back in his chair and tipped his chin up. It was as if he was thinking about them—as a couple—for the first time.

He shook his head. "I still don't think it's fair to phone in a relationship because you see us drifting apart. Don't you want to fight for us?"

Neither of them had been doing much fighting for their relationship lately, and deep down, Julia didn't want to fight—for him or with him. Bolstered by the realization, she pressed on. "I think we're past that point. You have been nothing but an upstanding guy, Milo, but this is what's best for me. And I'm sure, in time, you'll find it's best for you, too."

He leaned forward and reached for her hand. "Jules, please. You can't be serious."

She squeezed his hand before extracting her own. "I'm serious, Milo. I hope we can still be friends. We'll see a lot of each other in this town, and technically, you're still my landlord."

Julia shot him a good-natured smile, hoping her joke would ease some of the tension between them. Instead, her attempt at humor backfired. Milo's mouth thinned, and his face turned stony.

He stood, knocking his chair backward. "Well, if that's the way it's going to be, then that's the way it's going to be. I can't force you to stay in this relationship, but you're making a mistake. You'll see." He leaned down and pressed his pointer finger to the table, eyes narrowed at her. "Without us, what will you be?"

Julia's stomach churned. Milo had gone after her insecurities, and for a second, she wavered. Was she making a huge mistake?

When it came to their relationship, as much as she tried not to listen to the talk around town, even she couldn't ignore the way people looked at and spoke about her and Milo. Like they were some sort of power couple. And Milo *had* been a big part of her success. He'd been in her corner since the café's launch, yet here she was, giving up the status of being the Village Administrator's girlfriend.

Julia gave herself a quick mental shake. No. No matter how uncomfortable it was, this was the right thing to do. She steeled herself to get through the rest of the conversation, chewing on the inside of her cheek and waiting to see what Milo would do next.

Steadying his chair, he turned and looked to the door then back at her. "I hope you won't blame me for not hanging around for dinner." His voice cut the air with a hostile edge, and he spoke a little too loudly for her taste. The people at nearby tables didn't try to hide their curiosity.

"Of course not." Where was the nearest hole she could climb into? This was excruciating.

Milo gave a terse nod. "Okay, then. I'll see you around."

"Bye, Milo," Julia spoke to his back as he stalked to the exit.

When the glass door rattled shut, Julia sunk down in her seat and propped the menu up to shield her face. Trying to be inconspicuous, she peered around the diner. Most everyone had gone back to their dinner conversation, and they were at least pretending not to gawk, but Sally, the owner of Sally's Hair Salon, sat at the table nearest hers. She stared at Julia with a been-there-done-that expression. Julia gave her a weak smile. Sally was sweet, but she spread the town's news faster than a centipede scurries. If Sally saw what had happened between her and Milo, the whole village would know about their breakup before dawn.

·♥·♥·♥·♥·♥·

An hour later, Julia stood to leave Hal's. She'd gotten sucked into having dinner with Ted and Linda Koke, friends of her parents. When they walked in and saw her sitting by herself, they insisted she join them at their table.

Julia liked Ted and Linda. She did. They were sweet and funny, and they'd watched her grow throughout the years. So while she'd wanted nothing more than to escape to the quiet of her home, Julia sucked it up and joined the pair for dinner.

Now, the older couple stood smiling at her as they got ready to leave the restaurant.

"This was such a treat. You get home safely, dear." Linda hugged Julia.

Freedom was in sight, and Julia fought the urge to cut the woman off and race out the door. "I will, Mrs. Koke. Thanks again for keeping me company. It was nice to run into you both."

"Good grief, Julia. You're a grown woman. Call me Linda, for heaven's sake."

Julia chuckled, holding up her hands in a shrug. "Old habits die hard."

"I'm sure we'll see you around soon, kiddo." Ted patted her shoulder. He still treated her as if she were nine years old, playing third base on his softball team. No wonder she couldn't get on a first-name basis with them.

"I'm sure you're right. Take care, you two."

As they turned to go, Julia dug into her purse, pulled out her cell phone, and dialed Amanda.

Her friend picked up on the first ring. "It's about time! What happened?"

"Don't worry, I haven't been with Milo this whole time. The Kokes corralled me into having dinner with them post-breakup."

"Oh my gosh. Did Ted and Linda watch you break up with him?"

Julia pictured her friend's horrified expression. The two shared a similar desire for privacy. Amanda grew up in Mapleton, too, and knew people made it a point to keep track of everyone else's business.

"No, no. Thank goodness. They didn't walk in until after Milo left. He didn't want to stick around for dinner."

Julia stood on the sidewalk outside the restaurant for a minute and savored the feel of the damp evening air against her heated cheeks. She smelled the musk of the river and the smoke of a campfire, and the claw of tension gripping her back eased ever so slightly.

"Unfortunately, Sally was sitting at a table kitty-corner to mine. I'm pretty sure she watched the drama unfold, so it'll be all over town before I know it."

"Oh, girl, I'm sorry," Amanda consoled. "How did it go with Milo, though? Did he take it okay?"

"I don't know." She kicked a stone down the sidewalk as she walked down Mapleton Avenue toward her street. "He acted sort of strange."

"What do you mean 'strange'?"

"Well, he couldn't believe I was breaking up with him. There hasn't been anything to our relationship lately, so I'm not sure why he was surprised. We've only seen each other once a week for the past two months. Sometimes not even that often. But anyway, even if he couldn't believe it, what was weirder was how he got angry."

"Milo got angry?" Amanda's disbelief echoed through the phone.

"Yes...no..." Julia tossed her hand up in the air and let it drop to her side with a slap. "I don't know. He didn't start yelling or anything, but there was something in his voice I haven't heard before. He almost sounded menacing when he left. Like he'd be looking for payback or something. He basically said without him I'd be nothing." Julia blew out a self-deprecating scoff. "I guess that remains to be seen."

There was a pause on the other end of the line.

"Are you still there?"

Amanda cleared her throat. "Yeah. I'm here." She was quiet for another beat. "I'm sorry he treated you like that. Milo isn't used to people saying no to him or not doing what he expects. You caught him off guard. I'm sure you don't have anything to worry about. And you know you're amazing, right?"

"If you say so." Julia took a deep pull of night air and let it out in a rush. "I'm glad it's done—tonight's conversation and the relationship. Thanks for letting me vent. I'm almost home, so I'll let you go. You're okay to cover the morning shift solo tomorrow?"

With the Fourth of July in less than a week and a half, Julia planned to take one last day off before she'd be working non-stop to cover the holiday rush at the café and the ballfields.

"Of course. Maybe we can connect later after Nick takes over for me?"

"Sounds good. See you then. Night, Amanda. And thanks again." Julia's voice caught. It had been an emotional day, and she was really thankful to have a friend like Amanda.

Chapter 4

Samson

LONG EVENING SHADOWS DANCED across the street as Samson approached Julia from behind. Even from a distance, he could tell it was her from the tilt of her head and the shine of the setting sun reflecting off her golden hair.

She was on her phone, and Samson instinctively slowed his pace to give her privacy and avoid freaking her out, but all at once, she stopped walking to stow her phone in her purse. As if sensing she was being followed, she whirled around and faced him. She yelped in surprise.

A zing rattled through Samson's chest at the prospect of talking to her again. His long strides ate up the remaining distance between them. "Two meetings in one day. I'm a lucky man."

Julia scowled, looking up at him. "More like unlucky. You scared the living daylights out of me! What are you doing?"

"Wow, Julia." He annunciated her name, enjoying how her blue eyes widened in surprise when he used it. "You are quite the welcoming committee. Can a man not walk down his own street in this town?" He shot her a teasing grin. He couldn't help pushing her buttons.

"What do you mean your street?" Disbelief colored Julia's features, and she crossed her arms over her chest.

Samson gestured to his rental one block down. "I'm walking home after trying to get the lay of the land. I'm Samson, by the way. We haven't been formally introduced."

Julia frowned as she turned her whole body in the direction of his house. "You live there?" Her words came out sounding like an accusation.

Before he could answer, she whipped her head around and spoke again. "And since we haven't been 'formally introduced'"—she narrowed her eyes as she made air quotes to mock him—"how do you know my name?"

Samson put his hands into his pockets and grinned, enjoying the feeling of having the upper hand. Still, Julia was a firecracker. He may have surprised her, but as he learned this morning, she wasn't one to be walked all over. Verbally sparring with her was turning out to be the most fun he'd had in months. "Yeah, I rented a furnished place. And I learned your name from your boyfriend earlier today."

Julia's head snapped back. She glared at him, her eyes flaring with a series of emotions—embarrassment, dismay, and finally resignation—before she dropped her gaze. "So you've met Milo."

"Yeah, I was in his office this morning. I mentioned stopping at the coffee shop, and I saw a picture of you by his desk."

Julia turned and started walking down the street without acknowledging his explanation.

Samson didn't know what was going on, but he matched his pace with hers. They walked in silence for a couple paces before Julia puffed up her cheeks and blew out a full breath.

"He's not my boyfriend."

Samson caught his toe on a ridge of the sidewalk and stumbled. Recovering his footing, he glanced down at her. This was a new development.

Julia reluctantly met his eye. "Not anymore, anyway."

"It's none of my business." Samson shook his head. He didn't like her deflated tone. It didn't suit her the way her quick wit did. "We don't have to talk about it."

Julia gave a wry laugh. "Well, it'll be all over town in no time. Because this is Mapleton, Wisconsin. Population 2,133 of my closest friends. Scratch that. 2,132. I probably can't include

Milo in that number anymore since I broke up with him an hour ago."

Samson thought for a moment, puzzling over Julia. Even though she sounded exasperated at the thought of news of her breakup spreading through town, her fondness for Mapleton and the people here still rang out, loud and clear. He didn't understand it at all.

He tapped his chin. "This is an unusual place, isn't it?"

"What makes you say that?" Julia paid more attention to the stone she was kicking down the sidewalk than to him.

Samson told himself he was being ridiculous for wishing she'd bestow her sharp gaze on him instead of the ground. But he couldn't check his desire for her attention. Because when Julia looked at him, his synapses fired in bursts that rivaled a Fourth of July sparkler, all crackly, bright, and hot. Under her stare, he felt more alive.

Samson ran his hand behind his neck, massaging the skin with his fingers. He didn't know *what* had gotten into him with thoughts like that, but he needed to lock it up.

He peered to the side at Julia. She was staring at him now, likely waiting for him to explain himself. He cleared his throat. "There isn't a sense of personal space here, is there? You all know each other. And you have strong feelings about...things."

Julia looked down and kicked the stone hard, sending it scuttling into the road. She kept her head turned away from him. "It's a small town, Mapleton is. Most everyone who lives here has lived here for their whole life. People take care of each other. That's why we can spot a stranger or a newcomer from miles away."

"Like me, this morning."

Julia nodded once, glancing at him. "People here know each other's history. We're also very proud of our town's history."

"I gathered that." Samson tossed her a smirk but didn't press the issue of the mill. He was dying to find out why she, personally, was so against the development of the property, but nothing good could come from mentioning it now. He'd bide his time. "So, where are you off to?"

Someone who wasn't observing Julia as carefully wouldn't have caught her half-second of hesitation. It was like she debated lying before she raised her arm and pointed across the street. "That's my house over there." She motioned in the direction of a story-and-a-half gray brick bungalow with a detached single-stall garage. The white picket fence running between the house and garage matched the one surrounding the café, and old lantern lights flickered brightly on either side of the barn-red front door.

"You don't say?" Samson was shocked. Sure, it wasn't a big town, but what were the chances he'd be able to see Julia's front door from his front door?

"I do say." She tipped her head up to meet his eye, her tone cool and detached. "Bought it a few years back. Took some elbow grease to get it into shape, but it's coming along."

"Is it your first time being a homeowner?" His question forced Julia to linger with him for a moment in front of the walkway to his house. For some irrational reason, he didn't want to say goodbye to her yet.

"Yeah. When I moved back home after college, I lived with my parents until I got my feet under me." Julia blinked and gave her head a quick shake, as if unsure why she had shared that with him.

Samson wasn't complaining, but before he could say anything to try to keep her talking, she stepped away from him. "Anyway, I'm off."

"Can I walk you to your door?" Samson figured it was worth a shot to ask.

"No, that won't be necessary. There's nothing scary on these small-town streets." Julia scooted around him and rushed toward her house.

Samson watched her tall, lean figure for a minute before he retrieved his keys from his pocket and unlocked the door to his rental. With his hand on the knob, Samson took one more look across the street. Julia disappeared through the gate without looking back.

Samson pushed open his door, his mind whirring.

Julia was single now. Samson wasn't surprised by the breakup. He hadn't spent much time with either Julia or Milo, but from the little he had, the two didn't come across as compatible at all. Milo was a smooth-talker with a distinct *I'm-cooler-than-you* style. From what he could tell, Julia was principled and authentic. Judging by her modest home and her admission that she'd spent time living with her parents, Samson guessed she worked for what she had. Against his better judgment, Samson found himself thoroughly captivated by her.

Sinking into the couch, he pictured her clutching her chest when she spun around and faced him. She may have said there was nothing scary on the small-town streets of Mapleton, but she'd reacted to him as if something was out to get her. That got Samson wondering. What did Julia have to be afraid of?

A knock on the door interrupted his thoughts. Samson blinked. No one but Julia knew this was where he was staying. His belly flipped at the thought of seeing her again. No. That was preposterous. Those were probably just hunger pains.

He forced himself to take his time as he went to open the door. When he did, it wasn't Julia.

"Melly, what a surprise."

The matronly woman he met at the village offices beamed up at him, her mom-bob framing a heart-shaped, kind face.

"Hello, Samson. Don't mind my intrusion." She walked into his house without a second's hesitation. "I brought you a late dinner. I figured you wouldn't have much of a chance to get to the grocery store based on all the work you said you were doing today. I thought some home-cooked food might serve you well."

"Wow, thanks, Melly. That's so considerate of you." Samson took the dish from her hands and moved to set it on the kitchen counter. "When did you have time to whip this up?"

"I make it a point to keep my freezer stocked. You never know when a new baby is going to be born or when someone is going to wind up in the hospital, God bless 'em. I find it's best to be prepared." The woman stood with her hands gently clasped in front of her, surveying his space.

"I appreciate it."

Melly waved her hand. "It's nothing. I'm glad you can enjoy it. Sorry, I can't stay long. I've got to get home to the kids. Milo left the office early to get dinner with Julia, so I had to stay and lock up. That's why I'm a little late in my delivery. I checked the water department database and found your account. That's how I got your address. Hope that's okay."

"It's no problem." A little invasive, but what could he say? Melly didn't seem to think anything of it, and she didn't strike him as the type of person to use his personal information for unsavory ends. The woman brought him dinner, for Pete's sake.

Melly smiled. "I better hurry back before the kids start climbing the walls...or worse, raiding the refrigerator."

Melly was halfway out the door before Samson said goodbye.

He removed the tin foil from her pan and found some sort of cheesy noodle dish. His stomach growled.

See? Hunger pains.

Melly had taped baking instructions to the tin foil, and Samson preheated the oven as directed.

So, this was Mapleton. What had Julia said? *People here take care of each other.* Samson's mouth twitched. Melly had proven Julia's point. She was the epitome of small-town hospitality. Had he made his first friend in Mapleton?

After this morning, he'd take whatever—or whomever—he could get.

Chapter 5

Julia

SATURDAY MORNING DAWNED, AND the sun shone bright in the pale-blue summer sky.

Julia had slept terribly. It probably had something to do with Milo and the breakup. Or with the knowledge that Samson was just making himself at home across the street, completely thwarting her plans to avoid him.

She chugged her morning cup of coffee, and now she was wired. She needed fresh air.

"Come on, Mr. Waffles."

Her golden retriever galloped in her direction from where he'd been resting on the slip-covered couch in the living room.

"We're going for a walk."

Julia didn't bother showering. She shimmied into a pair of gym shorts and an old t-shirt from her days on the high school volleyball team and threw her hair into a messy top knot. She clipped on Mr. Waffles' short leash, letting it drag while she palmed her key and opened the side door off her kitchen.

Mr. Waffles bounded into the fenced-in backyard.

She followed him outside, turning to lock the door behind herself before bending to tie her shoes.

Mr. Waffles let out a happy bark and tore off through the slightly opened gate.

"Oh no!" Julia jumped off the stoop and sprinted after him. She must not have shut the gate firmly last night. "Mr. Waffles! Get back here!" She rounded the corner of her driveway and popped out onto the sidewalk, legs churning.

At the sight before her, Julia skidded to a halt. Across the street and half a block down, her white-haired golden retriever pranced around Samson.

"You've got to be kidding me." Julia stalked toward her dog, her heart suddenly doing its own version of a herky-jerky polka, which was just as ridiculous as it sounded.

Julia met Samson and Mr. Waffles on the sidewalk near Samson's rental.

"Sorry about that," she huffed by way of greeting Samson. "And you..." She eyed her dog. "What do you think you're doing?"

Mr. Waffles gazed at her.

Julia swore she detected a smirk in the dog's eyes. The traitor.

"I'm sorry. What did you say this guy's name is?" Samson's question interrupted her stare-down with her dog.

"Mr. Waffles." Julia frowned. "Why?"

Samson let out a bark of laughter.

Julia bent to tighten the laces on her shoe. "What's so funny? It's a perfectly good name for a dog. Isn't it, boy?"

Mr. Waffles' tail thumped against Samson's leg.

Samson raised an eyebrow at Julia as she stood up. "Seriously? Fang, sure. Spot, okay. But Mr. Waffles? Come on."

Julia stuck up her nose. Sure, she was slightly embarrassed Samson was making fun of her and her dog, but she wasn't going to give him the satisfaction of knowing he'd gotten under her skin.

"He's not your dog, so I don't see why it matters. And I happen to like the name."

Julia reached out to grab Mr. Waffles' leash. The sooner she got away from Samson, the better. She really needed to brush up on her avoidance skills.

As she grasped the leash, Mr. Waffles took off and sprinted in the opposite direction, dragging Julia into Samson.

Samson's strong arms engulfed Julia's waist, stopping her from toppling over. "Woah. I've got you."

She looked up, her mouth parting in surprise as Samson hurried to remove his hands, but Mr. Waffles circled, pinning the two together with his leash.

"Mr. Waffles. That's enough." Julia spoke sternly to her dog who sat down and appeared quite delighted by the spectacle. She shook her head. "I don't know what's gotten into him. He's usually obedient."

Julia stood chest to chest with Samson, and his broad shoulders dwarfed her smaller frame. All at once, her senses roared to life. The heat of their bodies pressed against each other made Julia's ears burn, and the intoxicating scent of his post-run sweat mixed with what smelled like bergamot soap was doing funny things to her head. She had to get out of his presence before she did something stupid—like buried her face into his neck.

Or dissolved in a fit of vapors.

She shifted her weight in one direction to let Samson get around, but he went the same way. She moved opposite of him, but he matched her step. Julia tried to lift the leash over his head, but he was a good six inches taller, and she ended up smacking him in the chin with her hand.

"Oh, gosh." Julia was certain her cheeks were as pink as Mr. Waffles' panting tongue.

Samson chuckled, a low throaty sound. It was one of those laughs. The kind that sent goosebumps tripping over themselves on their march up and down her arms.

"Why don't you let go of the leash and set me free."

"Right." Julia dropped the leash as if it were a snake.

Samson deftly stepped through the knot Mr. Waffles had created and picked up the braided rope. When he handed the leash to Julia, their fingers touched, and the goosebumps on her arms may as well have turned into mini volcanoes. It felt like they erupted, one by one, and sent melting lava cascading over her flesh in a terrifying sensation that was equal parts disconcerting and exhilarating.

Julia made the active choice not to think about it.

"What an interesting way to start my day." Samson's gaze snagged on hers, and his eyes gleamed with amusement. He began stretching his quads, balancing on one leg and then the other, as if to taunt her with his coordination.

Her mouth was suddenly as parched as in-field dirt. Julia forced herself to look away from the grooves of his leg muscles.

Leg muscles! Of all the things to be her undoing, her heart decided to accelerate to the point of no return over leg muscles.

"Yeah, well. Thanks for this." She held up the leash, croaking out the words. "We'll be going. Come on, Mr. Waffles." Julia yanked the dog past Samson and in the direction of Mapleton Avenue.

"See you around, neighbor," he yelled after her.

Julia ignored him and hurried away. Once she turned onto the avenue, she collapsed against the rough brick of the nearest building.

Her dog sat in front of her, cocking his head.

"Seriously, Mr. Waffles? You planned that, didn't you?"

The dog raised a paw and rubbed at his face.

"Oh, don't give me that innocent act. You knew what you were doing. Trying to reenact a sort of Pongo-and-Perdita scene, were you?" Julia was engaged in another staring contest with her dog when someone called her name.

"Morning, Julia!" Kenneth Wynert, the local mail carrier, crossed Mapleton Avenue.

"Hi, Mr. Wynert." Julia pushed off from the wall and tugged on Mr. Waffles' leash, encouraging him to move along down the street. She was still off-kilter and in no mood to make small talk with anyone, and Kenneth had a tendency to drone on and on about his predictions for the upcoming Green Bay Packers football season.

Why did her dog have to pick this morning, of all mornings, to run away while she laced up her shoes? He never did that. Ever. And why did he have to stumble upon Samson?

Samson, who looked like an actual athletic-wear model, with sweat glistening off his brow, his shirt pulled tight across his chest, and his shaggy hair flipping up ever-so-perfectly on the ends. He wasn't fazed by the episode at all, and she'd turned into a sputtering, incompetent mess. She had smacked him in the face, for crying out loud. How had she let *that* happen? All the while, he just stood there with a crooked smile on his face, radiating charm and ease. His swagger came so naturally.

She peered down at her rag-tag outfit and touched a finger to her makeup-free face.

Her swagger did not.

"Ugh." Julia let her head fall back. "Mr. Waffles, let's make a deal. Do not run into him ever again, okay?"

Mr. Waffles snorted, and Julia rolled her eyes. She was trying to reason with a dog.

And even as she scolded Mr. Waffles, she would be lying to herself if she said she wasn't still thinking about the way Samson's hands felt on her hips.

Chapter 6

JULIA

A WEEK AFTER MR. Waffles' 101 *Dalmatians* stunt, Julia loaded her dog into the back of her pick-up truck and drove to the baseball fields. She volunteered to work in the concession stand for the tournament the village was hosting, and if she didn't hurry, she'd be late.

The parking lot of On Deck Café was full as she passed by and drove through the entrance to Sunrise Park. Julia waved at one woman striding out of the café, balancing a carrier filled with four cups. In the back of Julia's head, a thought sprung up: a drive-thru window would add value to her business.

She tamped the idea down. It was a pipe dream. She was clueless as to how she'd go about making it a reality, and upsetting a good thing with unnecessary changes scared her. Unbidden, Milo's warning following their breakup rang in her ears—without him, without his connections, she was nothing. Not having an "in" at the village offices was a whole other reason why trying anything new with the café was a nonstarter. Julia couldn't risk it.

After giving her café one last glance, Julia turned her attention to the left, shoving the lingering fragments of the dream—the niggle of *what-if?*—aside.

The park was already hopping. The first weekend in July was the start of the busiest time of the year at the ballfield. She pulled into a parking spot that wasn't in foul ball territory and stepped out of her truck, taking in the array of manicured fields.

"Come on, Mr. Waffles."

The dog jumped out of the bed of her truck and took off.

"Heal, Mr. Waffles." Julia locked her vehicle and hurried after him. When she caught up to her dog, she clipped on his leash. "What did I say about running off?"

The image of Samson's cocky grin invaded her mind, trying to take up permanent residence, but Julia dismissed it. She'd gotten good at doing so this week. Samson popped into her head more than she'd like to admit, but she didn't spend unnecessary time dwelling on him—or on the ripples of his ab muscles, which she felt in all their glorious detail through his shirt last Saturday. Nope. She did *not* dwell on that. In fact, she gave herself a mental pat on the back right then and there because she'd succeeded in her efforts to avoid him—at least physically—for a whole week.

Julia walked Mr. Waffles to the small shed that served as the field's concession stand.

Two teams were warming up. One took the field, and the other utilized the open grassy space beyond it.

"Hi, Mr. Douglas," Julia shouted a greeting to the seasoned umpire. He wasn't from Mapleton, but he frequented her coffee shop after tournaments or between games.

"Ah. Good morning, Julia. Beautiful day!"

"It sure is."

Mr. Waffles tugged at his leash, trying to chase a butterfly that flew past.

A laugh gurgled up in Julia's chest at her dog's antics. She couldn't blame Mr. Waffles for wanting to seize the day.

There was nothing like a summer weekend at the ballfield. The energy of the teams and their fans was contagious. Parents were filling in the bleachers, and Julia's smile grew as the woman with the four coffees joined a group assembled behind one of the dugouts. The woman handed out the drinks, and they all bumped their cups together before taking a satisfying first sip.

Julia looped Mr. Waffles' leash around the metal pole at the corner of the concessions building. "Be a good boy." She ruffled the fur behind his ears and gave him an affectionate scratch.

In return, Mr. Waffles laid down in the shade and promptly fell asleep. What a life.

Retrieving the key from her purse, Julia unlocked the door, walked in, and got to work. She pulled boxes of candy from the hodge-podge of storage cabinets tacked to the back wall of the stand and set them up for display on the metal counter and on the shelf behind her. Skittles, licorice ropes, Blow-pops, sunflower seeds—the Sunrise Park concession stand stocked it all. Julia got her first batch of popcorn popping before opening up the metal garage door that covered the window. She was open for business. Craning her neck to see the field, she scanned the bleachers, which were now full.

"Julia, good. You're here."

Julia glanced to her right to see Marge Wilson. A stout woman with gray hair curled to within an inch of its life and a no-nonsense attitude, Marge ran the town from her position as volunteer coordinator of the baseball fields, the chairwoman of the Fourth of July Festival, a school board member, and gossip queen.

"I sure am." Julia saluted the woman, which got a tight smile out of the busy-body standing in front of her.

"I'm glad to see you. Don't forget to push these 50/50 raffle tickets." Marge shook the plastic container Julia had placed on the edge of the counter.

She fought an eye roll at Marge's reminder. This was not Julia's first rodeo; she knew the raffle tickets were a crucial fundraiser for the village festival. People never thought twice about throwing a couple of bucks in for a raffle. The village netted half the profit to roll into next year's festival, and the winner took home a chunk of change, too. Since you had to be present to win, pre-selling tickets was both a way to up sales and to encourage people to show up at the festival itself.

"We've got to keep attendance for the festival up if we want it to remain the premiere Fourth of July event for not only Mapleton residents but for those from the surrounding towns."

Julia pasted on a smile and shot her a thumbs-up. "You got it, Marge. I'll do my best to sell these tickets. You know you can count on me."

Marge nodded once. "By the way, I heard you and Milo broke up last week." Marge stared down at the ever-present clipboard in her hand as if her causal mention of Julia's personal life was completely natural.

Julia suppressed a sigh. "Who told you that?"

"I ran into Sally, and she overheard the two of you last week and said Milo had stormed out."

"Milo did not storm out!"

A few folks stared in Julia and Marge's direction.

Julia lowered her voice, the sudden sweat of her hands leaving streak marks on the cool metal counter as she dragged her arms up and crossed them over her chest. "Marge, there was no storming."

Marge didn't appear convinced. "I'm merely telling you what Sally told me. What matters is that you're here. I haven't seen you since the breakup and didn't know how torn up you'd be. I've got to get going now and check in at the other fields. I'll circle back as the morning goes on. Holler if you need anything." She pointed to the walkie-talkie clipped to her belt.

"Will do." Julia let out a heavy breath as Marge marched off.

Trying to control the narrative of her breakup was pointless. There were at least five versions bouncing around town, and one of them must've included the exaggeration that Julia was heartbroken.

She was spared dwelling on the public's perception of her romantic life when a little girl came up with two quarters and asked for help figuring out what to buy.

Julia rested her elbows on the counter, leaning down so she was at the girl's level, and began pointing out treats.

·♥·♥·♥·♥·♥·

Two hours later, Julia was popping her ninth batch of popcorn. She would reek of oil and butter for the rest of the day, but it would be worth it. She sold fifty dollars' worth of raffle tickets to a family from the neighboring town of Turner. They assured her they would be back to check out the festival.

Julia hummed to herself as she scooped popcorn into bags so it'd be ready for the hungry crowd. She heard the crack of a bat, and cheers went up from the stands. She turned to see if Mapleton was up to bat when Samson strolled around the corner. He did a double take, and his eyebrows shot up before he schooled his features and sauntered in her direction.

Julia groaned. And here she'd been so smug about how well she'd avoided him.

"Hey, neighbor!" He pinged her with the smirk she detested before his gaze settled on her dog. "Is that Mr. Waffles, himself?"

"Yes," Julia bit out. She turned to the popcorn maker, silently cursing every single drop of blood in her body for pulsing with so much intensity that she could barely hear herself think. Why was he here? And why did he make her so uncomfortable? "If I didn't know better, I'd think you were following me," Julia quipped.

"Following you would entail knowing where you were going to be. I had no idea you were going to be here. But what a pleasant surprise."

She turned to look over her shoulder and snorted in response, disregarding the way his green eyes glinted in the morning sun like blades of perfectly cut grass. "Pleasant is the word you'd use? Interesting."

"Woah. Now I feel like you don't like me." He gestured to the popcorn. "I'll take some of that."

Julia made a face, sneering at him. "Why wouldn't I like you?" She stuck her hand into the machine to pull out the last bag in the row she'd formed.

"Ouch!" She hissed and stepped back, dropping the bag of popcorn and scattering kernels across the floor. A mark started to form where she'd caught her arm on the scalding pot.

"Are you okay?" The tone of Samson's voice changed from playful to serious.

She met his gaze, and the concern darkening his eyes to emeralds made him even more handsome. Julia's heart skipped up her esophagus and took a seat in the back of her throat—an obnoxious position for it to be in, to say the least.

Oh no.

Kindness from Samson was not what she needed. She was perfectly content keeping him at a distance as the big-wig contractor and lousy—albeit annoyingly attractive—guy he was. There was no room in her head for him to have a heart. She blinked the thought away.

"I'll be fine." She fumbled for an icy pop from the freezer and held it on her forearm. "See, no big deal." She awkwardly collected a new bag of popcorn while still holding the red-colored frozen treat to her burn and scooted it over to him.

"Thanks." He tossed a dollar down on the counter.

She used her elbow to open up the cash register and deposited the bill with her free hand, hoping by the time she finished he would be gone. But Samson propped his shoulder up against the wall of the concession stand and started eating his popcorn.

"So, is this how you spend all your spare time? That is, when you're not chasing your runaway dog and getting tangled up with strangers."

"No." The heat of embarrassment rushed up her neck. She wished she could come up with a snarky retort, but she drew a blank.

Marge bustled around the corner, saving her from herself. Julia couldn't remember a time when she had been so happy to see her.

"How's it going, Julia?"

Samson moved aside to allow the two women to speak.

"It's going well, Marge. Lots of people here this morning," Julia assured her, discreetly ditching the cherry ice pop she was using to soothe her burn and kicking some of the spilled popcorn out of sight.

"Yes, yes. We're hoping for a record turnout. And the 50/50 raffle? Have you sold many tickets?"

"We're making progress." To prove it, Julia pointed to the nearly full canister holding the tickets she was collecting.

Marge barely acknowledged her efforts. Her gaze roamed about the field and through the bleachers, taking in every detail and what everyone was doing until it stopped on Samson.

"You. You're new. What brings you to the ballfield this morning?"

Samson stepped forward again as Marge drew him into the conversation. "You're right. Funny, everyone seems to be able to spot the new guy around here." Samson's eyes twinkled as he glanced at Julia. The smile and hint of mischief in his delivery made Julia's stomach flip all the way upside down.

She really needed to talk to her internal organs about staying in line.

"It's only my second weekend in town," Samson continued. "I thought I'd check out the park. It seemed like it was the place to be."

Marge beamed. "That it is! And now you've met Julia, I see."

Samson winked at her, but Julia ignored him, pretending to busy herself with restocking the shelves.

"I'm sure she's told you all about the 50/50 raffle and the village festival?" Marge asked.

"Actually, no, she hasn't."

Julia shot her head up, and if Samson would have been standing in front of a wall, she liked to think she would have pinned him to it with a murderous glare.

Marge turned and gave her an exasperated look. "Well, that will not do. Let me tell you about it then. I'm sure you'll want to join us this year. We throw the biggest party in a fifty-mile radius on the Fourth of July. We have games, food, live music, and a moonlight dance. And fireworks, of course!" Marge was in her element, schmoozing a potential patron.

"Sounds great."

"It is! And if you're going to be joining us, then you should definitely purchase some 50/50 raffle tickets. It's cheap to enter, and the pot is growing, as you can see." She motioned to the pile of tickets in Julia's container. "Here, Julia, sell this young man some tickets. I'm getting a call from the lower diamond. Someone got hit by a foul ball, and they need ice!" Marge hurried away with her walkie-talkie in hand.

"Wow. She's...something. Maybe you should suggest she take some popsicles down there." Samson kept a straight face.

Julia pursed her lips. "Very funny. I'm sure Marge has ice packs at the ready for just such an emergency. So, do you want to buy raffle tickets or not? No pressure."

"Sure, I figure I'll be here. How much?"

"Tickets are one dollar each. Or you can get six tickets for $5 or twelve for $10."

"I'll take $10 worth."

Julia counted out the tickets and ripped them in half. She put twelve into the pot and gave the matching stubs to Samson. "There you go. Good luck. Remember, you have to be present to win."

Samson nodded before grinning at her. "Careful. If I didn't know better, I'd think you wanted me there."

Julia stuck her nose into the air, summoning up her most indifferent expression. "Keep dreaming. But I can promise you the festival is a good time."

"I'll have to hold you to that promise."

Their gazes locked. Samson's eyes seemed less conniving and more cautiously optimistic—like he actually wanted to spend time with her.

The skin along her neck tingled, but a young mom and her kids approached the concession stand before Julia could string two thoughts together and respond to Samson.

"Hi, Colleen. Juney, what can I get you?" Julia leaned down to talk to Colleen's youngest daughter. Samson backed away, but she felt his gaze on her as she sold Skittles, licorice ropes, and another twelve raffle tickets. Julia put the money into the cash register and used her knuckles to swipe a stray hair out of her eyes.

Samson ambled up to the booth.

"Don't you want to watch any of the game?" Julia was growing desperate to get rid of him. What he did to her insides was...confusing.

"Nah. I can see fine from here. Besides, I know no one. And the bleachers are pretty full."

"Whatever." She couldn't argue with that.

A crack of the bat drew their attention to the field. Julia peered around the corner of the concession stand to catch the action. The third-base coach was waving a runner home, arm flying around in a windmill motion. The player from Mapleton tore around third base as the outfielder launched the ball to the catcher. The runner slid face-first, and Mr. Douglas, who had his face mask off, stood at the ready to make the call.

"Safe!"

Cheers erupted from the home-team side of the stands, and the visiting fans groaned and heckled the umpire.

"Wow. It gets intense down here. These guys are really good." Samson eyed the Mapleton dugout where players were still hooting and hollering as the fans retook their seats.

"These are the AAA high school teams. Their overall records matter, too. So not only are they trying to win this tournament, but they're trying to win as many games as possible throughout the summer to qualify for the state championship tournament in August."

Samson kept his attention on the field, and Julia took the chance to study him. He was tall. She guessed he stood around 6'2". He wore his thick mop of goldenrod hair a little longer, and it poked out from underneath a baseball cap. His square jaw was lined with a day's worth of scruff. He looked relaxed in shorts and a worn gray t-shirt. She'd kill to be as comfortable in her skin as Samson was in his.

Samson glanced in her direction and smirked.

Her heart raced, and she wanted to say something witty, but once again, nothing came to mind.

"So, if you aren't doing this in your spare time, or hanging with Mr. Waffles"—he nodded at her dog, who was currently chasing his tail—"what are you doing?"

"Mostly working," she said. Julia groaned as her dog toppled over in a heap of fur. Mr. Waffles was so embarrassing when he wanted to be.

"Is the coffee shop your only gig?"

"Yes." Julia stood up straighter. Was he trying to demean her business?

He held up his hands like a shield. "Easy! I didn't mean anything by that. I just didn't know if you worked there full time."

"I own the shop." Julia barely recognized her snooty tone. She downplayed the café to most people. Why did she feel like she had to prove herself to Samson? It shouldn't matter what he thought, but a surge of satisfaction hit her when his eyes widened.

"I had no idea. Good for you. So that's what you were doing when you lived with your parents? Getting the café off the ground. Clever name, by the way." He tilted his chin toward the ball diamond.

"Thank you. And yes, I had to build the shop from nothing. Well, not the actual building. The village owns that. But the idea for a café was all mine. I saw a need and filled it. We're in our fifth year now, and so far, so good."

"That's impressive."

Julia didn't detect any condescension in his voice. That surprised her, but not enough to stop her from feeling defensive. She threw back her shoulders and summoned as much doggedness as she could muster. "I'm no big-shot property developer, but I've done pretty well on my own." She stared him straight in the eye.

Samson's mouth dropped open.

Julia held her head a little higher, knowing she'd been the one to leave him speechless for once. She refused to break eye contact.

Finally, Samson blinked and turned to face the field.

The game must've ended because a flood of people rushed the concession stand. Julia was swept up in taking orders and handing out snacks. Samson ducked away from the booth without a goodbye.

Good. Amanda told her she needed to be more assertive when it came to her business, and this was a start. She'd defended it against Samson.

So why did she feel a little guilty—a little empty—when he was gone?

Chapter 7

Samson

THE AFTERNOON SUN BEAT down on Samson's back as he walked future lot lines on the mill property. It was a Monday that felt like a Friday since the Fourth of July was tomorrow. His first crew would arrive after the holiday. Samson was anxious to get down to actual business, but he was distracted. His mind kept wandering to a passionate barista with blonde hair who hadn't batted a cerulean blue eye when she put him in his place a couple days ago.

Initially, he'd chalked up his thrill at being around her to a playful flirtation and a fun way to pass some time. The more he talked to Julia, though, the more he *wanted* to talk to her. He wanted to get to know her, beyond finding ways to make her blush. So, when she called him out on his arrogance, it stung, and he'd tucked tail and ran. Now, she was all he could think about, and as much as his head told him to leave her alone, he was going to seek her out and try to win her over. He couldn't help himself.

Focusing on the task at hand, Samson scanned the property. A rundown gazebo stood off to one side. Samson made a mental note to see about getting it removed. He turned north toward the river. The lots along the water were the showpiece of this development. He needed to call his boss and make sure the architect drafted plans for two story homes. He was picturing dual-level decks facing the river.

He checked his watch. It was nearing four in the afternoon, but if he hurried, he could check in with the village to see if there were any restrictions on riverfront property. Afterward, he should still have enough time to get in touch with his boss before he left for the day. That was the beauty of a two-minute drive through town. It didn't take long to get anything done.

Samson trekked to his truck then drove to the administrative offices, thankful for something productive to do. He needed to reel in his thoughts about Julia before they flew any farther out of line.

"Hello there, Samson."

"Melly." Samson smiled as he approached her desk. "Nice to see you."

The receptionist tucked a corner of her hair behind her ear and returned his smile. "What can we do for you?"

"I was hoping to speak to the building inspector. Is he in?"

"No, sorry. He works part-time and by appointment only since he officially retired this spring. But I can get a message to him. Although, he's at his cottage with the family, so you might not hear back until after the Fourth."

Milo strolled out from the hallway that led to his office. "Oh, hi, Samson. Good to see you. Melly, can you take care of this for me?" He handed her a file before turning his full attention to Samson. "Anything I can help you with?"

"No. I was hoping to see the building inspector. But I guess he's not here."

"Come on back. Let me see if there's something I can do."

"Thanks. Maybe you can help me find some paperwork." Samson crossed toward Milo.

Melly's phone rang, and she spoke into the receiver before covering it with her hand and swiveling in her chair to face Milo. "It's Neil Schaumburg. Do you want me to send it to voicemail?"

"Nah, I'll take it. You don't mind, do you, Samson? Send the call to my office, Melly." He strode down the hallway, and Samson followed behind him. "I'll only be a minute. Take a seat here." Milo motioned to the same chair Samson sat in the last time he came in. Samson scanned the photos on the windowsill and wasn't surprised to find the one with Julia removed.

"Neil, you son of a gun," Milo said into his phone. "What's going on? Mmhmm. Mmhmm. Right, well, yes. The festival is slated to be bigger and better than ever this year. Yep. It sure is. Mmhmm. Well, I'm sure you do. But you let them know Mapleton has big plans for the coming years. Yes, that's right. I've put together a solid five-year plan, and we'll be growing and developing in ways no one saw coming. You can count on that. Alright. Yep. See you there, Neil. Okay. Buh-bye." Milo hung up the phone.

"Sorry about that, Samson. That's the Village President. He had lunch with a couple of guys from Turner who were running their mouths about Mapleton being landlocked and stalled, and Neil got his undies all in a bundle. I had to reassure him things will be quite alright here if I have anything to say about it."

Samson rearranged his expression to try to appear interested in Milo's peacocking. "I see. Well, I won't take up too much of your time, Milo. I was hoping you had a copy of your residential construction packet. I wanted to double check the sewer fee and the park fee. I've got some ideas for the riverfront property I'm going to run by my boss, but I want to have all the information in front of me before I do."

"I like the sound of that. New ideas are good." Milo's eyes took on a greedy gleam. He turned around and started rifling through the file cabinet behind his desk. "Here it is." He held up a collection of papers. "This should have all the information in it that you'll need for now. Melly will make sure Derek, our building inspector, calls you. Heck, you might even see him at the festival. You'll be there tomorrow?"

"I plan to check it out."

"Good, good. The town pulls it all together quite nicely. I'm thinking it's only going to grow in scale if my plans pan out as I think they will."

Samson's ears perked up as he skimmed the documents in front of him. "What sort of plans?"

"Well, I've been thinking for a while that the land around the baseball diamonds is prime real estate. You know the village owns nearly all of it?"

This got Samson's full attention. Any mention of "prime real estate" did that. But was Milo talking about the land Julia's café was on? She did tell him it was village-owned. "Is that right?"

"Yes, indeed. I can see lots of opportunities if we develop it. A small-scale hotel, a nice restaurant, that sort of thing. Lord knows we draw a lot of people in for baseball games and river recreation. Why not capitalize on that and give the people an even greater experience when they come to Mapleton? Keep them coming back for more. Anyway, it's still in the drawing-board phase, but exciting things are coming!"

"Sounds like it." Samson's voice sounded hollow in his ears as he tried and failed to match Milo's enthusiasm.

He stood, thanked the Village Administrator for his help with the packet, and said goodbye.

"See you at the festival, if not before," Milo called after him as he walked back toward Melly's desk.

She wasn't sitting behind her computer, and Samson was thankful he didn't have to make small talk. His head spun, and his stomach felt queasy as he digested what Milo shared with him.

He should be rushing to call his boss and tip him off to the prospect of Milo's plans. Any inkling of new development was a windfall for the company. But the idea of developing the land around the baseball diamonds didn't sit well. If Milo's ideas were as substantial as he described, there would be no room left for Julia's small, hometown café.

Something about that felt off. In the short time he'd been in Mapleton, he understood these people liked their traditions, and they were fiercely loyal to their own. Did Milo not see that? Or did he not care?

Samson shifted his jaw back and forth. That shouldn't be his concern. He had an obligation to share this lead with his boss. His confusing feelings for Julia aside, if there was an investment opportunity, Samson needed to pounce. He climbed into his truck and stayed parked as he hit his company's phone number and waited for the receptionist to answer.

"Hey, Victoria. It's Samson."

"Samson! Hi! How's life in Small Town, USA?" the perky secretary for Gabler, Burns, and Associates spoke with a teasing lilt.

Samson dragged his free hand through his hard-hat-mussed hair. "It's...interesting, that's for sure. Is Jerry in the office?"

"I think you called just in time. I'll get him on the line for you."

"Thanks, Victoria."

"Sure thing!"

Samson waited for a minute before his boss picked up the phone.

"Samson, what's the good word?"

Samson cleared his throat and gave Jerry a rundown of the status at the mill site. "We're in good shape. The electrical lines are marked, and we're ready to start digging the foundation on the multi-use facility as soon as our crew arrives."

"Excellent. Excellent. Right on schedule." Samson pictured Jerry leaning back in his chair, the epitome of corporate power and control.

"Listen, I have an idea for how to take some of these houses to the next level." Samson explained the riverfront properties and the added value the bigger houses and extended waterfront living space would provide. They'd have to shell out more money up front, but the payoff would be worth it.

"I like the way your brain works, Samson," Jerry said. "I'll get in touch with the architect ASAP. Although, this silly holiday is going to cramp our schedule a little bit. I doubt I'll hear from him today, and everyone is out of the office tomorrow for the Fourth. Let's hope he's not planning to take the rest of the week off. I'll let you know what I hear. And do me a favor? You keep your nose to the ground around town. Whatever you learn about interested buyers for our homes or potential tenants for the commercial space, I want to hear about it."

Samson squirmed in his seat. "I'll do that, sir. As a matter of fact, I just spoke with Milo Moore, the administrator here. Have you met him?"

"Not in person. We've communicated a bit via email. Why do you ask?"

"I was curious. He loves what we're doing, and he's very eager to see progress in his town. I was in his office, getting the details about the residential construction contracts we need, and he was going on and on about future developments in Mapleton. He's all about breathing new life into the village as a whole."

"Interesting." For a moment, his boss was quiet on the other end of the line. "Well, now that you have our foot in the door, maybe I should reach out and introduce myself. We might even be able to grow our partnership through future endeavors. Good work. Be in touch."

The phone clicked as Jerry ended the call.

Samson sat in the driver's seat and waited for the familiar surge of excitement at a new prospect to show itself.

It didn't come.

In its place, something gnawed at him. And that something was the opinion of the woman with eyes the color of the Atlantic Ocean and a dog named Mr. Waffles, of all things.

Samson scrubbed both hands over his face, trying to clear his head as he reasoned with himself. Milo gave him an opening. He walked through it, doing what any proper businessman would do. That was all. And he hadn't even said that much to Jerry.

Samson never let personal feelings get in the way of doing his job—and he wasn't going to start now. Milo and the village were going to do with the property what they wanted, and if Gabler, Burns, and Associates benefited from being tipped off, that was a good thing. If Julia's business was caught in the crossfire, he didn't have to like it. But it was the reality of the business world.

Then again, if this was "just business", why did he feel so unsettled?

He thought about what Julia told him—how she saw a need in her community and filled it with a quality service. He had to hand it to her. It wasn't easy to start a small business and be successful in a market this size, and yet she'd done just that. He appreciated that sort of tenacity.

But now, if Milo moved on his plans to develop and Gabler, Burns, and Associates closed the deal, he and Julia would be set up to go head-to-head, one against the other. The reality of that predicament crashed into him with the precision force of a bat connecting with a baseball. Julia wouldn't back down from a fight, and he wasn't sure he would win.

For the first time, he didn't know if he wanted to.

Chapter 8

JULIA

JULIA'S EYES CROSSED. SHE'D been up since before dawn, and it was now almost ten-thirty at night. She was at the café, working on last-minute preparations for the Fourth of July Festival with Marge and several other members of the festival committee—her mom included. What should have been mindless, manual labor had turned into an aggressive interrogation about her personal life.

To her right, Amanda stood in the corner, shoulders shaking, as she listened to Julia's mom pepper her with questions.

"I just don't understand what happened." Her mom, Gloria, tossed up her hands dramatically.

Julia turned her back to her mom and mouthed, "S.O.S.," to Amanda. The least her best friend could do was run some interference.

Amanda just shook her head, grinning.

Julia looked to the heavens, pleading for patience, before facing her mom again. She dropped her voice in an attempt to draw less attention. "Mom, we've been over this. I don't know what else to say. Like I told you on the phone last week, Milo wasn't the guy for me, so I broke it off. I'm doing fine. I'm sure he's doing fine. I'd hope you would be, too. I didn't think you even liked him all that much. Can we please focus on these baskets? I want to finish them up so I can get some sleep."

Julia stared down the particular beast of a wicker basket in front of her. The women were putting the finishing touches on the silent auction baskets that would be up for bid at the festival. Julia was always amazed at the community's generosity. Different businesses put together baskets that included gift cards and other themed items. It was remarkable what the town and surrounding communities pulled off. The baskets raised a ton of money for the festival and the charities it supported.

But charitable work or not, right now, all Julia wanted to do was get this pesky piece of plastic wrap to lay properly so she could tie it off with twine. She twisted it this way and that until, finally, her mom let loose an exasperated sigh and moved to help her.

"Here." Julia's mom bumped her hip, scooting Julia out of the way. "Let me do it."

In a few minutes, she had the plastic crinkled perfectly and a beautiful bow of twine tied. "Another one down." She brushed her hands together, looking pleased with her handiwork. "And dear, you know I liked Milo well enough. That is, except when he took his phone out at the dinner table. I swear, if he would have done that one more time, I'd have broken up with him for you. Anyway, I'm just trying to learn the details firsthand. I've gotten information from Sally and Linda, but you've been so busy I haven't spoken to you in person since the breakup. I'd think you would appreciate me coming to the source."

"I do, Mom. Really. But it's over and done with now."

And thank goodness for that. Fortunately, the buzz surrounding her failed relationship was finally quieting down. Julia was still on edge, though. She blamed a lack of sleep. She'd pulled a double shift, standing in for Seth who would cover the café on the Fourth of July so she could be on the festival grounds.

"Golly." Her mom moved to work on another basket. "It's been an exciting couple of weeks around here, hasn't it?" The rhetorical question was directed at no one in particular. "It's all I can do to keep track of my daughter, what with the festival and this new development happening at the mill. This is a busy time for our town!"

Julia thrust her chin down and out, narrowing her eyes at her mom. "You act like the new development on the mill property is a good thing."

"Who says it isn't?" Her mom turned to study Julia, her doe eyes blinking.

Julia pressed her palm to her forehead, shaking her head. "I can't believe you'd say that! After what losing the mill did to dad and to half the town?" Julia shifted her gaze, eyeing the rest of the folks in the café. The last thing she wanted to do was air the family's affairs in front of the particularly nosy festival committee members, but everyone knew the mill closing was a sore subject. She assumed most people agreed with her—her mom, most of all.

"Oh pish-posh. Sure, the mill closing was tough on us. Toughest on your father, indeed. But he landed on his feet. We all did."

"Still, I can't believe you think the new development is a good thing."

"Well, honestly, dear. What did you think was going to happen? Did you expect the town to leave the old building there for all of eternity? At least the village got some money when the land sold. And when they knocked down the old structure, I figured development was right around the corner. And now it's arrived. Come on. Even I knew that was the logical course of events. I think most everyone saw the writing on the wall. Now, Marge." Her mom turned and motioned for the committee head to join them, effectively cutting off an open-mouthed Julia.

Marge was at their sides in a second, her white, arch-support shoes skidding on the café's worn wooden plank floor. "What's up?"

"You said you ran into the person heading up the mill development. Tell me about him. Does he seem like a decent man?" Julia's mom leaned in, waiting for Marge to spill the proverbial tea.

Julia snapped her mouth shut and practically sprinted away from Marge and her mother. The last thing she needed was for someone else to give an opinion of Samson.

All day, she was jumpy, half expecting him to walk through the café doors. She wasn't sure if she was dreading it or looking forward to it, but she needn't have let it consume her. He never came.

Julia chewed her cheek as she hurried toward Amanda who was positioning items in one of the remaining baskets.

"Breathe," her friend ordered.

On command, Julia let the air rush from between her lips, and she slumped against the table. "I love my mom, but I think she's trying to kill me."

Amanda snorted. "Quit being dramatic. Gloria is the bomb. And she milked you for every bit of information you were reluctant to give to me and the rest of the town. So, I really should be thanking her."

Julia scrunched her nose and whimpered. "And now she's got me thinking about Samson again."

Amanda cut Julia a side-eyed look. "When's the last time you thought about him?"

Julia groaned internally. She'd walked right into that one. She tugged her top lip into her mouth, holding it between her teeth. She didn't answer Amanda's question, unsure whether or not she was ready to disclose her interactions with Samson to anyone—not Amanda, not her mom, and certainly not the town.

She'd replayed their conversation all weekend, and she hadn't been able to get the picture of his sandy-blond hair and dancing eyes out of her head. She was surprised by her own self confidence when she finally addressed him about her business, but she kicked herself for ending the conversation like she did.

They may not have agreed about the mill, but she should have been civil. And although she hated to admit it, what stuck with her the most was the instant concern he displayed when she'd stupidly burnt herself on the popcorn maker.

"Out with it, Julia." Amanda stopped messing with the basket and leaned against the table, staring Julia down. "Or I'll get your mother over here to pry it out of you."

"I don't know what you're talking about."

"Don't give me that. You are a terrible liar. What's going on?"

Trying to keep secrets from Amanda was pointless. When you'd known someone since grade school, it was impossible to hide anything from them. "Nothing's up. I just spent some time with Samson on Saturday. Completely unintentionally."

Amanda's eyebrows shot through the roof. "What? When?"

"He came by the ballfield while I was working concessions. It wasn't like I could walk away from him, or believe me, I would have. But he stood there and talked to me for over an hour."

"Oh, wow. I can't believe your cold shoulder didn't scare him off. That's actually sort of impressive."

"Hey. I do not have a cold shoulder!" Even as she said it, her mind instantly jumped back to how rude she had been on Saturday, and a hot flush of embarrassment trickled over her, like boiling water over coffee grounds.

"Oh, you *for sure* do. You blew him off the first time he came into the café. It was something to behold. And he hasn't been back. I thought he'd been completely shut down, but now I think he's coming at it from a different direction."

Julia gaped at her friend before slamming her mouth shut and taking a covert look around to make sure her mom and the other women were occupied. What was Amanda getting at?

"Coming at what?" she hissed. "There is nothing to come at!"

"Whatever you say, boss." Amanda shrugged, as if she was just going to leave the conversation hanging there.

Julia cocked her head. "Oh, no you don't. You can't just say something like that without an explanation. And don't call me boss. You know I hate that."

Amanda laughed, placing her hands on Julia's shoulders and squeezing. "I know. I only do it to bug you. And all I'm saying is, when Samson first walked into the café, his eyes lit up when he saw you. There was definite interest there. I didn't think anything of it because you were with Milo. But now..." Amanda dropped her arms and trailed off.

Julia opened her mouth to interject and tell her she was being absurd, but Amanda shook her head to stop her. "And you can't tell me you didn't notice how good-looking he is. Admit it. Up until he told you why he was in town, you were intrigued by him, too. Still, I figured your flat-out denial of his advances would stop him from getting to know you at all, but maybe I underestimated him. I need to reevaluate."

"There is absolutely nothing to reevaluate. You don't honestly think he's interested in me? Or I'm interested in him?"

"Too early to say." Amanda tapped her chin but shot Julia a sly look that said that was exactly what she thought.

"You are the worst." Julia couched her words in a chuckle so Amanda would know she was kidding. She really doubted Samson was interested in her—especially after the way she treated him. But to Amanda's credit, she'd read Julia like a book.

Julia looked on as Amanda tried to put together the basket. Her friend—God bless her—was a whiz when it came to making coffee, handling finances, and getting the scoop on the latest village gossip, but she had ten thumbs when it came to doing anything crafty.

"Here, let me help you with that, or we'll be here all night." Julia started pulling items out of Amanda's basket and helping her reorganize it so everything was displayed.

They worked side by side in silence, but Julia's thoughts boomeranged to Samson.

What would Amanda say if she knew about her interaction with him the night of her breakup with Milo? Or about running into him with Mr. Waffles? No use telling her friend now. That would only add to her speculation. And there wasn't anything to speculate about. She was newly single. Not interested in a man. And she couldn't possibly be interested in Samson. He was destroying the mill grounds. She disliked him on principle. She was frustrated with herself for getting so bent out of shape over him.

With a flourish, she tied off the twine to the basket.

"Done!" She spun the basket around to check it from all angles and held up her hand for a high five. Amanda slapped it.

"Time for bed. I've got to be up in"—Julia read the clock —"five hours."

Marge clapped her hands from across the café. "Okay, ladies. Things are looking good. Let's call it a night. I'll be handing out your assignment sheets as you leave this evening. Please report to your designated positions at least ten minutes early. We don't want to have any issues. After all, this has to be our biggest and best festival yet."

There was a general murmur of assent from the tired team of women as Marge continued to dole out bits of instruction as they all rose to head out.

Amanda rolled her eyes in Marge's direction before she shoved her curly hair behind her ear. "I'll fetch our to-do lists."

"Thanks." Julia turned and walked behind the counter of the coffee bar. She straightened the bean grinder and bent to check the under-the-counter refrigerator to be sure they had enough milk and ice stocked.

Yes, she was bone-tired, and yes, she'd be at the festival grounds in less than six hours to help with set-up, but Julia wanted to do a final check to make sure everything was in order at the café. The business would be in the capable hands of Seth and Amanda while she fulfilled her festival obligation, but this was her happy place, and tinkering behind the counter settled her racing mind.

Satisfied everything was as it should be, she leaned against the bar as Amanda and her mom approached.

"Here you go." Amanda handed her the assignment sheet Marge put together.

Julia stood upright and snatched the paper. "Ugh! I can't believe I got assigned to the dunk tank this year. Who makes these decisions? There is no way I am enough of a community figurehead for people to pay money to try to dunk me!"

"Cheer up, dear." Her mother tipped her head to the side. "Either way, it's a win for you. If no one pays to try to dunk you, then you stay dry. If people do pay, then you bring in money for the village."

"So, I'll either have my lack of popularity on full display, or I'll end up dunked and looking like a wet rat for the rest of the festival. That sounds perfect." Julia spread the sarcasm on thick as she scanned the rest of her assignments. "I have to go straight from the dunk tank to serving food? What did I do to Marge to deserve this schedule?"

Amanda laughed. "Come on. You're so tired you're delusional. Marge doesn't have it in for you."

"I agree, Julia." Her mom wrapped an arm around her waist as she came out from behind the counter. "Get home and get some sleep. You'll feel better in the morning."

The trio walked out into the dark, and Julia locked the doors behind them. Stars were splattered like white paint across the canvas of the night sky, and maple leaves rustled a familiar melody in the warm summer breeze.

Calmness washed over Julia. Maybe it was exhaustion. Either way, she loved this place, and though she didn't feel like it right now, she loved the festival and would do anything in her power to make it a success—even if it meant dealing with Marge.

She gave her mom a hug, and waited as she climbed into her Buick and drove off before walking with Amanda the rest of the way to their parked cars on the far side of the building.

"I'll see you tomorrow afternoon." Julia yawned.

"I'll think of you in the morning while I'm serving and sipping coffee as you're taking your orders from Marge." Amanda slid her key into the lock on her old Toyota Camry.

"Remind me again why I like you?" Julia said playfully. "Especially since I fear I might be losing out on my Jules-and-Manda time thanks to someone by the name of Seth."

Amanda whirled around and narrowed her eyes at Julia.

"You're not the only observant one in this friendship." Julia smirked and gave her friend a pointed look. "Don't think I haven't noticed your willingness to pick up shifts with him. You didn't complain once about having to work the morning of the festival as soon as you found out he was working, too. And you two certainly didn't mind shopping together for new ceramics for the café."

Amanda's sheepish expression gave her away, and Julia grinned. Two could play at this game.

"Night, best friend," Julia sung.

Amanda stuck out her tongue and laughed as she opened her car door. "Night, Jules."

Chapter 9

SAMSON

COFFEE MUG IN HAND, Samson surveyed his modest backyard on the morning of the Fourth of July. It was a gorgeous day: warm, but not unbearably so, and not a cloud to be seen. He had only been in town about a week and a half, but he knew the Mapleton Festival meant a ton to the village. This sort of weather meant an increase in the number of people attending. No one would sit through fireworks in the rain.

Samson shielded his face from the sun and gazed at the powder-blue sky. A corner of his mouth turned up. He didn't know why he cared, but he felt weirdly happy for Mapleton and the people who worked so hard to pull off the festival. It should be a good day for everyone.

He took a swig of his home-brewed coffee and frowned before downing the rest with a grimace. It didn't come close to the quality of the cup he'd had from On Deck Café, but after a restless night, he needed the caffeine. His dreams were filled with weird visions of Julia, the café, bulldozers demolishing it, and Milo cackling. All the while, Mr. Waffles was snoring beneath a maple tree, completely unfazed. Samson wasn't sure what to make of it.

His heart and his head were at war. His head told him getting involved with Julia beyond being neighbors wasn't smart. He should keep his distance and not get attached to anything or anyone in Mapleton. That was how he operated in the past, and it worked for him. Besides, this place chewed him up and spit him out in disgust within five minutes of his arrival.

But he couldn't ignore that Julia made him feel...something. Something different than he was used to feeling. She challenged him. She made him smile a real smile, not the kind he put on when there was a job to be done. And he was sure she felt something, too. Whether those were feelings of interest, hatred, or something else entirely, Samson couldn't tell, but he wanted to explore whatever was going on between them. If he could keep business out of it, he might have a shot to clear the air and get acquainted with her. Against his better judgment, he wanted to give it a try.

Samson stashed his empty mug in the sink, got himself ready for the day, and walked out of his rental, locking the front door behind him.

Across the street, Julia's house was dark. He'd hoped to catch a glimpse of her—maybe try to strike up a conversation—but she must have been working at the café or already at the festival.

Samson eyed his truck in the driveway but decided to take advantage of the nice weather and walk the mile and a half to the park.

He fell in stride with the residents crowding the sidewalks. The grassy terrace along Mapleton Avenue was adorned with American flags. The wrought-iron flower baskets hanging from the ornate light poles spilled over with peak-colored blooms. Hal's Diner, which appeared to be the only restaurant in town, had red, white, and blue cloth swags hanging from its windows. The old-school, felt letter board sign out front read *God Bless America. Closed for the Fourth. See you at the festival!*

The July air was thick with more than humidity. The extra energy floating around was palpable. It pressed into Samson, filling him with excitement and added anticipation for the day to come. It was bizarre to feel such a connection to this place and these people, but he couldn't deny it. Mapleton was like a flame and he was a moth, helpless but to get sucked in.

Men, women, and children were dressed in their finest patriotic garb. American flag t-shirts, military veteran baseball caps, and red-and-white-striped overalls were among the festive ensembles. He hadn't thought much about his own outfit, but now Samson was glad he picked a white polo shirt. He would have stood out like a sore thumb if he had chosen to wear green.

"I want to play Plinko!" A couple paces ahead of him, a little girl tugged on her mother's arm. She was dressed in a red, white, and blue handkerchief dress with ribbons tied around curly pigtails. "And the duck game!"

When she glanced over her shoulder at him, Samson offered the child an amused smile, but she turned away from him shyly and continued to pester her mom and dad. He got caught behind an older couple who was shuffling along and lost sight of the family before he could figure out what the duck game was.

Samson looked across the street. Groups of teenagers were walking in the direction of the festival, jumping and skipping around, getting into all sorts of tomfoolery, no doubt. It was a party for all ages, and he was thankful he left his vehicle at home. He'd underestimated the crowds and now realized parking anywhere close to the grounds would have been a nightmare.

As he approached the park entrance, Samson saw Mr. Waffles sitting outside the front door of Julia's café. The dog lapped up the attention of passersby who stopped to give him a pat.

Samson cut across the street to the café. He could really go for some better coffee. Seeing Julia was only part of his motivation for making a pit-stop—a major part, but still.

He reached the door and held it open for a group of chattering teen girls. They were sipping coffee drinks, and when he flashed them his trademark grin, they fell quiet and hurried past him before bursting into giggles.

If only it would be so easy to charm Julia and the rest of the town.

He readied himself for battle and turned to face the café's main counter. As he walked forward, the barista behind the register looked up and did a double take before smiling at him.

"I'll be right with you!"

She wasn't Julia, but Samson recognized the woman from his first visit to the café.

He nodded and stepped to the side, allowing a larger group who had just collected their drinks to exit.

The volume inside the small dining room decreased. A couple of people sipped drinks at the window seats, and a crowd was gathered on the deck, which Samson caught a glimpse of out the rear door.

The curly-haired barista slid behind the register. "Alright, what can I get ya?"

"A cup of your house roast would be great. Thank you."

"No problem." She reached for a to-go cup and poured his coffee. "You ready to see what a Mapleton Fourth of July Festival is like?"

This woman wasn't icing him out. Hope ballooned in his chest. "Ready or not, here I come, I guess."

"It's pretty intense, but it's a lot of fun, too. I'm Amanda, by the way."

"Samson."

"I know."

"That much of an impression, huh?"

"Don't flatter yourself." Amanda turned her back to him to secure the lid on his drink, but she kept talking. "You are pretty memorable, though. You had Julia off her game the first time you came in here. And I've heard you've seen her since."

The door to the deck slammed, and Samson's breath caught as he waited for Julia to appear. A coat of sweat formed on his back, and he swallowed a couple of times. How would she react to seeing him? What could he do to make her smile? To make her like him? Samson's thoughts raced in circles before skidding to a stop when a man with a black apron joined Amanda at the register. This guy *definitely* wasn't Julia. Samson let out a breath. He needed to chill.

Amanda tipped her head in the direction of the new arrival. "Seth, this is Samson, the guy I was telling you about."

The male barista held out his hand. "Oh yeah? Hey, man. It takes a lot to throw Julia off, so you must be something."

"I don't know about that. She must just really love the mill."

"Something like that." Amanda smirked.

Samson stared at her, trying to figure out what she wasn't saying.

Amanda's eyes glinted as she stared back.

He raised his eyebrows in silent question.

She pressed her lips together as if she had a secret and handed him his coffee. "Here you go."

Samson chuckled. "Thanks." He took his first sip and involuntarily sighed. "This is so good."

Amanda grinned. "I'm glad you think so. It's the best around."

"I believe that. Well, I'm sure I'll be seeing you."

He turned to go, but Amanda spoke up. "Maybe we'll run into you at the festival. We close at two this afternoon so we can enjoy the evening concert, fireworks, and dance."

She shot Seth a look at the mention of the dance. He glanced up from wiping the countertop and smiled.

Amanda's face glowed when she turned back to Samson. "We have to run Mr. Waffles home for Julia. Then, it should be a great rest of the day. And hey, Julia's in the dunk tank for another half hour. You know, in case you were wondering."

The bell over the door rang, and a group of patrons hurried in, laughing and talking. Samson looked to Amanda who winked before turning to take the orders of the new customers.

"Thanks for that." He held up his coffee. "And this."

"You got it. See you later."

Samson had gained an ally, and he walked into the park with a smile on his face, his heart pounding out an eager beat at the thought of seeing Julia again.

Chapter 10

Julia

JULIA WAS GOING TO kill Marge.

While she sat perched on a tiny wooden seat suspended over a giant tank of cold water, the older woman stood on the solid ground at the base of the tank, shamelessly recruiting everyone within earshot to come and take a chance at dunking Julia.

Currently, there were a few little kids who were trying. Their parents must have been rich, because they kept handing over ticket after ticket.

Julia survived her first hour without anyone hitting the mark and sinking her, but she had thirty minutes to go, and she was afraid her luck wouldn't last—especially with Marge drafting everyone in sight.

"Marge!" she hollered down. "Maybe you should go check on the food tent. It is lunchtime, after all. The volunteers might need you."

"No need, Julia. I've got it all under control. Kristy checked in on the walkie-talkie, and they're in good shape. Sales are up, too."

"Great. That's just...great," Julia sighed.

She shifted in her seat, and scanned the festival grounds. That was the one benefit of her predicament. The dunk tank was positioned at the highest point of the park, so she had a panoramic view of the festivities. The atmosphere snapped and sizzled with good cheer and shouts of greeting between neighbors and friends.

Music blared through the loudspeakers on either side of the stage. A local band entertained the lunch crowd with old school country hits. Beyond the amphitheater, lush trees swayed in a light breeze, and the blue sky was clear above her. A group of teenagers walked down the main drag, holding coffee cups from her café. Julia glowed with pride.

After panning the grounds once more, she looked to her left and inhaled sharply as Samson sauntered into the park. He looked like he belonged on the streets of Nantucket in a pair of navy-blue boat shorts and a white polo shirt. His baseball cap cast his chiseled features in dangerous shadows. Julia turned away so fast she almost lost her balance.

Why was she afraid to make eye contact with him? Was she embarrassed by her position, propped up above the dunk tank? Yes, but it was more than that. What Amanda said to her last night was eating away at her. She liked the man. Not the man who acted arrogant and was responsible for developing the mill site. No, that was something that hung her up. But she couldn't deny she was attracted to the man who was ready with a kind look when she needed it and who complimented her on her business. Judging from the café cup in his hand, he had good taste in coffee, too.

Julia decided then and there she needed to be nicer to him. After all, if he was going to be in town for a while, then the two could exist as cordial acquaintances...friends, perhaps. Even as she thought it, a strange sort of hope sparked in the depths of her heart—hope that maybe they could be more than friends.

"Not possible," she muttered.

"What's that?"

Julia didn't realize she'd spoken out loud.

"Nothing, Marge."

Samson made his way over and grinned at her as he stopped to talk to Marge. She gave him a weak smile but was spared having to make conversation when another group of youngsters approached the dunk tank to take a shot at her.

After handing Marge the tickets, the first kid launched a ball at the target. Julia closed her eyes, but his pitch thudded into the base of the tank.

One ball down.

Maybe she'd escape another round. From her perilous position, she listened with half an ear to the conversation Marge was having with Samson as the young boys trying to dunk her talked strategy.

"I'm so glad you made it," Marge said. "Isn't this wonderful?"

Julia didn't look down but pictured Marge surveying the park as if she was a queen looking out over her domain.

"It is something. There's so much to do," Samson said.

"We pride ourselves on having something for everyone."

Another ball thudded into the base of the dunk tank.

Two down. One to go.

"Oh look!"

At Marge's directive, Julia peered down to see what had caught the woman's attention. Marge waved her arm furiously, signaling to someone. Julia followed Marge's gaze and spotted Milo striding toward the dunk tank.

Julia gripped the wooden seat with both hands.

The only way this could get any more excruciating was if she got dunked in the presence of both Samson *and* Milo.

"Milo! Great to see you!" Marge's voice trilled.

Samson stepped to the side, looked up, and his eyes found Julia's. She turned toward the dunkers-to-be but not before she saw a splash of emotion streak across Samson's face. Was it empathy?

Huh. Was it possible Samson, a relative stranger, was more in-tune to her potential embarrassment than Marge was?

Before Julia could think too much about it, one of the kids wound up and launched a baseball at her. It sailed wide right. Julia breathed a sigh of relief.

"Better luck next time, kiddos!" She waved goodbye to the boys as they grumbled and trotted off. Hopefully, they wouldn't be back.

Since no one else was in line, Julia turned her attention to Marge, Milo, and Samson.

"Marge." Milo beamed as he bent and kissed the woman on her cheek. "Looks like the day is off to a smashing start. And Samson, good to see you again. What are your first impressions of our festival?"

"Seems like a good time. I haven't had much chance to explore the grounds yet, but—"

"I see you made it to the most exciting area of the festival right away, though, eh?" Milo cut Samson off before he could continue, and Julia frowned from her perch. Why hadn't she taken note of his rudeness when they were dating?

Milo tipped his chin and shot her a conniving smile. "Julia looks too dry, though, doesn't she? That won't do."

Julia rolled her eyes. "I'm fine up here, thanks, Milo."

"No, no. What good is it to have a dunk tank if no one gets dunked?"

"Well, I'm raising a lot of money for a good cause." Julia smiled sweetly, but a pit of dread formed in her stomach. He wasn't going to try to dunk her, was he? That would be a new low, even for Milo.

The problem was Milo had a strong arm. He was the star pitcher on his high school baseball team. It was one of the reasons Mapleton was on his radar when he started searching for a job a few years ago—he had played traveling tournaments at Sunrise Park growing up.

"What do you say? Should I give it a shot, Jules?"

"Yes, yes," Marge answered for her, clapping like a schoolgirl. "We need some excitement around here."

Julia ground her teeth together so hard that, for a second, she was afraid she'd chipped a molar.

"Isn't this a kid's game?" Samson glanced around at the three of them.

It was difficult to tell from where she sat above them, but Julia liked to believe it was a look of support he offered her when his gaze traveled to hers.

"Nonsense. Anyone can take a chance to dunk our community figureheads." Milo dismissed Samson's question as he rolled up the sleeves of his button-down shirt.

Why he wore slacks, a button-up, and a tie to the Fourth of July Festival, Julia would never understand. He once told her he needed to give off the impression of consummate professionalism and civility at all times. Too bad that civility didn't apply to dunking his ex-girlfriend.

She gave Samson what she hoped he took as an appreciative shrug before turning her focus to Milo.

To her dismay, the crowd around the dunk tank grew as festival-goers realized what was going on. Now she'd have an audience for her water adventure.

Maybe Milo would miss. Maybe he'd gotten rusty with age.

He grabbed three baseballs and juggled them effortlessly, putting on a show for the onlookers.

So much for being rusty.

Milo took in the crowd before turning in her direction. What she wouldn't give to wipe the smug expression off his face. Julia wasn't confrontational, but Milo was making her feel like scum.

"At least pay before you toss." Julia motioned to the bucket of tickets at Marge's feet. "This is a village fundraiser, after all." She kept her voice steady even as a wad of apprehension clogged the back of her throat. The last thing she wanted to do was give Milo the impression he had gotten to her.

"Of course." Milo dug into his pocket and got out three tickets. He handed them to Marge before strolling to the line sprayed in the grass.

Someone hollered from the crowd. "Let's see what you've got, Milo!"

"Patience, friends. I've got to make this worth it." He stretched his arms above his head, milking the situation for as much attention as he could.

Julia crossed her right leg over her left and bounced her toe. She was ready to get this over with. She eyed her waterproof smart watch. It would have been too good to be true to escape her hour and a half unscathed.

Below her and off to the side of the crowd, Samson stood with his hands in his pockets as he took in the scene. To his credit, he didn't appear as elated as everyone else who gathered around.

"Alright, Milo. Batter up."

Leave it to Marge to attempt an applicable reference only to miss the mark.

Milo dropped two of the balls, stepped behind the line, and stared down the target. He didn't give her a second look. He wound up and fired his first pitch.

Julia closed her eyes as he released it and prepared to get wet.

Thud.

A scream rang out from the spectators. "Strike one!"

She cracked an eye, and a couple of people groaned while a few started clapping. She wasn't sure if they were cheering Milo on or if they were in her corner.

"Just getting warmed up." Milo plucked the second ball from the ground and studied it for a beat before tossing it back and forth.

"Ready for this, Jules?" Milo finally looked up at her.

Julia raised her empty hands to demonstrate she was utterly helpless in this situation. It wasn't like she was going to climb down and deny him his shot. "I don't have many options here, do I, Milo? Go ahead and take your pitch."

"Okay. I just wouldn't want you to get cold feet and back out on me."

His double meaning hung in the air between them, and Julia tensed. Was he really going to indirectly talk about their relationship in front of all these people? How dare he.

Julia's next words came out clipped. "I'm just fine."

Milo wound up and fired.

"Strike two!" Compounding squeals of anticipation spread through the onlookers like ripples in the river.

For all of his faults, Milo sure drummed up a crowd.

"Last ball, Milo."

"Thanks, Marge." Milo's voice was tight. He wasn't gloating anymore. He wasn't trying to be chummy with those who were watching him. He was focused.

He palmed his final ball and shook out his arm. He raised his head, determination written all over his face.

Out of the corner of her eye, Julia saw Samson take a step closer to the side of the dunk tank. There was no way Milo would miss three times in a row, was there? Julia held her breath for the wind-up.

Milo released his pitch, and before she registered the thud of the ball on the target, she was dumped feet-first into the massive tank of water. She resurfaced to the happy shrieks of the crowd.

Milo turned away from her, his arms raised in victory. People surrounded him on all sides, but he looked over his shoulder and smirked at Julia before slapping hands with his admirers. "Anything for the town!"

Julia bit the inside of her cheek and waded over to the stairs to climb out of the tank. She wouldn't have cared so much about getting dunked, but because it came at the hands of Milo, in front of half the town, it smarted. It felt like another example of him holding the power, just like he implied he would when she broke up with him. Julia didn't like it one bit.

She climbed the ladder and hoisted herself out of the water. Her clothes stuck to her skin, and pieces of her hair clung to her cheeks.

"Here."

Julia sucked in a surprised breath when she looked up and found Samson holding out a towel for her.

"Thought you could use this."

She grabbed it and wiped off her face. "Thanks," she mumbled, ducking her head.

"Don't mention it."

Marge shoved Samson aside, vibrating with glee. "Well, Julia. I'd say your time here was well spent. And your shift is over. Off to the burger tent you go."

"Gee, thanks, Marge."

"You're welcome." Marge turned to greet the high school principal, Mr. Kinnickinik, who was taking over the dunk tank.

Julia glared at the woman's back before rolling her shoulders. It was the Fourth of July Festival, one of her favorite days of the year. She was not going to let Marge or Milo or anyone else ruin it for her. No matter what they threw her way.

Turning from Marge, she took off but stopped herself before she ran smack into Samson's chest.

"Ope, sorry," she gasped. Her wet face grew warm with embarrassment. Leave it to her to almost run into him...for the second time. In this case, she couldn't blame her dog. "I didn't realize you were still here."

"No problem." Samson stared down at her, holding her in place with the intensity of his gaze. A drop of water slid down the brim of her nose, and she dabbed it away without breaking eye contact.

A twinkle flashed in Samson's eyes, but it wasn't a mocking glow. If she didn't know any better, she'd say it was affectionate. Like maybe he liked what he saw.

How was that even possible? She'd been rude to him, and now she was a mess. She was *always* a mess when he was around. She shouldn't care what he thought, but she did.

He cleared his throat, and the moment passed. "So, you have to work some more?"

"Yeah." Julia glanced at the red-and-white-striped food tent, happy to have something else to focus on. "I'm supposed to serve food over there for the next hour and a half. I'm going to run over to the café to dry off and change clothes first, though."

Samson nodded. He hesitated for a second before he spoke again. "Maybe I'll see you around. I'm going to go grab a bite to eat."

"Okay."

Without another word, Samson strode across the grounds to the food tent.

Julia stood rooted in place, staring after him. She wrapped the towel Samson gave her snugly around her shoulders. It warmed her—on the outside and the inside. What was she supposed to make of *that*?

And who was Samson really? A big-shot businessman or a considerate gentleman? She shook her water-logged head. She'd have to figure it out later. Right now, she needed dry clothes.

She cut behind the festival rides and kids' game trailers so she could walk to the coffee shop undisturbed. She'd like to save any further interaction with the town for when she was no longer sopping wet.

She snuck into the café through the door off the deck and heard the murmur of Amanda's voice in conversation with Seth. Their heads swiveled her way as she walked into the dining room, leaving a small stream of water in her wake.

Amanda covered her mouth to hide a laugh. "Oh, man. You got dunked."

"Laugh it up. I'm a disaster. I came here to change before my shift in the food tent. I seriously must've offended Marge in some way. This schedule is bonkers." Julia hurried behind the counter where she kept a fresh white t-shirt and some jean shorts handy in case of a coffee spill.

"Who managed to dunk you?" Seth questioned as she dipped into the storage room and peeled off her wet clothes.

"Milo."

"What?"

From behind the closed door, she noted how Amanda's tone had gone from spirited to sympathetic.

"Yeah." Julia didn't know what else to say.

"What a jerk!"

"Amanda!" Even as Julia scolded her, she agreed with her best friend. She hated how he made her feel. But saying so out loud would only fuel Amanda's protective streak, and Julia wanted to forget all about Milo.

Julia emerged from the closet in her dry clothes, refreshed. "It's fine. It's good for the town, so I can't complain, can I?"

Amanda hugged her.

"Thanks, girl." Amanda would always have her back. They didn't have to talk about her annoyance with Milo or that she was embarrassed. Amanda knew without Julia having to say a word. Julia said a silent prayer of thanksgiving for good friends before she changed the subject. "Now, it must be almost time to shut this place down for the day, right?"

Seth nodded, looking out over the deserted café. "We'll close at two like we said and get Mr. Waffles safely home."

Julia arranged her wet hair in a messy bun on the top of her head. "Thanks for doing that. I'll see you guys over there in a bit. Just follow the smell of charred hamburger."

Amanda and Seth laughed and spoke at the same time.

"Sounds good."

"We'll find you."

With a wave, Julia was out the door to take on the rest of the day.

Chapter 11

SAMSON

SAMSON HAD EATEN A lot of mouth-watering food in his life, but there was something next-level about the Village of Mapleton's fried peanut-butter-and-jelly sandwich. He contemplated having another. It was the Fourth of July, after all. And nothing said *freedom* like the gooey, crunchy goodness of a messy, fried PB&J.

"Samson!"

He turned at the sound of someone calling his name. Melly waved and made her way toward him with three men trailing behind her. Samson stood, wiping the remaining peanut butter from his hands onto the red-checked tablecloth covering the picnic table.

"Melly. It's good to see you again." A genuine smile widened across his face as the woman hurried over, her mom-bob ruffling in the wind.

"You too! I wanted to introduce you to my family. This is Lucas, my husband. And Andy and Petey, our sons."

Samson shook hands with the three. "It's nice to meet you all."

He spent ten minutes talking to Melly and her family. When they wandered off to meet up with their friends, Samson returned to his seat.

He perused the grounds, and spotted Julia. Her wet hair was stacked up on the top of her head, and she wore a sun visor. She bustled from the grill to the service counter with an oversized black apron tied around her waist. The smile on her face drew him in. Samson wanted to be near her...to try to talk to her.

Then again, he had barely gotten a word out at the dunk tank because of Milo. Honestly, what was he supposed to say? *Hey, Julia. I got wind of your ex-boyfriend's plan to usurp your land. My company's probably going to buy it. And by the way, I like you and want to get to know you.*

That wasn't likely to go over well.

She turned in his direction to greet a patron, and Samson looked away, ducking his head under the picnic table and pretending to search the grass for a lost item.

Apparently he was ten years old now.

Samson usually knew what to do and when to do it, but with Julia, he may as well toss his entire playbook into the Squirrel River.

"Hey, stranger!" Amanda plopped down next to him, and Samson banged his head on the picnic table.

Amanda looked at him funny as Seth took a seat across from him. "Fancy meeting you here."

"It's the place to be, isn't it?" Samson rubbed his head and forced himself to relax.

"How's it going?" Amanda scanned the crowd and waved to Julia.

Julia smiled in return. When her eyes bounced in his direction, an arc of electricity crackled between them. She tore her gaze away before he could determine if she was happy or annoyed to see him with her friends. He was afraid she would think he was stalking her, what with his always being around wherever she was. He swallowed, realizing Amanda was waiting for his response.

"It's going fine. I've been sitting here listening to music and people-watching since I came in—after I saw the dunk tank spectacle, that is."

"What do you mean by *spectacle*?" Seth questioned.

"Didn't you talk to Julia?" Surely she would have told her friends about Milo.

"She told us she got dunked. And that Milo did it." Amanda said Milo's name with a hint of irritation lacing her tone. "What else is there?"

"I don't know. There was a whole group of people, and Milo was pretty outspoken. He said something about Julia getting cold feet, and he gloated when he finally dunked her. Marge was thrilled, of course."

The corners of Amanda's mouth sunk.

Samson stared back and forth between her and Seth, trying to get a better feel for the situation. Maybe he was making a bigger deal out of it than it was, but he thought Julia was affected by Milo's behavior. He assumed the dunk tank would be a fun, carefree thing. But the way Milo acted indicated some serious unspoken tension.

"She didn't tell us any of that." Amanda balled up her hands and pressed her fists against the table. "I could punch Milo."

Seth scowled. "I'll beat you to it."

He was built like a linebacker, and Samson was sure Seth could take Milo down if he wanted. The Village Administrator was suave, but he didn't appear to be very strong.

"Yeah, he seemed a little over-aggressive to me, but I don't know the guy that well." Samson shrugged.

He had to have a working relationship with Milo, so he shouldn't openly condemn the man his first month on the job, but even if he put Julia out of his mind—which was becoming more difficult by the minute—there was something about Milo that rubbed him the wrong way.

Amanda sighed. "He's a good guy. At least I think he is. He never treated Julia poorly when they were dating. But I feel like he's been a little different since she broke up with him. And I only know what she's told me, so I don't have the full story. Either way, I'm glad she's not dating *him* anymore." She wiggled her eyebrows at Samson.

Samson's heartrate kicked up. "Oh yeah? Is there someone else you'd rather see her with?"

Amanda smiled innocently and took a sip of her iced coffee. She was going to make him work for it. Fine. He appreciated that Julia had cool friends. And he appreciated that Amanda was in his corner. Seth, for his part, only chuckled at her.

Samson leaned his elbows on the table, hands clasped, and cocked his head in Amanda's direction. "Because for the record, I'm interested."

"Yes!" Amanda threw her fist in the air before high-fiving Seth across the table. "I *knew* it. I think she's 'interested' in you, too." She winked as she made air quotes.

Samson stilled, waiting for her to say more, but Amanda turned her attention to Seth. "Do you know that country music is my favorite?"

Seth smiled. "I had a hunch."

They all faced the main stage. The band was playing the Toby Keith patriotic classic "Courtesy of the Red, White, and Blue."

Amanda and Seth got lost in their own conversation, and Samson took a minute to collect his thoughts.

Around him, laughter and chatter buzzed like a swarm of bees. Samson recognized several familiar faces as he took in the growing crowd. He'd been in town for less than two weeks, so that was a definite testament to the size of Mapleton—there weren't many people to confuse.

Near the stage, a man who Samson was sure had been at Julia's café the morning he arrived in town was talking to a woman with snow-white hair and getting animated as he pointed to the river and held his hands up, shaking them defiantly. The grandpa-aged man turned in Samson's direction and glared at him for a second before being slapped on the arm by the white-haired woman.

"Ow!" Samson heard him exclaim over the music. "What was that for?"

As the song ended, the woman responded in a loud enough voice it carried to where Samson was sitting.

"There's no use being obvious. And besides, you don't know anything about him."

When the band picked up, the elderly couple's conversation was drowned out again, but Samson guessed what it was about. The man was a mill supporter.

Thank goodness Samson had thick skin and a practiced poker face, because charming the residents of Mapleton was turning out to be a brutal, uphill battle. At least Melly liked him. And so did Amanda and Seth. And Milo—though he wasn't sure if that was worth much.

He wondered about Julia. He wanted her to like him now more than ever, but he'd have to be cautious if he was going to keep his business interests separate from his personal interests where she was concerned.

Seth interrupted his thoughts as Amanda stood up. "We're going to check out the music on the side stage. Want to walk with us?"

"Are you guys sure you don't mind?"

"Of course not." Amanda dismissed his concern with a wave of her hand. "Besides, Julia's got another thirty minutes before her shift is up. Then she'll be able to relax and enjoy the rest of the day." She chucked him on the shoulder. "You should hang around."

Samson laughed. "Twist my arm, why don't you."

Chapter 12

JULIA

AMANDA, SETH, AND SAMSON vacated their table, and as Julia looked on, her belly twisted. Amanda and Seth were spending time with Samson, and if she didn't know better, she'd say the curdling feeling in her stomach was...jealousy.

She wanted to be the one to spend more time with him.

"Hi, honey."

Julia jumped.

Her mom and dad waved as they saddled up to the food counter.

She'd been staring after Samson and was so lost in her own bubble of thoughts she hadn't seen them approach. "Hi, guys! Ya hungry?"

"You know I can't turn down a festival burger." Joe Derks rubbed his slightly rounded belly.

"And even though Dr. Mortinson said he should watch what he eats, I can hardly withhold festival food from your father, can I?"

A smile spread over Julia's face as her dad dropped a kiss on her mom's forehead.

"That's why I love you, Gloria."

This was her parents' brand of playful banter, but her dad meant what he said, too. Her parents were always on the same page. It was like they could read each other's minds. They supported and respected each other, and darned if they weren't adorable at it.

Julia longed for the type of relationship they had. She and Milo never got close to their level, which, even if she didn't realize it at the time, was probably one of the reasons she broke up with him.

Julia blinked and returned her focus to the food tent. The Fourth of July Festival was not the time to dwell on her lack of a love life.

"One burger, coming right up," she said cheerfully. "And what can I get for you, Mom?"

"I ate before I came." Julia's mom looked past her dad and pointed to a group of people congregated in the grassy area beyond the tent. "Look, Joe! There are Charlie and Lorraine over by the stage. Golly, they shouldn't sit so close. The speakers are going to blow out their hearing aids."

"I haven't seen Charlie in a while. We should go chat." Her dad rummaged around in his pocket for money to pay for his burger. "Keep the change." He let out a laugh, but then his face turned serious. "Wait, do those tips go to you or the village?"

"Dad! They go to the village, of course." Julia tucked his extra dollar into the Mason jar Marge strategically positioned on the food counter.

"Well, I guess I'll have to stop by that café of yours to leave a tip for you, then. Excellent service." Her dad rubbed his hands together as she put a plate with his burger on the counter in front of him.

"Thanks, Dad."

He strode over to the stage, armed with a hamburger and a smile.

"Charlie!" her dad shouted. Heads turned in his direction, but Charlie remained oblivious until Joe placed a hand on his shoulder. Then, the older man's face lit up.

"Charlie and your father always did have a special bond." Her mom followed Julia's gaze.

Julia nodded. "I remember going to Charlie and Jeanne's house for dinner all the time as a kid." Jeanne lost her battle with cancer years ago, and Charlie had leaned heavily on Julia's parents. His more recent friendship with Lorraine had been good for him.

A wistful smile played across her mom's face. "Those two made quite the pair. Sometimes, I think Jeanne ran the mill more than Charlie. She definitely kept him in line!"

Given the conversation they had the night before, Julia was anxious to talk to her mom. "Does the mill property being developed really not bother you?"

Her mom shrugged. "Of course it stings a little, Jules. That's because that place and what it stood for held such value for our family and the town. It was our livelihood and a pillar of the community. But the mill itself has been long gone. You know that. We've adjusted our course, and things turned out fine. The people who made up the mill are still here, and that's what matters. Just because the land is being developed now doesn't mean we're disrespecting what the mill stood for."

"But—"

Her mom held up her hand. "Like I said yesterday, did you think that site was going to sit vacant forever? I, for one, would rather see something beautiful in its place."

Julia pressed her lips together. Her mom made a valid point. If charming and well-crafted homes went up along the river, families would get to enjoy living in them and experience life in Mapleton, which was a good thing—for those families and for the community as a whole.

"You look like you swallowed a lemon, dear."

Julia unscrewed her mouth. "Just thinking about what you said." She paused. "They better not mess with the old gazebo, though."

"Ah, well. It's a good thing that's a historic landmark, isn't it?"

Julia grinned at that. "Sure is. I'm going to finish up here." She turned to survey the counter. The lunch rush was over, and most people were out on the festival grounds, playing games and listening to the band. "You go catch up with Dad. I'm sure we'll meet up later."

"Sounds good, dear. See you soon."

Her mom walked off, and Julia glanced at her watch.

Fifteen minutes to freedom.

·♥·♥·♥·♥·♥·

When her shift finally ended, Julia went in search of her friends. She spotted Seth and Amanda with Samson at the bottom of the hill that led down to the river. They were standing with a group of people gathered at the side stage. A high school punk band was entertaining the crowd. It sounded like a lot of screeching to Julia.

Questionable music aside, it was time to enjoy the day. Julia took a deep breath and skipped down the hill. Amanda saw her first, and Julia waved at her friend.

"There's the cutest little waitress of all." Amanda opened her arms and embraced her in a hug as Julia skidded to a stop.

"I don't know about that. But I do know I've punched out. Time to have some fun!" Julia leaned away from Amanda and gave Samson a tentative smile. "How do you like your first festival?"

"So far so good. Seth and Amanda were explaining to me that this is the sledding hill in the winter." Samson shouted over the band and motioned to the hill Julia had descended.

"Yeah. The locals love it here after a heavy snow."

"Come on," Seth yelled. "We were just going to make the rounds."

Julia fell into step with Samson as Seth and Amanda led the way. No one tried to talk over the punk rockers as they hiked up the hill, and Julia used the time to try to get her head on straight about Samson—a difficult task since every time their shoulders brushed, her brain short-circuited. The hints of his cedar cologne and citrus soap were dizzying.

Still, by the time they crested the hill and the four stopped to assess the festival grounds, Julia had vowed to herself she wasn't going to overthink what Samson was thinking or what he was doing hanging around with her and her friends. She wasn't going to focus on the way the hair on her arms stood up every time she caught him looking at her when he thought she wasn't paying attention. Or on the feeling of her heartbeat in her pinky finger after his hand grazed hers. She was just going to be herself.

"What should we do next?" Amanda asked.

"Why doesn't Julia decide?"

Julia turned her head toward Samson and arched her brow.

Hands in the pockets of his shorts, looking as cool as a modern-day Danny Zuko, he shrugged easily back at her. "You're the one who's been a slave to Marge for most of the day. And besides, you promised this would be a good time."

"Oh no, don't give her that power," Amanda warned Samson.

Julia made a face at her friend before rounding on Samson. His eyes shone with mischief, and she read the silent challenge he issued.

Challenge accepted.

She'd show him they knew how to throw a party in small-town Wisconsin. She shoved a hand against her hip and cocked her head at him. "You sure you're ready for this?"

Samson nodded. "I can handle it."

"Alright, hot-shot. Let's do it. Tilt-a-whirl!"

Chapter 13

SAMSON

THE FOUR OF THEM hit the tilt-a-whirl—twice—before moving on to balloon darts, putt-putt golf, and squirt-gun spray away. Seth turned his squirt gun at Amanda and doused her when she wasn't expecting it.

Samson eyed Julia and pointed the water gun in her direction.

"Don't even think about it." Julia pointed at him, daring him to disobey her order.

He held up his gun in surrender.

"I've had enough water for one day," Julia mumbled, but a smile played across her face before she marched off and proceeded to kick his butt in corn hole.

He'd managed to beat her in touchdown toss, and now she sat with the giant pink bear he won perched on the corner of their table.

Samson folded his long legs under the picnic table. He was beat but, at the same time, energized. He couldn't remember the last time he'd had so much fun. Julia definitely fulfilled her promise of a good time as she led them on a tour of the festival.

In between games, they stopped to chat with pockets of friends Julia and Amanda knew from high school or around town. Samson received a few funny looks when Julia introduced him and told people he was in town for work. Fortunately, much of the heat was taken off of him because Seth was new to a lot of these folks, too.

"I'm exhausted," Amanda moaned from across the table as she laid her head down on Seth's shoulder.

"Oh, come on." Julia laughed. "What's a festival without some games? Besides, we had to work up an appetite. What do you think, Hank?" She turned to the pink bear. "Will it be the fried PB&J or a French-fry-wrapped hot dog?"

Samson shook his head. "Woah, woah, woah. Did you say Hank?"

Julia narrowed her eyes at him. "Yes, what's wrong with Hank?"

"That bear's a girl."

"No, this bear is Hank." The way Julia said it left no room for argument. Their eyes locked in a stare-down, and Samson decided then and there he could look at Julia forever.

He gave himself a mental shake. *Dude, no need to be creepy.*

Out loud, he said, "You know. You have a very interesting taste in names. Hank, Mr. Waffles..." Samson let his voice trail off.

Julia's eyes sparkled. "Alright, out with it. What do you have against Mr. Waffles?"

"I've got nothing against the dog. He's actually quite endearing. But his name?" Samson shrugged, holding his hand up and moving it side to side.

Julia scoffed. "Apparently, you're too closed-minded to appreciate Mr. Waffles' name. But you can't tell me Mr. Waffles' fur is not the exact color of waffle batter, can you?" Julia stared at him with a smirk on her face.

She was daring him to dispute her.

He wasn't used to people standing up to him, and the corners of his lips quivered as he fought off a smile. She was something else, and the more he thought about it, the more he realized Mr. Waffles' fur *did* remind him of creamy waffle batter.

He blinked first and found Amanda and Seth staring at them from across the table. Amanda looked triumphant.

Samson cleared the sudden spasm out of his throat, rubbing the back of his neck. "Fine. You win this one. The bear can be

Hank. Now, I'm going with the fried peanut butter and jelly."

Julia clicked her tongue. "Excellent choice."

"We'll stay here and hold our spot at this table. Why don't you guys go get your food, and then we'll swap." Amanda shooed them away. "Don't worry, Jules. I'll take good care of Hank."

Samson laughed as he stood and shadowed Julia to the food booth. The humid air under the tent was charged. Kids were screaming and racing around, trying their hands at different games. Samson spotted what he assumed was the duck game across the way, and he smiled to himself, hoping the little girl from earlier had gotten her chance to play.

In the center of the tent, the rows of people lining the paddle board table had grown deeper since lunchtime. With each repetitive tick of the spinner, the anticipation swelled only to burst forth with raucous cheers and dismayed groans when the winning number was called. All around, groups of friends stood huddled together, leaning in to be heard over the din.

Julia expertly crossed the crowd, jostling her way to the food counter. All he had to do was follow her top knot as she bobbed and weaved among the festival-goers. At one point, she threw her head back and laughed at someone across the way, and that was when it hit him. These were her people. This was her town. Watching her navigate it—with all its quirks and interesting personalities—gave Samson pause.

These people all had stories and lives that were connected, and Julia knew them and cared about each one. But none of them—not Julia or anyone in Mapleton or anyone anywhere, really—knew him. Did he want to be known? Did he want to get to know the people of Mapleton?

He found himself thinking about his previous jobs, about the places he had been. He was always busy doing what he needed to do to get a job done. There was no time to care about the town or its people. He moved from one project to the next, focusing on his career and on winning people over to his side. But deep down, he wondered if it was time to admit to himself the real Samson wasn't the one on display there—that was the persona he put on to get the job done. And he'd been fine with that. But now he wondered...was it enough? To act his way through life? Or was it time to be his real self?

Julia stopped in front of the counter where Marge stood with her arms folded, surveying the tent.

"How's it going, Marge? We're hungry," Julia shouted to draw the woman's attention.

The sound of her voice effectively ended Samson's deep thoughts, which was a relief. Shaking his head, he wedged himself into the only free space at the wrap-around food counter. He stood shoulder to shoulder with Julia, and his pulse quickened as their arms touched.

"What'll you have?" Marge asked.

Julia nodded for him to go first, so he went ahead and placed his order for a fried PB&J.

"I'll have the same," Julia echoed.

"You two have good taste," Marge said. "I'll have that right up."

As she hurried off, Samson bent and rested his elbows on the bar so his face was beside Julia's.

"So..." Samson blanked on anything else to say. He shifted when Julia turned in his direction. Heat radiated from her side as she looked at him expectantly.

"Is this a pretty good crowd by Fourth of July Festival standards? It seems busy."

It wasn't much of a conversation starter, but at least it was something. She looked so gorgeous. He should get a medal for getting any words out at all.

Julia nodded. "You'd have to ask Marge for the actual numbers, but based on what I can tell, this is one of our bigger years—at least since I've been on the committee. The weather couldn't be better."

She gazed over Samson's shoulder and out the opposite side of the tent to where the sun was glistening on the grounds. When she looked back at him, her blue eyes mirrored the brightness of the sky, and her fresh face glowed. She was radiant, and it took everything in him not to reach out and trace the perfect curve of her neck. An urge to kiss her rose up in his chest like the puck soaring to the top of the high-flyer game outside.

Samson broke eye contact and looked around. Kissing Julia right now would be a terrible idea and solely the result of getting caught up in the atmosphere of the tent. At least, that was what he told himself.

He cleared his throat. "Are all these people from Mapleton?"

"A lot of them, yes." She nodded. "But I'm guessing the number of out-of-towners is up this year, too."

"Here you are." Marge placed two sizzling sandwiches in front of them.

"Thanks, Marge." Samson smiled at the woman as Julia dug into her purse. "I've got it." Samson placed his hand on her forearm to stop her from getting out her wallet. A shock jumped from her skin to his, and Samson gulped. Her gaze flew to his, and he absently licked his lips.

"That's not n-necessary." Julia's cheeks were red, and she looked down and continued to shuffle through her purse.

Meanwhile, Marge's head swiveled from Julia to Samson and back again like she was watching a tennis match, and Samson could practically see her wheels turning as she worked to figure out what was going on between the two of them.

That was all they needed: to have town crier Marge breathing down their necks. Samson wouldn't be surprised if the woman sniffed out Milo's plans for the park. The thought made his heart race for a whole different reason. Samson needed to get out of the tent and to the open air where Hank sat waiting for them. Where things were less complicated.

"I insist. Consider it a thank you for showing me around the best Fourth of July celebration I've ever attended." With that, Samson cast Marge a full smile, and she tittered.

He felt Julia's eyes on him as he handed Marge the money to pay for their meals.

"Keep the change for the village fund."

Marge tucked the money into the till. "Thank you, Samson."

He nodded and turned to Julia, who'd given up the desperate hunt for cash in her purse to reach for their food. From her quick movements, Samson determined Julia wanted to be out from under the scrutiny of Marge as much as he did.

"Shall we?" He took one of the plates from her, placed his hand on her back, and turned her toward the picnic tables. "Good to see you again, Marge." He tossed the woman another full-throttle smile over his shoulder.

"You do that a lot, don't you?"

Samson looked down at Julia. "What?"

"Charm people to get your way in situations."

He squirmed. "I don't know what you mean."

Julia snickered. "You don't even know you're doing it, but that happy-go-lucky act you put on for Marge? That's not the real you. You tried it with me your first morning here, too."

Samson should have been offended, but she wasn't wrong. Hadn't he been thinking the same thing?

To hide his discomfort, he changed the subject. "What's the deal with her?"

"Who?"

"Marge. Is she, like, an alien?"

Julia shook her head and laughed. It was the sweetest sound Samson ever heard.

"I'm serious," he said. "She's freakishly organized, demanding, domineering, and a little scary."

Catching her breath, Julia looked up and drummed her fingers across her cheek. "I don't know. Marge has always been this way. She's been in charge of the festival for as long as I remember. It's like the woman doesn't age. She looks the same now as she did when I was a kid. She does seem a little more intense than usual this year. I'm not sure what has gotten into her." Julia turned to him and shrugged. "You'll get used to her. She's got the town's best interests at heart. Sometimes her delivery is a little extreme."

"I'll have to take your word for it. For now, I'll steer clear."

Julia laughed again, and Samson relaxed.

If he could make his living by making her laugh, he was starting to think he'd do just that.

Chapter 14

JULIA

"SO, TELL ME ABOUT your history with the festival." Samson's palms rested on the picnic table bench a few inches from where Julia's fingers were spread out on the weathered wood. He sat, casually listening to the band serenade them from the mainstage. He looked good like that. Like he belonged.

Julia stared at their hands—so close to each other, yet so far. Something had ignited between them under the tent, and she wasn't sure what to make of it.

Samson kept her on her toes, and she found it challenging to read him. Earlier at the dunk tank, he was considerate and kind. He liked to have fun, which he proved when he'd matched her, game for game, all afternoon. But every once in a while, it was like he was someone else.

Like when he'd charmed Marge. Sure, she was glad to be out from under the woman's watchful eye, but Samson transformed so easily into his smooth-talking businessman self. It was unsettling.

Also unsettling? The way she found herself leaning toward him, like a sunflower seeking the sun.

Julia tucked her hands into her lap and forced herself to sit up straighter. "What do you want to know?"

"How'd you get so good at festival games, for one?"

Julia laughed, letting her muscles go slack. "I loved attending the festival as a kid. I'd run from game booth to game booth with my friends and rack up all the stuffed animal prizes I could. So I've had a lot of experience."

Samson chuckled but didn't say anything.

"The village lore grows with each year of the festival, too. Some years, the festivities go off without a hitch. Other years, it feels like everything that could go wrong does. Like the time the tent stakes let loose and the giant red-and-white canvas blew into the river."

Samson balked. "No way."

Julia held her hand over her heart. "On my honor. Or the time when some meddling teenagers thought it would be clever to let the baby goats out of the petting zoo area."

Samson narrowed his eyes at her, and Julia's stomach fizzled under his gaze. "Were you a particularly meddlesome teenager?" he asked.

She quirked one half of her mouth up, lifting her shoulder with it. "Not me. I'm a straight-up rule follower."

Samson laughed. "For some reason, I believe that."

Julia smiled. It was easy to talk to Samson, and he seemed to genuinely care what she had to say. He was a good listener. It made her want to open up to him even more.

"One thing is for sure," she said. "The festival is always memorable, and it's pretty great to have the shared experience with the people around here. As I grew older, the festival was a chance to reconnect with the town. When I was away, working summer internships in Eau Claire, near where I went to college, I always made it a point to come home for the festival. I would get to see my friends from high school and catch up with all the village residents who've known me since I was born. Oh, and I love any excuse to dance."

"Is that right?" Samson raised a brow, but his mouth softened into a smile. A real smile this time. It flooded his face, enhancing his already too-handsome features with an irresistible dash of authenticity.

A familiar laugh drew her attention, and she broke eye contact with Samson. They turned at the same time to observe Amanda and Seth.

"See, their technique is all wrong..." Seth narrated to a captivated Amanda. He was pointing to a group of teenagers who were trying their luck at balloon darts and failing miserably.

Amanda was smitten, and it delighted Julia to no end. Seth was a great guy—smart and charismatic when he opened himself up.

"Have those two been an item for long?"

At the tickle of Samson's breath near her ear, Julia shivered. She hadn't noticed he moved closer to her. Now the whole festival grounds faded away as she locked eyes with him again. When he looked at her, Julia felt like she was the only person in the world. It was both terrifying and thrilling.

"Want to go for a walk and give them some space?" Samson stood and held out his hand for her.

She stared at it for a beat and shot a glance left and right. The last thing she needed was some nosy townsfolk getting wind of her running off with the new guy. They'd be all up in her business before she knew it.

But Julia would be lying to herself if she said she didn't want to explore the spark between them, no matter what anyone else thought. Besides, the rest of the town was busy having fun. Nobody was paying her the least bit of attention—except for Samson, who was paying her and only her attention. Now was the time to take a chance. She may as well get to know him.

"Let's do it." She took his hand and let him effortlessly hoist her up.

Julia looked down at her hand in Samson's. His fingers were calloused from work, she assumed, and she liked that about him. Milo's hands were always soft and manicured to perfection. Julia used to be self-conscious about her short nails and the steam burns lining her arms. She shouldn't compare Samson to Milo, but it was tough not to when he kept surpassing her expectations at every turn. It had taken her years to give Milo a chance, and yet here she was, already more comfortable with Samson after one afternoon.

Julia wanted to throw caution to the wind and hold on to Samson for dear life, but she needed to get to know him more before she did that. She worried her heart was zooming too fast in his direction, so she dropped his hand.

Across the table, Amanda and Seth were oblivious to anything but each other. Julia contemplated leaving unannounced, but they'd worry if they realized she and Samson were gone. She waved and got their attention. "Hey, you two, we'll be right back. Don't have too much fun without us." Julia shot a pointed look at Amanda.

Amanda's mouth dropped open in surprise, but she recovered herself and winked. "Right back atcha, girlfriend."

Julia couldn't help but laugh at her friend. Turning to Samson, she said, "Let's go."

Chapter 15

SAMSON

SAMSON FISTED HIS FINGERS, trying to hold onto the fleeting warmth from Julia's grasp for a second longer.

He suggested going for a walk because he wanted an excuse to be by her side. He wasn't sure where Julia was taking him, and at this point, it didn't matter. All that mattered was the fact that Julia was next to him. Her hand would feel good in his, but she kept some space between them, and Samson wasn't going to push it.

He sensed a change wash over Julia over the course of the afternoon. Samson didn't know what caused it, but something had shifted since the dunk tank. There, she was timid and a little shy in his presence. Now, she walked confidently, smiled boldly, and there was a glimmer in her eye that had him believing if she didn't know his deepest secrets, she'd learn them soon.

Gosh, he hoped not.

To this point in the day, steering clear of touchy subjects had been easy. They were just two people having fun at the festival. Samson wanted to continue to learn more about her as the night progressed without ruining everything by discussing the mill or disclosing Milo's potential plans.

"Let's go this way." Julia pointed north. "We can walk around the ball diamonds, and if you want, I'll take you through the trees on my favorite path. We'll end up down by the river."

"Sounds perfect."

They walked side by side in silence for a minute. The farther they got from the main stage, the quieter it became. While the laughter from the food tent and yells from those riding rides and playing games echoed through the early evening air, the sounds were muffled, and only decrescendo strains of melody from the band reached them on the breeze.

"So, Seth and Amanda." Samson figured that was a safe topic. "Is it a budding relationship I'm sensing?"

A smile cracked across Julia's face, and she seemed happy to pick up the conversation where they had left off at the picnic table. "I don't know for sure. But I'm sensing it, too. I hired Seth a year ago. He and Amanda didn't work together much for the first several months. I trained him, and he worked the opposite shift with another guy named Nick. But recently, Amanda and Seth are together more and more when they're at work and during off hours. I mean, they definitely enjoy each other's company, right? If it is obvious to you, then I'd say it's obvious."

"Yeah," Samson concurred. *Kind of like I'm enjoying your company.*

"I'm hopeful for the two of them. Seth is a good guy. He's soft-spoken but incredibly witty. He'd make a good match for Amanda. She's a character."

"Yeah, I've gathered that. I popped into the café on my way to the festival and officially met her there."

They stepped off the path to make way for a group of middle-schoolers.

"I know." Julia turned her body and faced him as she walked sideways along.

That surprised him. "You do?" He wondered what Amanda told her.

"Yeah. I saw your cup when you arrived at the park. I'm astute, remember?" She tapped her temple.

"I remember." Samson grinned at her, loving the way her mind worked. "I couldn't resist the best coffee in town."

"You're just saying that to butter me up." She turned forward, elbowing his side with a sort of comfortable familiarity he could get used to.

He held up his hands in mock surrender. "Hey, I speak the truth. The coffee is delicious, and Amanda and Seth are also excellent company. So are you."

The second his words registered with her, Julia's eyes flew wide, and she glanced up at him, as if to make sure she heard him correctly. When he didn't look away, she ducked her head but not before he saw a slow smile spread over her face.

Samson was a tad shocked at how bashful she was at his compliment. Her reaction made him wonder if she wasn't used to receiving praise. Milo was a fool if he hadn't been showering her with his affections. After one afternoon in Julia's presence —plus a couple run-ins—Samson could already tell she was something special. If it was up to him, Julia would never go a second without a reminder that she was awesome.

He swallowed. "Anyway, Amanda told me she'd catch up with me later and help show me around the festival. She hinted that you'd be around, and that was that. Now, here I am."

"Remind me to thank Amanda." Julia winked, rose-colored dabs blossoming on her cheeks. She clapped her hands once. "But now that we can hear ourselves think, you have to tell me about yourself. I want to know more about you. The good, the bad, and the ugly."

"I don't know about that." Samson laughed and readjusted the brim of his baseball cap, trying to hide his sudden panic. He couldn't remember the last time he had told someone about himself outside of a job interview.

"Come on. It's only fair."

"Why is it fair?"

"Because you already know a ton about me."

Samson doubted that. He had a feeling he'd only scratched the surface with her. "I do not."

Julia snorted and held up her fingers as she started listing things off. "For starters, you know all about my town. You know about my house, my job, and my dog. And you've spent the day with two of my best friends." She leveled him with a look that said, "Don't even try to argue."

Okay, so she had a point. Samson rubbed his clammy hands against his shorts as they walked along.

As if sensing his hesitation, Julia pointed to a break in the trees about two hundred meters ahead. "Take your time. See up there? That's the entrance to a wooded path. It'll wind us down and around, and we can walk along the river and come up on the other side of the café."

"Wow, so time for the full life story then, huh?"

Julia looked at him, her eyes warm and expectant. He couldn't say no to her, and his mind jumped back to what he'd been thinking about in the tent—how it might be nice to feel known. He decided to take a chance.

As they wound their way down the path and into the opening to the woods, Samson described his childhood. He told her about moving from military base to military base as his dad was transferred to different air stations around the country.

"My dad is active-duty Navy, though he'll probably be retiring soon. My mom does all her work for the military on a volunteer basis. Weirdly, she reminds me of Marge. Just a little less scary."

Julia laughed, and her delight propelled him to continue. She stopped him to ask questions, and she truly seemed interested in where he came from.

The trees arched over the top of them, creating the illusion of a cocoon. It wasn't yet dark outside, but it was much darker under the branches than on the walking path. The rest of the world was shut out as they picked their way through the woods. A creek bubbled ahead, and the grass rustled at their feet. It was easy to relax as they moved deeper into the woods.

Julia glanced over her shoulder as she led the way down a slight hill. "You lived in more places by the time you were six years old than I have my entire life."

"Yeah. Military life is crazy." Samson stepped on a twig, and it snapped beneath his foot. "Not always a good crazy, but I can't complain about my childhood."

"What made you settle in Wisconsin?" Julia dipped nimbly under a low-hanging tree branch and around an overgrown bush. He matched her route, and after they crossed a makeshift wooden bridge over the small creek, they were out in the open. "Here, we'll go this way toward the river." Julia motioned ahead before turning right on the gravel path that ran along the creek.

Samson followed her. "I came to Wisconsin for school. I knew I wanted to build things, and the university here had the most academic options based on what I was looking for. My dad was stationed in North Dakota when I was in high school. He was in charge of the ROTC program at North Dakota State, so I had my eye on schools in the Midwest because they were close to where I was living at the time. Then, I never left Madison."

Julia nodded. "A lot of people who attend UW-Madison stay in the area. Are most of your friends still around there?"

"They used to be. Slowly but surely, they've settled elsewhere. Now, I mostly socialize through work. I guess that's why it wasn't a big deal to move up here."

When he said it out loud, Samson's life sounded pathetic and lonely. He hadn't thought about making friends after college. He'd been focused on his job.

It dawned on him then that he had inadvertently led the conversation toward his work in town. Samson cringed. He didn't want to dive into a discussion about the mill if it would change the pleasant and carefree exchange they were having. But maybe if they cleared that hurdle, everything else would work out okay.

Julia grabbed for his hand and, for a second, all other thoughts escaped him. He let himself enjoy the feel of skin-on-skin contact with her as she steered him directly into another bunch of trees.

"Come on over here. There's a little bench. We can sit for a minute."

Sure enough, as they wedged themselves behind a fence and into what looked like a clump of overgrown foliage, Samson was surprised to find a small clearing with an old, stone bench facing the river.

Samson reluctantly let go of her hand and waited for her to sit before settling next to her. The bench was just big enough for two, and the sensation of Julia's right arm resting against his left arm felt like the best sort of tattoo.

Out of the corner of his eye, he glanced at her profile. Her eyelashes fanned out like warm sunbeams across her face, and a stray tendril of hair had escaped her bun. Samson wanted to tuck it behind her ear and feel her soft skin under his fingers again.

"So, you like what you do?" Julia spoke into the stillness, keeping her eyes facing the river.

Samson said a quick prayer. This conversation might ruin the best thing to come out of his time in Mapleton. But it had to happen.

"I do."

Chapter 16

JULIA

JULIA HELD HER BREATH and waited for Samson to continue. She didn't dare look him in the eye, but when she felt his gaze boring into the side of her face, Julia reluctantly shifted to meet it.

Samson seemed to choose his words carefully. "I try not to get too involved in the politics of acquiring land. I do my job, which is to develop what my company acquires, but what I love most is the process of building something from the ground up."

Samson's face transformed with boyish enthusiasm as he discussed construction work. He looked like a kid who was thrilled to be gifted a new Lego set. It was obvious he was passionate about his work. Julia listened intently as he went on.

"My background is in construction site project management, so ventures in their infancy—buildings or land on the cusp of being molded and transformed into something new—are my bread and butter. I know my way around a job site, and I like working with the crews." Samson's voice didn't hold conceit. Instead, he spoke like a guy who was confident in his skill set.

Julia nodded, encouraging him to continue.

"Three years ago, I applied for a position with Gabler, Burns, and Associates, an up-and-coming real estate investment and property development firm based in Madison. They hired me after one interview, thanks to my experience in construction and my people skills. My boss likes that I keep jobs on schedule and can navigate community dynamics."

Samson sucked in a breath as if he was afraid what he wanted to say next would offend her. Julia braced herself.

"The site here is exceptional. Riverfront property in a landlocked town? That is incredibly valuable. The homes and properties we're planning to build will fit well here, and the end product is going to be wonderful for Mapleton. Lots of people from the town could end up moving in there, and maybe some outsiders will find a place to call home, too."

He hesitated, and Julia could tell he was studying her face for her reaction. His green eyes held her blue ones in place, and all the blood rushed to Julia's head. Breathing was proving tricky under his concentrated gaze.

She swallowed and broke eye contact. From everything he said, Julia gleaned he was a hard worker who was well-versed in dealing with people. Nothing sinister.

"Tell me about the mill, Julia—if you want to," Samson spoke quietly. "I want to know about it. And about why you hated me when I showed up."

She glanced up. "I didn't hate you when you showed up."

Samson shot her a *Yeah, right* look.

"Okay, fine. So I wasn't the most cordial when it came to welcoming you to town." She winced as Samson chuckled.

All of a sudden, it seemed silly that the mill site was such a big deal to her. Would he understand her attachment to it? After listening to her mom and hearing Samson's plans for the grounds, was preserving the space as important as she thought it would be? And what was she hoping would be preserved, after all? The old building was gone.

Julia's mind was as muddled as the muddy river's water, but she owed him an explanation.

"The mill was the heartbeat of this town." Julia sat back as she reflected on a time that was still so fresh in her memory. She let her mind take her back to what it felt like to be seventeen years old.

"I was working as an administrative assistant at the village offices for my summer job when I took the call from a representative for the company who owned and operated the mill. He wanted to speak to the Village Administrator. I didn't think anything of it. I transferred the call back to my boss. Five minutes later, he walked out of his office and dropped a bombshell. He told us they were closing the mill. After that, village residents and mill workers protested for months. You have to understand."

Julia took his hand in hers, hating the catch in her voice. "The mill was a fixture in town. People didn't know what would happen to Mapleton if the mill shut its doors for good. Most importantly, what would happen to the hundreds of workers who would lose their jobs?"

Samson inclined his head toward her but stayed silent, giving her the chance to continue.

Julia pulled in a deep breath. "That's where it gets personal. My dad had worked at the mill from the day he graduated high school until the day they shut it down. He lived and breathed millwork. He rose through the ranks and became a manager of his team. He worked harder than anyone I knew. I went home the day the news broke and found my parents holding hands on the couch. I saw the tear stains on my mom's face and my dad's set jaw. One look at his weathered skin and graying hair was enough to send me spiraling. I didn't know what he was going to do. He was too young to retire, but he didn't have any other experience. I wondered if we'd have to move. My dad told me it would be okay. And it has been—for us, at least. But it was hard."

Samson stared back at her, his face full of sympathy.

"My dad struggled for a while. He felt like a failure, I think." Julia held herself stiff, closing her eyes and giving her head a quick shake. "The memory of him in those early days after the mill shut down makes me physically hurt. He was only a shadow of his real self. Fortunately, my mom put him in touch with a therapist she knew through the school district, and he worked through his feelings. That was ten years ago. He ended up finding a job at a facility specializing in manufacturing military equipment parts. He took a pay cut, but his new position pays the bills. And he's doing much better now. Although he doesn't get to lead his team, he's content with his current role. I'm sure he'll work there for a few more years until he's ready to retire."

Samson nodded, and Julia let the rest of the story spill out around them, filling the quiet cove with the weight of the town's—and her family's—history.

"Since it shut down, the old mill sat empty for nearly a decade. In a way, it was sort of like the coffin at a funeral. Every time you drove past the shell of what was once a humming, prosperous business, you couldn't help but bow your head and pay your respects. The abandoned building turned into almost as much of a fixture around town as the working mill had been. Then, about six months ago, bulldozers showed up, and slowly, over several months, they destroyed the big, blue building. As piece by piece crashed to the ground, the town experienced the death all over again."

Julia stopped to consider her next words. She didn't know how to convey to him the connection between the mill and the café, but she wanted to give it a shot. "A lot of the people who patronize the café are former mill workers. I try to make sure they're taken care of. It feels like it's the least I can do."

Samson sat quietly, looking thoughtful and compassionate, not at all like the arrogant, insensitive outsider she'd pegged him as when he had first shown up in her café. He hadn't said anything as she rambled on, just listened.

Now, she rolled her lips inward and waited for him to reply.

Finally, he flipped her hand into his and squeezed her fingers. "I appreciate you explaining this to me. And I am sorry that closing the mill was handled that way. I can only imagine how tough it was."

Julia's eyes welled. *He got it.* Whether or not he thought she was crazy was another thing, but at least he understood why it was difficult for her—and much of the town—to see the mill site messed with. That was a change from their first meeting.

"Please don't cry."

The desperation in his voice and the expression on his face was enough to make Julia laugh through the tears clouding her vision. He looked like Mr. Waffles during a thunderstorm.

"Come on, you can't tell me a few tears are all it would take to knock you off your game," Julia kidded as she pulled her hand back and swiped away the tears pooling along her lash line.

"You could knock me off my game pretty easily."

"I—"

"Julia."

Her mind spun at the implications of what he said, but she made herself listen. She liked the sound of her name on his lips.

"I understand why the mill site being turned into something else makes you sad. And I'm so sorry about what your dad went through. I admit, I hadn't thought much about the personal impact of the shutdown before. But you do know I'm not the one who closed the mill, right? I didn't force your dad out of a job. It wasn't even my company."

She grimaced, bowing her head. He spoke kindly but firmly. And he was right. Of course he wasn't responsible for the loss of the mill, but she took out her pent-up frustration and anger on him. It was wrong of her.

Julia nodded, her downturned chin tapping her chest.

"So, are we good?" Samson questioned, his gaze full of such gravity she could see it out of the corner of her eye.

She dragged her head up. "We're good."

Samson rested back against the bench as if the weight of the world was off his shoulders.

She hadn't realized he was nervous about her answer until he visibly relaxed.

He looked out over the water. "Good."

As Julia turned, they were shoulder to shoulder again, and Samson went on. "So, is Milo a tool or what?"

His sudden subject change and subsequent dry delivery made Julia snort, and she clamped a hand over her mouth.

With her other hand, she smacked Samson on the shoulder. "That's not very nice!"

"Well, sorry." Samson didn't look apologetic. "I'm trying to get a handle on the guy. I have to work with him, and I figured you'd be as good a source as anyone."

That was fair, but how to describe Milo?

"Gosh, I don't know. I don't think he's a tool. He's done a lot for the town, keeping it moving forward and all. And he was a good boyfriend. Funny. Helpful. Attentive. Until..." Julia trailed off.

"Until what?" Samson asked after she paused.

Julia shrugged. "Until he wasn't. A part of me thinks I only saw one side of Milo. I feel like I don't know him as well as I thought I did. We dated for almost a year, but since breaking up, I see him in a different light. He seems self-absorbed and mean now that our relationship didn't go his way. He hasn't been very nice to me."

She stopped short of telling Samson how Milo made her feel like she was worthless when she broke up with him. Her cheeks burned. She wasn't sure what compelled her to share all that she had, and she hurried to try to save face. "I don't mean to air my dirty laundry to you."

"Not at all. We can talk about something else. It's private, and I don't want to pry into your relationship. Milo seemed fine to work with when I first arrived. He's excited about the mill project. But today, he was a little aggressive for my taste."

"What, at the dunk tank?"

"Yeah."

"Yeah. That was...uncomfortable."

"I'm sorry he treated you that way," Samson dropped his voice. An emotion flickered in his eyes that she couldn't fully decipher. Whatever it was made her stomach drop with a satisfying whoosh into her belly.

"Thank you for saying that." Her voice came out higher than usual, and she had to work to even out her tone when she spoke again. "Breaking up with Milo was the right move. But it's never easy breaking up in a small town. Especially when I'll have to be around him quite a bit, and everyone and their brother is analyzing the situation. I'd give anything to lay low."

"That's understandable. Like I said to you the other day, this town is something else. I've never been on the receiving end of anything like it. Everyone is very invested in everyone else, which is cool, but I imagine it's not the greatest when you're trying to keep a low profile."

"Exactly."

They lapsed into comfortable silence.

The sun was a giant ball of orange, slowly setting over the Squirrel River. Its rays cast sparkling lines across the choppy water, making the current shimmer like a mirrorball. Being by the water calmed Julia, and she felt sheltered in the moment.

She inhaled the mossy smell of the river and closed her eyes. She couldn't hear the noise of the festival, which meant they were away from the listening ears of the town. She could stay on this stony, uncomfortable, small bench—with Samson by her side—all night and be perfectly content.

For a moment it was like Julia was out of her body and looking down on the two of them. They fit well together, if she did say so herself, and she marveled at the transformation her opinion of him had undergone. She'd gone from hating his guts to hoping to be his friend to wanting so much more. The intensity of that want startled her.

Samson shifted.

Julia glanced in his direction in time to see him check his watch.

"I want to be conscious of your time. Do you have anywhere you need to be before the fireworks?" Samson asked.

She sighed. Staying in their little tree-covered hideaway would be easier, but the real world was just that—real.

"We should probably head back." Julia peeled her legs off the bench, stretched her arms over her head, and turned to the opening that led to the path behind the ball diamonds. She fought the urge to reach for Samson's hand. She wanted to, but at the same time, she didn't want to complicate things. She sensed Samson liked her, but she needed time to think. And walking into the heart of town, hand in hand with him, would not be the best way to fly under the radar after her breakup with Milo.

Samson trailed behind her along the path. As they walked, worry crept in, stronger and stronger with each step. How would people react to her and Samson together? Would those devoted to the mill call her a turncoat? Would anyone judge her for moving on from Milo so quickly? How would it affect her business?

Julia told herself to relax. She wasn't in a relationship with Samson.

Yet.

She could try to shush the little voice inside her head all she wanted, but the truth was, she hoped she *would* be in a relationship with Samson soon.

And that scared the bottle rockets out of her.

She was thankful Samson didn't try to make conversation as they walked along. She led him on the quicker route up the hill and past the café before circling and entering the festival grounds from the front.

The crowd was growing as the time for fireworks approached. The sky had faded from indigo blue to pale black, and the two of them were able to slip in practically unnoticed.

"Do you see Amanda and Seth?" Julia rose up on her tiptoes, trying to spot her friends.

Samson gave the grounds his own thorough search. "I don't."

Before Julia could say anything further, a familiar voice sounded from too close by.

"Take a seat on the hill, folks! The best of the fest is yet to come!" Marge's rally cry crackled through the squeaky speaker of a blow-horn as she walked in their direction, encouraging people who were milling around to find a spot to view the fireworks display.

Samson ducked his head down and scooted behind Julia.

"Coward," she coughed.

Samson smiled a disarming smile, and Julia lost herself in the look of his face—all laugh-lined and enchanting—until they got swept up in the crowd being ushered toward the grassy hill. People scurried about, trying to find the best seat to lay out blankets and watch the fireworks.

"Hey, Jules!"

Crap.

"Mom, Dad!" Panic seeped into her voice as her parents crossed toward them. Julia didn't want to explain Samson to them right now. Not when she was trying to sort through her own thoughts and feelings about him.

She shot him a frantic look. "Do you think you, uh, could leave me alone for a minute?"

The carefree expression he wore fell away, and his face closed in on itself.

"Yeah, I guess I should go. Excuse me." Samson gave her a formal nod before striding in the opposite direction as her mom and dad approached.

Julia stared after him, a tug-of-war of relief and dismay raging in her head and heart, until her parents stepped into her line of sight.

"How's it going, Jules?" Her dad bent to kiss her cheek.

"Who was that?" Her mom swiveled her head and followed Julia's gaze.

"What? No one. It's going fine." Julia's words came out in a rush. Her mom arched a brow, but Julia ignored her, speaking instead to her dad. "How was your festival burger?"

"Better than ever." Her dad patted his belly. "Did you try one?"

Julia fielded her parents' questions about her afternoon and evening, leaving out how she'd spent the past hour.

Guilt at ditching Samson in front of her parents welled up inside her. She shouldn't have done that.

Then again, she *really* didn't relish the idea of getting the third degree from her mom and dad in the middle of the festival. A little space from Samson would be good. And he'd understand, right? He'd said as much down by the river.

Still, Julia hated the way they had parted, and she couldn't deny she wanted to be by his side again.

Like, right now.

Her whole body stung with the awareness that she'd made a mistake, and the fear that she might not get a chance to rectify it sent her nerves chattering.

"You coming with us to watch the show, Julia?" her dad asked.

Julia pasted a fake smile on her face. "Lead the way!"

She scanned the crowd as they took their seats, but she didn't see Samson in the hordes of people collected on the hill.

And as the first firework lit up the sky high above her, disappointment rolled around in Julia's gut like a rock.

Chapter 17

SAMSON

MAPLETON PUT ON A spectacular fireworks show for a town of its size. Samson had been to the nation's capital for several Fourth of July events, so he had high expectations, and if Julia had been by his side, this display may have topped them all.

Samson would be lying if he said it hadn't stung when she'd panicked at the sight of her parents, but he'd taken the hit to his pride and bailed.

Now, he was spending the entire fireworks show warring over one question: did he really *want* to meet them, anyway? It would only complicate things.

Granted, everything was complicated as it was, so what harm could adding parents to the mix cause?

Samson took off his baseball cap and dragged a hand through his hair. He'd almost blown it when he mentioned Milo down by the river. Julia sensed her ex was acting strangely. Was Milo's behavior due to his plans to wipe her business out from under her?

The familiar pit of dread returned to Samson's stomach. He'd been able to forget about Milo's schemes for most of the day, and what he realized in the meantime was he liked Julia. He *really* liked her. Keeping business and personal separate was going to be more of a challenge than he anticipated.

Lost in his thoughts, Samson stayed close to the food tent and observed the crowds as they oohed and ahhed at the fireworks display. The grand finale complete, he stood watching as people got up and stretched after the half-hour show, the scent of black powder lingering in the evening air.

"Check, check. Check one, two."

Samson pivoted to face the amphitheater where the final act of the night had taken the stage. A banner above the drum set read *Buffy and the Streetcats*. A woman whom he guessed to be Buffy stood at the mic.

"How are y'all doing out there?" Her deep, sultry voice was answered with cheers from the crowd.

When the Streetcats began playing, Samson looked for Julia, and after panning back and forth twice and not seeing her, he thought maybe she had called it an early night. But she would have found him and said goodbye, wouldn't she have?

Samson shoved his hat back on his head, tugging it into place. He'd never felt this sort of connection to anyone—this urgency to be near her and to see her face. And it wasn't like he hadn't dated. He'd had a steady girlfriend for his entire sophomore and junior year of college. But when Tisha Green studied abroad the summer before their senior year, neither she nor Samson missed each other, so they mutually ended things.

Since Tisha, Samson had gone on several dates and been in a couple short-term relationships, but nothing came of them. There certainly hadn't been anyone who had made him feel the way Julia did. He missed her more in the past hour than he missed Tisha the entire time she'd been in Japan. The thought sent his stomach catapulting forward.

"Well, what do you think?"

Samson spun around to find Marge standing with two other older women.

"P-pardon me?" he asked.

"What do you think about the festival thus far? Keep in mind the dance is often the best part, and that's yet to come." As if to prove Marge's point, Buffy and the Streetcats struck up a lively number.

The two other women standing with her looked at him curiously. The blonde strongly resembled Julia, and it dawned on Samson that this was Julia's mom, the same woman who had approached the two of them earlier. She looked like he imagined Julia would look in twenty or thirty years, and Samson couldn't help but stare.

She eyed him with interest, eventually raising a brow.

Samson gulped and let his go-to grin spread over his face, rotating back to Marge. "The festival has been wonderful, Marge. Thanks so much for inviting me."

Marge beamed at him.

Samson had fallen back on his charm. If Julia were here, she'd see right through him and call him on it, but she wasn't around.

He dipped his chin to Marge's companions, plowing ahead. "And who are these lovely ladies?"

"Samson, meet Gloria Derks and Linda Koke. They are on the festival committee with me. We have a couple items to tend to before we enjoy the dance ourselves."

Samson shook hands with Gloria and Linda. "I'd say you've earned some enjoyment. Everything ran smoothly. The fireworks were impressive, and the food has been better than anything I've tasted in a long time." No matter what Julia said, Samson was going to butter Marge up every chance he got. He'd rather be on her good side than not.

"All in all, I'd say it was another good year," the woman named Linda spoke in response. "What brings you to town, Samson?"

Samson cleared his throat. "I'm here for work."

Marge rested her hands on the utility belt she wore around her waist. "Samson is with the firm that's bought the mill land. He's working on the new properties going up."

Samson kept his expression smooth even though he wanted to grimace. So much for being discreet.

Gloria's eyes bugged before she settled her features, and a slow smile slid across her face.

Linda stared him down, not bothering to hide her appraisal. "Oh, you're him. I heard you caused quite a stir at the café when you arrived. My husband, Ted, came in shortly after you were there and said the folks inside were all in a tizzy. Did Julia mention anything to you, Gloria?"

"We've talked about the development, yes." Gloria's gaze bore into him. It was like she wanted to ask a question of him or say something else but never got so far as opening her mouth. Instead, she blinked and turned to Marge. "Should we gather the rest of the committee?"

Marge checked her watch. "Yes, yes. It's time." She rounded on Samson and clarified. "We always do a little meeting to make sure everyone knows their roles for clean-up and take-down. So we must be going. You enjoy yourself. Dance like there's no one watching. Let the rhythm move you. All that jazz. You know." Marge was on a roll.

Samson suppressed a smile.

Gloria was less successful and let out a laugh that she covered with a fake sneeze.

Marge stuck up her nose.

"Nice to meet you, Samson." Gloria smiled at him, dodging a dirty look from Marge. "I'm sure we'll see you around. Oh, there you are. Julia!" Gloria held her arm high and waved.

Samson sucked in a lungful of air and turned to find Julia approaching.

"Hey, Mom." She joined the circle. "Hi, Samson." Lines of apprehension creased her face, and his heart convulsed.

"Hello, Julia." His greeting came out sounding robotic and formal. It wasn't at all how he felt—he longed to go back to the familiar and easy rapport they'd developed—but he figured it was best to let her take the lead. These were her people.

Gloria's head twisted between the two of them. If she was anything like his mom, she was undoubtedly reading the scene as only a mother could. His hunch was confirmed when Julia's cheeks turned pink under her mom's scrutiny.

Marge clapped her hands. "Good, Julia, you're here. We need to find Amanda, Sally, Mable, Colleen, and Therese. Let's round 'em up, ladies. Meeting under the tent in five minutes." With that, she whipped out her walkie-talkie and marched off, oblivious to the undercurrent of thoughts and feelings rushing between the other members of her party.

"Mable is over by the main stage. I'll grab her." Linda headed toward the amphitheater, cutting through the lines of dancers and stopping to say hello to a few people along the way.

Gloria squared her shoulders. "Well, then. I'll check around for Therese. Her group usually has a table over by the porta-potties. Jules, can you find Amanda, Colleen, and Sally?" She waited for Julia to nod before turning to him. "Nice to meet you, Samson. I trust we'll be seeing you around." With a finger wave, she left them alone.

Samson slid his hands into his pockets and let his attention rest on Julia, waiting for her to say something first.

She nibbled her lip and eventually dragged her gaze up to his face. "So, you've met my mom."

"Marge introduced us. Sorry, I know that's not what you wanted." Samson told himself he was silly for feeling wounded over it, and yet here he was.

Julia sunk her chin, scuffing a white-laced shoe back and forth in the grass. "That's not entirely true." She took a full-body breath and met his stare again. "I have to go now, though."

Did she sound reluctant? Or was he only hearing what he wanted to hear? Samson's heart hammered with hope, the pain of being ditched by her suddenly scabbing over with the potential promise of more time together. "Okay."

"I'll find you later?"

He checked his enthusiasm and nodded. "Sure, I'll look for you."

"Okay."

"Okay." Julia turned on her heel and walked off into the crowd.

Samson missed her before she was even out of sight.

Chapter 18

JULIA

JULIA BOUNCED HER KNEE under the table where she sat with the rest of the festival committee members. All the villagers and guests were now over by the stage dancing to Buffy and the Streetcats, so aside from the chirping of Marge's voice, this was the quietest spot in the whole park.

Except for the knoll by the river.

Julia's mind flitted to Samson. If only the two of them could have stayed on the stone bench—alone. If only things weren't so complicated. If only she didn't have to deal with other people's opinions and over-bearing committee heads who wouldn't stop talking. She'd had enough orders barked at her to last a year, and she could barely focus on what Marge was saying since she was so fed up with the woman.

And so distracted by Samson.

Amanda poked her in the side and shot her a questioning look. "What's going on?" she mouthed.

Julia picked at a sticker that was stuck to the edge of the table. "Nothing," she whispered.

Amanda rolled her eyes.

Julia arched her brows. "You're one to talk. You look smitten."

Amanda blushed. "Seth kissed me."

Julia reached over and squeezed her hand. She couldn't wait to hear all the swoony details.

"Is that okay with you, Julia?"

Julia sat up straight, whipping her head around to face the front of the make-shift meeting space.

Marge's hands were on her hips, and she tapped her foot, waiting on Julia's response.

Julia reached up and squeezed her top knot, trying to act nonchalant. They were busted, and the only way to cover for her lack of attention was to go along and agree with whatever Marge asked of her. "Sure, Marge. That's no problem."

"Brilliant. Thanks so much. I'll find you thirty minutes before the dance concludes, and you can help us move the money to the village office safe."

Julia's arm dropped to her lap, and she stifled a groan—barely—when she realized what Marge had asked her to do.

The woman *must* have a vendetta against her. Not only would she have to leave the grounds early, but she'd be required to go with Marge and the money bag to the village offices. Milo would be along for the ride to ensure the money was safely stored in the vault until it could be deposited in the bank in the morning. That meant, not only would she be spending the end of her night with Marge, but also with her ex-boyfriend. Peachy.

"Alright, I think that's everything. Let's enjoy the rest of the festival and bring it home, ladies. It's been another good one."

The committee members stood and whooped. Most hurried off to meet up with their friends and families, but Julia's mom hung back and approached Julia and Amanda.

"Jules, I'm surprised you were willing to do the money this year. I can't imagine you want to spend extra time with Milo."

Amanda snickered at Gloria's no-nonsense delivery.

Julia, too, couldn't help but laugh. She slung her arm over her mom's shoulder.

"No, Mom. I don't really want to. But you know Marge. What was I supposed to say? Besides, you guys have all paid your dues. I don't mind taking one for the team."

Her mom stared her down. "Well, that's nice, but it seemed to me like you only agreed because you were caught passing notes in the back of the classroom." She dropped her voice and leaned in. "What did they say?"

Amanda and Julia laughed.

Julia pitched her voice with a sing-song inflection. "I'll never tell." She directed her mom to the grassy field where the dance was in full swing. "Come on. You need to find Dad. He owes you a dance for letting him have that festival burger earlier."

"You're right. He certainly does. I imagine he's found a seat with Charlie. I'll have to go hunt for him." Her mom glanced over the crowd.

"There he is." Julia pointed to her dad and caught his eye.

He waved to her and her mom, and a warm smile spread over her mom's face.

"Alright. I'm off then. If I don't catch you before you leave with the money, Happy Fourth of July, Jules. You, too, Amanda."

Amanda gave Julia's mom a hug, and Gloria took two steps before stopping and turning to pin Julia with a look.

"You know, Samson seemed like a nice young man. Maybe you should find him."

Amanda sputtered next to her.

Julia wanted to bury her head in her hands. Only her mom would be able to see right through her.

"Maybe I should."

It was a noncommittal response, but her mom's expression said it all. She already knew everything she needed to know.

"Maybe you should. Night, dear." With that, she floated off, and when she made it across the crowd, Joe pulled her down into his lap, and Julia's mom wrapped an arm around his neck.

Julia sighed. Her parents were so comfortable with each other, so content in one another's presence.

She looked around, listening as Amanda pointed out friends and familiar faces. Everyone was laughing and enjoying themselves. It was that sort of night.

The band struck up the tune of "American Girl" by Tom Petty, and Buffy was killing it on the vocals. A group of high schoolers were huddled together, dancing nearest to them. Some thirty- and forty-somethings broke it down in the middle of the crowd. Along the front row were the die-hard Buffy and the Streetcats groupies, singing every word with their hands in the air.

"Hey."

Julia jumped and turned to find Samson walking her way with Seth. He had his hands in his pockets, and his baseball cap shaded his eyes. Her whole body heated at the sight.

"Hey yourself."

Next to Julia, Amanda laughed as Seth grabbed her hand and pulled her out onto the dance floor without a word.

Her gaze lingered on the happy couple as she worked up the courage to apologize for her behavior before the fireworks and ask Samson to dance.

"If you want me to leave you alone, you should say so now."

Julia's spine stiffened, and she shot him a look. "What do you mean?"

Samson clenched his jaw and spoke through gritted teeth, like he didn't particularly like the taste of the words he was forcing himself to say. "I get the sense that you're conflicted, and I wanted to give you an out. If there are other people you want to see, or if you'd rather not be around me, tell me. I'll leave you alone."

His voice was thick with nerves and a type of vulnerability she hadn't expected, and it took Julia exactly one second to determine her answer. She knew in her heart she didn't want to distance herself from him, no matter what her head—or the town—said. She tilted her chin up and hooked his gaze. "No. Listen, I'm sorry for how I acted before. I get caught up in what I think other people think of me sometimes, especially in Mapleton, but I was being cowardly and stupid. You don't have to leave me alone. The truth is I like your company."

The defined angle of Samson's jawline eased, and he shot her a wicked grin. "Good. Then you said you like to dance, so let's dance." He put his baseball cap on backwards, reached for her hand, and dragged her into the crowd.

"What?!" Julia hurried to keep up with him. "You didn't tell me you danced."

"There's a lot I haven't told you." A dimple flashed in the side of his cheek, and Julia inhaled sharply. She was in big trouble with Samson.

The toe-curling, can't-get-enough, good kind of trouble.

They joined Seth, Amanda, and the throng of villagers, who all transitioned to dancing to Buffy's rendition of the cult favorite, "Paradise by the Dashboard Light."

Samson spun Julia around, and a laugh bubbled up. Trouble or not, she let go and let herself have fun.

He was a good dancer. They juked and jived together with the group, many of whom she recognized and who welcomed them and their dancing antics with open arms.

"This is the longest song ever!" Julia shouted to Samson.

In response, he twirled her out and pulled her back toward him. Her hand landed on his arm, and her mind went blank except for one singular thought: BICEPS.

By the time Buffy wrapped up the eight-minute song, Julia's side ached from laughing and dancing. They didn't get any reprieve as Buffy went right into "I Want to Dance with Somebody", as made famous by Whitney Houston.

After a few more tunes, Buffy smiled into the microphone. "We're going to slow it down a little for y'all."

The crowd collectively sighed, some in relief and some in despair, as Buffy's band played the opening chords to "Heaven" by Bryan Adams.

Samson held out his hand to Julia, and she gladly let him draw her in close. Julia stretched up and placed her opposite arm around his broad shoulders, marveling at the ripple of muscle she felt along his upper back. Not many men made her feel dainty at 5'8", but Samson did.

He tucked one hand around the small of her back and held her other hand tightly in his, resting it against his chest. She didn't look into his eyes, just turned her head and breathed him in—cedar and citrus. Samson-scented air was the best kind of air, and with his arms wrapped around her, she felt like she could breathe easy. The realization should have been jarring, but instead, it made her feel settled.

He moved her in time with the gentle music, and his cheek skimmed against her hair as she pressed herself closer to him. Samson's heart beat strongly through his shirt, and Julia allowed herself a small smile at the knowledge that he wasn't unaffected by her, either. For a second, she thought about who was watching her, but the thought passed. Safe in Samson's arms, she didn't care. She trusted him to take care of her.

Samson shifted, dropping her hand and settling both of his arms around her waist. She draped her hands around his neck and looked up at him.

"What?" she asked.

"You're smiling."

"I'm happy."

"I'm glad about that. Julia…"

She pressed her lips together, not daring to make a sound and miss what Samson was going to say next.

"This has been one of the best days I've had in a long time. Thank you."

His gaze cradled hers, full of a combination of kindness and desire. It made Julia shiver. He spoke with control and conviction. Based on everything he'd told her earlier in the evening, Samson was a man who knew what he wanted and went after it, and right now, as far as she could tell, he wanted her.

That knowledge grounded Julia—made her feel some sort of invincible.

"I'm glad you're here." Julia stared at Samson and willed him to believe her words. She could barely believe them herself. If someone had told her a month ago that she'd be happy someone was in town to work on the mill site, she would have laughed out loud and called that person a liar. But tonight, gazing into Samson's eyes, Julia could say it was the honest truth.

"You promise you mean that?"

"I promise."

Samson pulled her closer. "Well, then. I was hoping maybe we could have more days like this."

"What did you have in mind?" Julia's chest tingled at the thought of spending time with him.

"I don't care as long as you're there."

His gravelly voice made her knees turn to applesauce. "Ditto."

With aching tenderness, Samson trailed his hands up to cup her face.

He was going to kiss her. All the breath seeped from Julia's lungs. The other dancers around them faded to muted gray. Her sole focus was the man in front of her, standing there in piercing color. He gently pulled her mouth closer to his, hovering with his lips a mere inch away. She closed her eyes, her heart pounding.

"Julia!" Her eyes snapped open in time to see Samson drop his hands to his sides. Stunned, she followed suit. Marge stood directly to her right with Milo a couple of paces behind her, irritation written like a horrible sunburn all over his face. "It's time for us to go."

Julia shoved a flyaway behind her ear while she worked to unstick her tongue from the roof of her mouth. She craved Samson's touch and longed to tell Marge and Milo to take a hike while she captured Samson's lips with hers. But in this case, her head prevailed over her heart—at least for now. There would be more time for kissing—she hoped.

Julia's cheeks flamed from a mixture of frustration and yearning as she flashed Samson an apologetic look. "I guess I have to go."

"Okay." Samson searched her face.

Julia leaned in, angling her head toward his and giving his bicep a quick squeeze. Because, *come on*. "I'll see you soon, though. I promise."

Samson's lips quirked when he caught her last word.

"See you around, neighbor." He held her gaze for a little longer than was customary before turning and walking in the opposite direction, not giving Marge or Milo the satisfaction of a second glance.

Julia took a deep breath to try to control her racing heart before squaring her shoulders to face Marge and Milo.

"Alrighty, then. Let's go."

She trailed them to Milo's car, trying not to dwell on the awkwardness of it all. As she scooted into the backseat with the zipper bag full of festival money, she said a silent prayer of thanks that she'd had the courage to end things with Milo when she did. The depth of feeling she'd experienced with Samson in one night—both emotionally and physically—highlighted how much was lacking in her previous relationship.

When Milo turned onto Mapleton Avenue, he shot her a scathing look through the rearview mirror, almost as if he was expecting some sort of explanation from her.

She raised her brows but kept her mouth shut. She didn't owe him anything. Had he forgotten the way he acted at the dunk tank? If he wanted her to be cordial in the wake of their breakup, well, he should have considered that before he threw that third baseball.

And before he told her she would amount to nothing without him.

Marge rescued the car from the depths of uncomfortable silence by engaging Milo with small talk. "I'd say it was a successful day."

"Can't argue with that."

"Weather was perfect."

"Couldn't have asked for a better turnout."

Julia looked out her window, tuning them out and fighting off a grin as she absently touched her lips, her memory caught up in Samson and the way it felt to be held in his arms.

The flags that lined the avenue blew gently in the sticky night breeze as they approached the village offices. When Milo parked, Julia hopped out of the car, anxious to secure the money and be on her way. She was tired and ready for bed, and she had a feeling her dreams would be happy tonight, despite the grumbly expression on Milo's face.

Chapter 19

SAMSON

THE DAY AFTER THE Fourth of July Festival, Samson put in eight hours of work, but any time he had a minute to himself, his mind found its way to Julia—to the sound of her laugh and the way she bit her lip when she was thinking.

So when he turned into his driveway that night, his heart rate ratcheted up at the sight before his eyes. Julia sat perched on his front stoop. Before he could stop it, the thought crossed his mind: *I could get used to coming home to her.*

"Hey, neighbor." The tilted grin on her lips was adorable, and a desire to finish what they had started at the festival and kiss her hit him hard and fast. He told himself to chill.

"Hi there." He slammed his door and skirted the front of his truck.

"Is this weird?"

"What, you on my front porch? Or the fact that we're neighbors?"

Julia snickered. "I don't know. All of it."

Samson walked up to her, bending to scratch an excited Mr. Waffles behind the ears. "I've never minded weird things."

"Really? Like what?" Julia's blue eyes twinkled.

"Hmmm, let me think." He stood upright, and Mr. Waffles ran in a circle around him before taking a seat on his porch. "Dipping grilled cheese sandwiches in ketchup," he finally said.

Julia burst out laughing. "That's the weirdest thing you can think of? That's not that weird. Ketchup is basically like tomato soup."

"You go then. It's harder to think of your own weirdness on the spot."

"I'm very weird, so it's not hard for me. Let's see. I smell every book I open. I read the labels of my shampoo bottle every time I'm in the shower. I often think in Taylor Swift lyrics. Oh, and I put cinnamon in my black coffee."

"Yikes. That cinnamon thing is going to be a deal breaker," Samson deadpanned, eliciting another laugh from her.

He wasn't one to banter, but with Julia he wanted to.

"Do you want to come in for a minute?"

"Sure." Julia tied Mr. Waffles' leash to his porch rail and followed Samson inside. "This is a nice place." She turned around in a circle to take in his modest accommodations. "I've never been in here before."

"Yeah, it's working out well so far. Can't beat the proximity to the job site, and I hear the neighbors are pretty cool...when they aren't being weird."

"It's their weirdness that makes them cool," Julia said without missing a beat. "I don't have your phone number," she added. "And if I want to keep my promise of seeing you again, I need to get it."

"So, you're a girl who keeps her word. Good to know." He slid his phone across the kitchen counter to her. She entered her number and pushed it back.

"I think I proved that by showing you a good time at the festival. Text me so I have yours." She motioned to his phone.

"You entered your first and last name, and for company name, you put *weird neighbor*?"

"So you don't forget me."

Not possible.

Samson texted her, and when it went through, she typed away, presumably adding him as a contact.

"Dare I ask what title you gave me?"

"Samson was all I needed." She broke eye contact, running her hands along the Corian countertop. "So, what did you do today?"

He allowed the change in subject even as a current of electricity sizzled between them. "I actually swung by the café this morning."

"Really?"

"Yeah, but then I saw the sign on the door saying you weren't opening until noon."

Julia nodded. "It's always a long day at the festival, so we take it easy on July 5th."

"That's understandable, though I missed my morning coffee. And seeing you."

Julia's mouth curved upward. "And then what'd you do?"

"Just worked." There wasn't much to report on that end, at least not much she'd want to hear about.

They fell into silence until Samson decided to go for it. There were rules about this sort of thing. He was sure he was supposed to wait a few days to call her to set up a proper date. Oh well. She was the one who showed up on his porch.

He cleared his throat. "So, do you have plans for tonight? I'm pretty beat, but it would be great to spend some time together."

Julia scooted out one of his barstools and took a seat. "I'm all yours." She gulped, blinking a couple times. "I mean, yeah, let's hang out."

Samson smirked, loving the swath of red covering her cheeks. He couldn't resist teasing her. "All mine, huh?"

Julia rolled her sparkling eyes. "You wish. I've got an idea, though. You get changed or do whatever you have to do. Then we'll go for a ride around Mapleton. I'll drive so you can relax."

Samson didn't know if he should explore Mapleton with her as his guide, because he didn't know what to make of his growing attachment to this quirky little town. But despite his reservations, spending time with Julia won out. What harm could a simple drive around do, anyway?

"Okay. I'll be right back."

Samson hurried to shower. He changed into jeans and an ocean-blue crewneck t-shirt.

When he was ready, he followed Julia outside. Mr. Waffles leapt into the bed of the truck and stuck his head through the window into the cab.

Samson grinned as he opened the passenger side door. "Did I steal your seat, Mr. Waffles?"

"No," Julia answered for the dog as she climbed into the driver's seat. "He's always back there. I love him, but he sheds like crazy. If he sat up here, no one else would want to."

Samson looked around the cherry-red Ford Ranger. "Nice ride." It was worn but looked to be well taken care of. He reached behind him to buckle his seat belt.

"Thanks. It used to be my dad's." Julia smoothed down her shoulder strap and started the ignition. She rolled down her window with the manual knob before directing her attention to the radio, which was currently blaring static.

Samson followed her lead and rolled down his window. He used the time she spent messing with the radio to observe her. She was a natural beauty. She wore little makeup, and her blonde hair was down tonight with layers that fell across her face as she leaned forward to turn the dial this way and that. She bit her tongue in concentration, and Samson loved how normal she was. He felt privileged to see her relaxed like this without a festival going on in the background or a café to run. Just her, in her truck. She wasn't trying to impress him. She was being herself, without pretense. Around her, he wanted to be himself, too.

Before Samson could overthink *that*, music started blaring.

"Yes!" Julia stopped fiddling with the ancient buttons and sat up with an exultant look on her fresh face. "Sorry. The old radio is touchy, so you have to set it exactly right to get it to play. It hasn't played all day. But what's a drive without some music, right?"

Samson could count on one hand the number of times he'd taken a drive solely for the sake of taking a drive, but he nodded. They weren't even out of the driveway, but he already considered drives with Julia his new favorite hobby.

Julia angled her truck toward Mapleton Avenue. "So, where should I take you tonight? Not in a creepy way."

The corners of Samson's mouth tugged upward. "Well, we've already established you're weird, so we may as well add creepy to the list."

She laughed, and he vowed to do whatever it took to keep her happy. He glanced left and right as Julia came to a stop at the intersection of their street and the avenue. "I don't know. It's your town. Show me the good stuff."

"My café is the good stuff." Julia didn't hesitate as she delivered her one-liner. For a second, Samson was concerned he had offended her, but she cracked another smile. "But there's other good stuff, too. We'll take the long way around town, and I'll show you."

The easy conversation between the two of them dashed away any lingering doubt Samson had about exploring the town—and a relationship—with her...at least for the time being. They chatted about their favorite books and movies as Julia turned left and took another quick left two streets down. They drove down a hilly road that became less and less populated with houses as they went. The few buildings in this part of town sat off the road at the ends of gravel driveways. They passed what appeared to be a Christmas tree farm, and when they crested an unusually large hill, Samson was surprised to see an expansive blacktop parking lot and a state-of-the-art school ahead.

"Wow, I didn't expect this to be out here. It seemed like we were driving into farmlands."

"We were. Mapleton is surrounded to the south by farms. To the east and west are other towns, and to the north is, well, the river. But this land is owned by the Mapleton Area School District, and it's where they built our high school. It was built a few years before my freshman year, so it's still relatively new." Julia scrunched up her nose as if doing the math in her head before giving up with a shrug. She threw her truck into park, hopped effortlessly down onto the blacktop, and opened the tailgate for the dog. "Come on, Mr. Waffles."

Mr. Waffles darted out and started chasing his tail around in a circle. When he wasn't sleeping, that must have been his thing.

Julia studied her dog. "He's very intelligent, I promise. But he has a funny way of showing it."

"If you say so." Samson's smart-alecky comment earned him an elbow to his ribs.

He reached over and caught Julia's wrist, pulling her to him and tickling her side.

She shrieked and jumped away, laughing. "You cut that out!"

It didn't take her long to fall back into step next to him, and they walked along toward the school, knocking shoulders in a way that seemed unintentional but, at least on Samson's end, was completely intentional. The parking lot was deserted, and Samson felt like the luckiest guy in the world to have Julia all to himself.

"Mapleton High School, Home of the Paper Shredders." He read the stone-etched sign in front of the building and turned to Julia.

She stood, smiling at the sign with pride flickering in her eyes. "This is where I went to school."

"I figured, but is your mascot really a paper shredder?"

She shot him a don't-mess-with-me look. "Yes, it is. Do you have a problem with that? I'm proud to be a paper shredder."

Samson couldn't help laughing. "Seriously?"

"Of course! Why? What was your high school mascot? Something annoyingly unoriginal like a wildcat?"

"No. I was a crusader." Samson beat one hand against his chest as he said it in the way they used to do as part of their rally cry at school. He always thought crusader was an imposing and smart mascot—certainly it beat paper shredder.

"Wow. That's a whole thing, then?" Julia motioned to his fist where it was planted on his chest.

"Indeed." He chuckled. "I haven't done that in years, though. High school was a while ago for some of us."

"What are you, like, old?" Julia asked as they walked to the right of the building.

Mr. Waffles trotted in front of them.

An outdoor commons space extended out from a side exit of the school and overlooked the farm fields to the west.

Samson shrugged. "Probably older than you. How old do you think I am?"

"That's not fair. I don't want to guess wrong." Julia hoisted herself up and over the low fence that went around the commons. "It's okay if we sit up here for a bit. I've done this before."

With Milo? The question popped into Samson's head without warning and was followed with a rush of displeasure. Samson had never been the jealous type. Then again, no one had given him a reason to be. Until now. Now, he wanted to be the one Julia made memories with. Plain and simple.

Samson pointed to Mr. Waffles, who had taken off around the fence and into the fields. "Is it okay for him to run like that?"

She nodded. "He'll stay close."

He wasn't sure if he trusted Mr. Waffles' dog IQ, but Samson scaled the fence and joined Julia at a picnic table on the side of the commons, facing the farm fields behind the school. "Alright. Go ahead and guess my age. I won't be offended."

She looked him up and down as he dropped into a seat next to her, tapping her fingers along her slim jaw. "Let me see."

Samson sat up straight under her gaze, loving how her blue eyes danced and glistened like waves in the late-day sun.

"I'm the worst at this. I think you're thirty-two," she said after a minute.

"Final answer?"

"Yes."

"Close. Thirty. But I turn thirty-one on the fourteenth of July."

"You *are* old then," Julia teased. "I'm only twenty-seven."

"Wow. I'm ancient." Samson kept his face straight.

When Julia laughed, another unfamiliar sensation coursed through him, and if he didn't know better, he'd say it was love.

Chapter 20

Julia

OPENING UP TO SAMSON was as easy to do in her truck as it had been at the festival. Julia told him about her time on the debate team, and how her experience in DECA—the business, marketing, and entrepreneurial club at school—made her want to be a business major. Her former DECA advisor was retired now but came to On Deck Café at least a few times a week. Julia was proud of that, and Samson understood why it was cool to her. In their whole year of dating, she hadn't gotten around to explaining the connection to Milo.

"Okay." Julia drove on, glancing over at Samson. "Have you seen the swim lake, yet?"

"I thought Mapleton had a river. You have a lake, too?" His eyebrows drew together in a V-shape, making his green eyes glint.

Julia laughed at Samson's obvious confusion. To be fair, not many places could boast an in-town lake.

"Yes and no. It's man-made. I'll show you." She drove through Mapleton proper, turning left onto the avenue and cruising by her café. Only a couple cars were left in the lot this late in the evening.

Past the woods of Sunrise Park, she made a slight right turn then a quick left turn. She drove for a half mile as Samson peered out the window.

"Is this still Mapleton?" he asked.

"Yes. These are the outskirts of town. And this is the swim lake." She parked her truck in the deserted lot and pointed ahead at the body of water. It was surrounded by a chain-link fence. No one was swimming now, as the lake shut down at the dinner hour each night. The two of them were alone. "Let's go so you can take a closer look. Sorry, boy, you have to stay here."

Mr. Waffles whimpered but settled himself into the bed of the truck.

Samson followed her, and they walked toward the lake.

"Everyone knows about Mapleton's baseball diamonds and the river, but this is more of a local secret."

They approached the chain-link fence, and Samson peered through. "I've lived in a lot of places, but I've never seen anything like this."

Julia nodded. "It's a one-of-a-kind establishment. Give me a boost." She lifted her hands up and grabbed hold of the fence.

Samson gave her a quizzical look. "You're hopping the fence?"

"Only if you help me." She laughed. "Don't worry. There's no one else around."

He chuckled. "I thought you said you were a rule follower." Samson bent down and made a step for her by cupping his hands.

Julia pulled herself up. "Ehhh." She grunted as she swung one leg over the fence before dropping down onto the other side, brushing her hands together. "I take calculated risks." She stared through the fence at him. "Besides, the guy who manages this place is a family friend. You coming?"

Samson smirked and vaulted himself up and over the fence, landing next to her all in one fluid motion. He winked when he caught her staring at the line of skin along his waist where his shirt had ridden up, and his pleased expression heightened the allure of his handsome face.

Julia cleared her throat and jerked her head toward the water, a surge of both sweat and chills sweeping over body. "Right. Well. This is the lake! Complete with sand on all sides. The locals come here from Memorial Day to Labor Day to cool off. We staff it with lifeguards, like yours truly."

Julia kicked off her flip-flops, and Samson did the same. They walked in the damp sand along the water's edge.

"You're a lifeguard?"

"I was. In the summers throughout high school until I took a desk job at the village offices. I have a lot of happy memories here. The lifeguards were some of my best friends. Amanda was one, too. We loved hanging in the guard house." She hooked her thumb toward a small hut set away from the water. "And I got my first kiss right over there." Julia tipped her chin to the old swing set that sat along the grass beyond the sand.

"Your first kiss was on a swing set?"

Julia's heart fluttered at the sound of the word 'kiss' on Samson's lips. She wasn't sure why she had brought up this part of her history, but she guessed that, at least subliminally, it had something to do with the fact that she really wanted a kiss from Samson. Yesterday. She wanted a kiss from him yesterday. Literally.

She swallowed hard and charged on with her story. "Yep. With Curtis Houston. His family moved to Mapleton when we were in sixth grade. I had the biggest crush on him, and finally, the summer before my freshman year of high school, we met here with a bunch of friends. We were swinging and talking, and he asked if he could kiss me. I told him yes, so he did. It would have been romantic if we hadn't had an audience of all of our friends. So it ended up being sort of embarrassing." Julia laughed at the memory.

"Does Curtis still live in town?"

Out of the corner of her eye, Julia studied Samson. He looked at ease as he shifted his gaze out over the water, but the trace of jealousy in his tone made her insides swirl—all sweet and delicious like a chocolate and vanilla twist soft serve ice cream cone. "Oh, no. He and his family moved away when we were sophomores in high school. I forget what his dad did, but they bounced around a lot. We never even dated. We met up here a couple of times that summer before our freshman year, but that was it. Last I heard, he was married with two kids. He was a good guy. Not a terrible first-kiss story, I suppose."

Samson shrugged his wide shoulders. "Better than mine."

"Care to share?" When Samson shook his head, she nudged his arm, and a jolt shot up her spine at the contact. It was incredible her hair wasn't permanently standing on end given all the electricity passing between them. "Come on. I told you mine."

"Fine," Samson relented. "Her name was Cassidy Lessing. We were both thirteen. Her dad was a Marine, and we lived on the same street on base. She dared me to kiss her after we had been hanging out together one day, so I did. Her mom peeked out to the back patio to check on us at that very moment. I was humiliated and left. But then it got worse because her mom knew my mom, and the gossip surrounding our kiss spread like wildfire. Thank goodness we moved to North Dakota two months later."

Julia couldn't help but laugh, picturing a young Samson sprinting home with his tail between his legs. "First kisses are so silly. It's not like they mean anything, but we all remember them, don't we?"

"Definitely."

They walked on in silence and eventually angled to the fence. Julia slipped on her shoes, and Samson helped her scale the chain links. Back at her truck, they found Mr. Waffles snoring.

Julia rolled her eyes at her dog and tried not to let the idea of a first kiss with Samson affect her driving.

From the swim lake, she took him through the old part of Mapleton where the original neighborhoods stood—close to Julia's bungalow and Samson's rental unit. A lot of the homes in this part of town were run-down. Several were uninhabited. It always broke Julia's heart to see them sitting empty.

"I dream of these homes getting made over and restored to their former glory." She peered out the window and eased her truck down the street. "Not sure how that'll happen, but it would be nice if this part of town underwent a sort of revival.

The building where I opened the café looked like this before I got my hands on it."

She pointed to an old, brown shingle-sided house. The pale-yellow paint on the front door was peeling. The windows were shuttered, and the middle digit of the house number was dangling upside down. It was a cosmetic nightmare, but you could tell what good bones it had and what a charming house it could be.

"Really? I can't imagine your café looking like that. It's so nice now." Samson pointed to another house as she turned onto Mapleton Avenue. "You can't replicate this kind of charm and character with new construction. I've seen architects try. Those porches are to die for." He stared at the wrap-around porch on the first level of the two-story, white-clapboard house. Expertly manicured hedges lined the driveway and gave the house a sophisticated air, even in the twilight.

"Oh, yes. That's Mary Ellen and George Vander Kempen's house." Julia smiled as she thought of the middle-aged couple whose son she'd gone to school with.

"It's nice you know pretty much everyone in town."

Pride for Mapleton and its residents flooded Julia. "It is. This town has been so supportive of me through the years. Lesser people might have raised an eyebrow at a young, twenty-something kid trying to launch a business. But if they had their doubts about me, I never knew it. They showed up and bought coffee. I'm thankful to be a part of this community."

She glanced to her right, and Samson was studying her intently. "What?"

Samson turned to face forward and ran his hand along the lip of the truck's open window. "Nothing. It's just...well, the community is probably pretty glad to have you, too."

"Why do you say that?"

"You do a lot for Mapleton. Even an outsider like me can tell that. And your business brings people in and gives them a reason to stay around. I'm sure you could have been successful launching On Deck Café somewhere else, too. But you chose Mapleton."

"Huh." She hadn't thought of it that way. She'd been busting her butt to serve her patrons because she loved what she did. She didn't think twice about working hard and giving back to the community, and she certainly never considered herself a particular asset. She squeezed her hands on the wheel of her truck, a pleasant glow from Samson's compliment settling over her like morning dew on summer grass. "Thanks for saying that."

Julia drove past Hal's Diner and the water tower, and the open expanse of the mill grounds came into sight.

The night had turned black. It was a new moon, and only a handful of stars dotted the onyx sky.

"I have one more place to show you—if you're up for it." She looked at him out of the corner of her eye. He nodded, so she drove on until she was able to pull over into the gravel that led to the new construction site Samson was preparing. She threw her truck into park, ignored the question marks in Samson's eyes, and hopped out.

She didn't linger near the gaping void of leveled ground where the mill used to sit, instead crossing over to the old gazebo. The crunch of Samson's footsteps on the loose dirt and gravel produced a staccato beat a couple paces behind her.

Julia took the two small wooden steps up and walked to the middle of the structure. The white paint was chipped and peeling off. Many of the old wooden beams were damaged from the elements over the years, but the gazebo would always be perfect to her. She tipped her head up, closed her eyes, and took her time turning around in a circle. When she opened her eyes, Samson was standing on the top step, watching her. She walked over and reached for his hand, tugging him closer.

"Come all the way in." The skin-to-skin contact made each of her pulse points pound. She stood for a minute, soaking the sensation in. The only sound was their breathing and the chirping crickets. If she listened closely, she could hear the faint rushing of the river, but the gazebo was set a good distance off the water.

"I saved the best for last. This..."—Julia motioned with her free hand—"this is my favorite spot in town."

Samson squeezed her fingers, but he didn't let go as he took in the scene. "Tell me about it."

"This gazebo is where my dad proposed to my mom." Her parents had told her the story so many times she felt like she had been there.

"The two of them have known each other since they were knee high. They went to the same elementary, middle, and high school here in town. They were always good friends, but never more. My dad started working at the mill directly out of high school, and my mom went to college to get her degree in teaching. They didn't see each other until Christmas break of her freshman year. Four months. Which was four months longer than they'd ever been apart." Julia grinned as the story came to life in her mind, details so clear it was as if she was watching it unfold in front of her.

"My dad says he was on his lunch break and decided to get some fresh air. He grabbed his jacket and stepped outside of the mill and into the cold of a Wisconsin December. Mapleton had been hit with six inches of snow the previous night. It was the week before Christmas, so nobody minded. He strolled around the front of the building until it was time to get back on the floor. When he rounded the corner, this gazebo came into sight." Julia tapped one of the old wooden columns for effect. She frowned when the whole structure shook.

"It's seen better days."

Julia followed Samson's gaze to the roof. He wasn't wrong.

"True. But this is where the magic happened. When my dad looked into the gazebo that day, he stopped in his tracks. The way he describes it, he saw a woman standing in the center of this gazebo"—she pulled Samson to the middle of the gazebo—"right where we are now."

Samson shifted so he was standing directly in front of her. He was so close. The dark night engulfed the two of them, as if they were wrapped up together, hidden in their own little world. For a half second, Julia wondered if Samson would try to kiss her. Her lips tingled with anticipation, but instead of making a move, he spoke again, his voice low and husky.

"Then what happened?"

Julia swallowed, returning her thoughts to her parents' love story. "Well, the woman's back was to my dad. She was wearing a red pea coat and a white quilted stocking cap. He thought to himself, *She looks like a cardinal in the middle of the snow.* When she spun slightly, he caught a glimpse of her profile, and his breath hitched. He realized it was Gloria Van Epren. The sight of her made his heart flip-flop in his chest. He approached her, and her smile made him feel so warm he could have shed his parka right then and there. She wrapped him in a hug, and they got to talking. Thirty minutes later, my dad was late for his afternoon shift. Before he hurried back into the mill, he secured a dinner date with my mom for later that same night.

"Turned out, that was the first of three consecutive weeks of evenings they spent together, reconnecting and getting to know each other. When my mom went back to college, they were officially dating. My dad visited her several times in Oshkosh over the next semester, and when she came back to Mapleton for spring break, he brought her here to the gazebo one night when the stars were like this in the night sky. He got down on one knee and asked her to marry him."

Julia's eyes misted as the story touched her heart. She didn't think it would ever get old to her. She loved her parents' love. She loved that they were friends until, one day, they were more than that. And at that point, they just knew.

Did she know about Samson? The question popped into her head without warning. She tried to reason with herself. This wasn't the same thing.

Then again, was it?

Chapter 21

SAMSON

SAMSON WAS MESMERIZED BY Julia as she got caught up in the memory of her parents' courtship. Her voice drifted through the night, flowing over him and everything it touched as smoothly as melted chocolate over strawberries. She commanded his attention, and it was as if the crickets quieted their chirping while she spoke. Now, they took up their cries as Julia stood, lost in thought.

Samson spoke quietly, wanting to acknowledge what she had shared but hesitant to break the spell she'd cast over them. "That's one of the best stories I've ever heard."

At the sound of his voice, she blinked and tipped her chin up at him, unshed tears glistening in her eyes. The scattered starlight kissed her cheeks and cast her in a heavenly glow.

"It's my favorite story of all time. That's why this is my favorite spot in all of town."

He took another look around. The gazebo was in rough shape. Emotional stronghold though it may be, the actual physical structure was almost dangerous to stand in. The floor sagged, the pillars supporting the roof were crooked, and boards along the railing of the stairs were missing, not to mention all of the rot from years of rodents and termites.

"You know, I wondered about this place when I first got to town." Samson said it and then immediately clamped his mouth shut, as if that would allow him to take the words back. The only reason he even acknowledged the gazebo when he arrived in Mapleton was because he wanted to know whom to talk to about getting rid of it. Why had he thought *that* would be a pleasant conversation to have with Julia right now?

"Really?" Her striking blue eyes seemed to see right through him.

Avoiding tough subjects with Julia would be futile. They'd come out in the end. Samson's skin pricked as a sense of foreboding washed over him. "Yeah. I wanted to know why it hadn't been torn down." Samson grimaced when Julia's brows knitted. "Now, I'm so glad it wasn't demolished," he hurried to add.

"Actually, it's a historic landmark. Here, you can see a plaque on this side." She wandered over to the west side of the gazebo.

Their hands were still loosely clasped together. It felt so natural to Samson. He let her lead him to one of the exterior pillars.

Sure enough, tacked onto the outside, he saw an official marker. "That explains a lot. I'm thankful for that, especially after hearing your parents' story. I wonder how many other stories this gazebo has been a part of." His mind spun, trying to figure out the best way to repair the old structure.

"Probably too many to count. When early settlers sailed down the Squirrel River, they stopped and built a shelter here. The gazebo was erected in place of that, and it's been here ever since. That's what, like, several hundred years' worth of stories?"

"Too many to count." Samson was relieved Julia's spirits were high after his mention of the mill being demolished. Somewhere in his brain, a vision was forming of a way he could share his own once-in-a-lifetime experience and create his own story with her in a spot like this one. Maybe not tonight, but hopefully someday.

He forced himself to be present in the moment.

"So." Julia's melodic voice cut through the silence. "There you have it. That's my official tour of Mapleton. Think you'll stay awhile?"

"Yeah, I think I'll stick around." Samson smiled before turning serious. "Thank you for sharing all of this with me."

It would have been easy for her to wash her hands of him. They'd gotten off to a rocky start. He was in town to mess with something she had strong feelings about. He was an outsider, and he'd definitely given her a hard time with his teasing—at least initially. She didn't owe him anything. And yet, she was taking time for him.

Julia made people feel valued. When he was with her, he felt like he was the only person in the world. Like what he shared with her was the most important information to ever be shared. Conversations, people...they mattered to Julia. She made him feel seen and heard, and he knew one thing. He wanted to be her guy. All he could do was hope that, like him, she believed they had a growing connection and would give him a chance.

"It's been a good night." Julia's voice broke into his rapid-fire thoughts. "I should get going, though. I work early tomorrow."

"Of course."

They walked hand-in-hand to her truck. He opened the driver's side door for her, and she slid into her seat. He jogged around to the passenger side, letting his eyes take in the job site he'd return to in the morning. Like the rest of town, he'd see this place with a fresh perspective, thanks to Julia.

It was amazing how he'd started to think of his time in Mapleton as split into two categories: *before Julia* and *after Julia*. He didn't want to go back to before; he couldn't wait to see what came next.

Samson climbed up into the seat, and Julia pulled out onto the deserted road. The radio stopped working, and she didn't bother adjusting it. An easy silence settled over them until they pulled up in front of Samson's rental.

"Thank you for spending the evening with me." Julia put the truck in park in his driveway.

"The best night I've had since last night," Samson quipped, keeping his voice light and friendly. No use baring his soul to her yet.

Julia rewarded him with a quiet chuckle.

"Can I see you again?" he asked more earnestly.

Julia's eyelashes fluttered. "I'd like that."

He wanted to kiss her—gosh, he wanted to kiss her—but something stopped him. He was suddenly nervous, afraid of going too fast and damaging their fledgling relationship before it even had a chance to grow wings.

Samson cleared his throat and looked at his dark house before looking at her. His gaze dropped to her lips, but he willed his eyes up. His mind was a jumbled mess of emotion and desire, and he was way out of his depth. "I'll call you to set something up."

"Okay."

Samson searched her face, uncertain of what he hoped to find. Finally, he reached for his door handle and opened it. "Good night, Julia."

"Good night, Samson."

He slammed the door and walked to his front stoop. He paused, pivoted, and waved to Julia. She smiled before putting her truck in reverse and driving the half a block to her bungalow. Her garage door opened, and she disappeared.

It took Samson less than two seconds to come to his senses.

He took off in a jog down the street. Hopefully, none of the neighbors looked out the window and called the police about a strange man running around after dark. That would be his small-town luck.

He made it to Julia's driveway before she reappeared. He slowed to a walk and tried to control his breathing. He was a smidge light-headed, but his mind was set.

"Julia," he said her name quietly as she emerged from the garage, Mr. Waffles on her heels.

She pulled up short. "Samson. What's wrong?" She opened the gate for Mr. Waffles then turned to Samson, taking a step in his direction and peering at him with worry fogging her eyes.

"Nothing." He walked toward her. All he wanted to do was to erase her concerned look. Well, that and kiss her senseless. "Except, I didn't do this."

He cupped her face, spearing her silky golden hair with his fingers and tipping her head up toward his. Her skin was soft against his calloused hands, and he gently stroked her cheeks with the pads of his thumbs. Julia's mouth opened on a slight gasp. Her blue eyes darkened to navy, and in their depths, a spark burned. He closed the gap between them, and when their lips touched, it was magic. She was magic.

Full-blown, out-of-this-world magic.

Kissing Julia was, at once, like exploring a mysterious, new land and like coming home to where he belonged. She held a hand against his chest, and her other arm reached around his back as she clung to his shirt. She leaned her body into his, as if she couldn't get close enough to him—as if she wanted to sear herself against his skin. He traced one of his fingers down the column of her neck before wrapping her in his arms and holding her tight. He wasn't sure how long they stood there, lost in each other's embrace, their hearts beating in time.

When he finally backed away, her eyes remained shut for a beat, and a slow smile spread over her slightly swollen lips. Samson didn't think he'd ever seen anything so beautiful.

"There." He ran his hands up and down her arms to ward off the chill in the night air. "Now nothing's wrong."

Julia's eyes danced when she looked up at him. "No, I'd say that felt pretty right."

Samson placed a kiss on her nose, and Julia giggled. "Alright. I've kept you long enough. Sweet dreams, Julia. I'll call you."

She turned and tossed a grin over her shoulder. "Can't wait. Night, neighbor."

Chapter 22

JULIA

"HERE YOU GO, Susan. Have a great day!" Julia set the iced latte on the high countertop in front of her and chuckled at the woman reaching for it like a lifeline.

Susan Tillersand took a sip and let out a contented sigh. "You have been sent from the angels, Julia Derks. This stuff gets me through the day. Gotta run!"

Julia laughed and turned to the counter to tidy up her mess before shoveling ice into a cup for another drink.

"Gee, someone is in a good mood this morning." Amanda stood with her hands on her hips, staring Julia down.

"Who? Susan? I know. She always has so much energy." This earned her a swat from the towel Amanda kept slung over her shoulder.

"You know that's not who I meant. You haven't been able to keep the pie-eatin' grin off your face since I first saw you at five this morning. That's almost two and a half hours of straight smiling. Should I be worried?"

Julia hadn't told Amanda about her evening with Samson. She was waiting until after work when they'd have time to dive into and analyze all the details.

And she was reveling in the new feelings she had for him.

If she was honest, it scared her a little—to feel this vulnerable and attached so soon. Once she shared it all with Amanda, it would only become that much more real, and like it or not, Julia would have to answer the tough questions that needed answering. Her best friend would ask, and she wouldn't be able to dodge addressing them. After all, Samson was leaving town in a month or two. They hadn't talked about that. Nor had they defined their relationship. But that kiss—that mind-blowing, spine-tingling, heart-stopping kiss—spoke for itself. Surely Samson wanted to explore the connection between the two of them as much as she did?

Julia bent to reshuffle coffee mugs that didn't need reshuffling. "No, there's no need to be worried. How about we do lunch when we get off here, and I'll tell you all about it?"

"Deal! I can't wait."

The bell over the front door jingled, and Kristy Klink walked into the café. Kristy had been a couple grades ahead of Julia in school. She'd married and settled with her husband, Ashton, in Mapleton, and her pregnant belly hadn't stopped her from tearing up the dance floor at the festival.

"Hi, Kristy."

"Julia. Great to see you again. Hey, Amanda." Kristy turned to Amanda, who moved to stand behind the register. "I'll take a medium decaf iced coffee. Trying to limit my caffeine."

Amanda rang up the drink, and Julia got to work preparing it.

"How are you and the baby feeling?" she asked.

"Oh, pretty well. Although my ankles hated me after the Fourth. Standing behind the food counter and all that dancing? I'm paying for it! But like I told Ashton, I've got to get this kid to like music as much as we do. If that means rocking out to Buffy and the Streetcats, then so be it."

Julia laughed. "You were the hottest mama on the dance floor." She meant it. Kristy's pregnancy glow, coupled with her constant kindness, made her seem ethereal.

"That's sweet of you to say." Kristy moved closer to the counter. "And between the two of us...care to share about the cutie you were dancing with?"

"Yeah, Jules. Care to share?" Amanda piped up from the register.

Julia rolled her eyes. This was classic Mapleton, but of all the people in town, she trusted Kristy and Amanda.

"His name is Samson, and he's a very, *very* good dancer." Julia dropped her voice in a conspiring whisper, and Kristy and Amanda looked at each other and then back at Julia.

"And will there be more dancing in your future?" Kristy asked.

"I hope so. Kissing, too." She wiggled her eyebrows at her friends.

After a shocked second, Kristy and Amanda squealed. Amanda pointed victoriously at Julia. "I *knew* it. I get to take partial credit for setting this up."

"Fair." Julia conceded the point, relishing the warm feeling of joy bobbing up and down inside her chest.

"I'm happy for you, Jules." Kristy beamed. "I heard you broke up with Milo not too long ago, but sometimes, when the time is right with someone new, it's right. You know, Ashton was my brother's best friend. And he was deploying almost immediately after we reconnected. Not ideal timing or circumstances, but we worked it out."

"I had forgotten that, but yeah. I think you're right." Julia's attention was taken up when the bell over the door rang. "Here's your decaf iced coffee, Kristy. Thanks for stopping in."

"Thank you! I'll be back soon. Still two more months before the baby arrives, and I feel like I have to take full advantage of my independence while I can. I expect updates!" she said over her shoulder as she walked out of the café.

"Updates?" Seth questioned as he approached the counter from the front door.

Amanda walked around and greeted him with a hug.

"Hey, Seth." Julia shifted toward the register.

"How's it going, Julia?"

"Can't complain."

"Ha. Can't complain? More like can't keep from singing." Amanda turned to Seth, cupping her hand around her mouth in a feigned attempt at secrecy but speaking in a loud whisper. "I think our efforts on the Fourth paid off. I'm still waiting on the full story. I'll let you know when I get it." She stepped away from Seth and brushed down her black apron.

"Now, I've got to get back to work before my boss finds out I'm seeing my boyfriend while I'm on the clock and fires me." Amanda winked at Julia and sauntered around the counter.

It was Julia's turn to toss a towel at her. "As if." She poured Seth a to-go cup of coffee before turning serious. "I will need you both to sign an agreement about working together. Obviously, you disclosed it, but this way all our bases are covered."

"You got it." Seth took the cup from her. "Thanks for this. I'm going to head out. I'll be back at midday for the shift change."

"Bye!" Amanda smiled as he waved to them. When the door closed behind him, she clasped her hands to her chest. "My very own prince."

Julia stared down Amanda, who kept a straight face for all of five seconds before burying her head in her hands and bursting into laughter.

"Okay, fine. That was a little much."

"A little?" Julia caught Daniel Smith's eye. The writer and café regular was seated a few tables away from the front counter. From the way he was attempting to cover his grin with his coffee mug, she guessed he'd heard their conversation.

"See? Even Daniel thinks that was over the top."

"Yeah. Yeah." Amanda huffed with mock offense. "You guys are right, but Seth has been nothing short of amazing. And he is charming, so he's got that going for him in the prince department, too."

Amanda hadn't dated much over the years. Most people couldn't keep up with her energy, or they tried to be domineering. Seth offered Amanda support while also leveling her out. If Amanda found her prince in Seth, Julia would consider that a wonderful development.

"You're right. You know I think it's great." Julia gave Amanda a side hug. "Sorry for the disruption, Daniel. We can let you get back to work."

"No problem. I'm happy for you, Amanda," Daniel said.

Amanda shot him a brilliant smile. "Thank you!"

Julia was struck for the second time in ten minutes with the goodness of the people in her town—first Kristy, and now Daniel. They cared about those around them, and it showed.

The doorbell tinkled, and Julia passed the rest of the morning chatting with new customers and making drinks. When the noon hour rolled around, she and Amanda worked seamlessly together with Jimmy to prepare sandwiches for the hungry folks who stopped by to order a bite to eat, and when Seth and Nick took over for them, Julia spilled her guts to her best friend over lunch.

Amanda did an extensive happy dance before sobering. "So, what's next for you guys?"

Julia's brain stuttered at the question. If she was being honest, she'd wondered the same thing. She'd shoved it aside and focused on how great it felt to be with Samson—and to be kissed by him—but she knew she had to think details. Her life was in Mapleton. His wasn't—at least not permanently. His company was based in Madison. He wouldn't be around for much longer. They had to decide if they were going to have a long-distance relationship.

"I don't know. I haven't thought that far ahead. Maybe I should, but I'm so happy when I'm around him that's all I keep focusing on. We texted a little this morning. He's got a busy rest of the week with work, and I'm working here." She shrugged. "I'd like to see him more. Maybe this weekend."

"Well, you did just share your first kiss, so it's not like he's going to propose tomorrow."

"Yeah. Nobody said anything about a proposal. That is way too premature."

Amanda shrugged. "Sure, but don't forget what Kristy said. When you know, you know!"

Julia sat quietly, chewing on that. There was no way she could know about Samson already—was there? He was different from anyone she'd dated before, and that was turning out to be a good thing. He challenged her and championed her. Julia closed her eyes and took a deep breath. When she blinked, Amanda was giving her a knowing smile.

"No use worrying about it all right now, Jules. You've got time. Enjoy being happy. Enjoy being with someone who makes you feel like you've felt today, you know? It's a good thing. The details will all come out in the wash."

Chapter 23

JULIA

THE NEXT MORNING, JULIA opened umbrellas on the deck and used the broom they kept inside the back door to do a quick sweep of the wood-plank floor. She doubted anyone would choose to sit outside in the drizzly weather, but she wanted to be prepared in case the sun came out.

As she turned to go inside, she saw a worker with a tripod across Mapleton Avenue. He looked like he was packing up. Julia squinted to get a better look but couldn't make out who it was. Giving up, she opened the door, stashed the broom, and walked to the front of the café, shaking water droplets from her ponytail.

"Showtime!" she hollered to Seth, who was in the kitchen, prepping breakfast bagels.

She unlocked the front door and flipped the homemade sign hanging from the window from *Closed* to *Open*. Peering out the glass, she saw the man with the tripod climbing into a car.

"Did you see that guy out there?" she asked when she joined Seth behind the counter.

"What guy?"

"Somebody outside, measuring something. I don't know. He was across the street."

Seth stopped pouring himself a cup of coffee and looked up. "I didn't notice him before. It was probably somebody from the village street department. They are always out surveying or doing something."

Julia nodded, and the bell over the door chimed. It was time to get to work.

·♥·♥·♥·♥·♥·

Two hours and several drenched customers later, Julia forgot all about the man outside. She took a sip of her now lukewarm coffee and inspected the café. The drizzle had turned into a full-blown summer thunderstorm. Raindrops ran in rivers down the glass of the café windows, and her gutters were having a difficult time keeping up. Julia's head spun all morning, toying with the idea of how to add a drive-thru window to the building.

Maybe it was time to take that leap of faith. It would come in handy on days like today. She could tell their customer count was down. A lot of her regulars did without their coffee on mornings when they'd get soaked coming in. Those who had braved the early-July rain sat with pools forming at their feet while they drank, or they grimaced before darting across the puddle-filled parking lot to the protection of their cars. Julia walked around the counter with a carafe of their house blend to top off anyone's mugs.

"Here you go." She refilled Val Marshall's drink.

"Mmm, thanks, Julia." Val raised her mug to her mouth for a satisfying sip before launching into a discussion of the schedule for next week's baseball tournament.

The bell over the door jingled, and Julia glanced up as Samson strode in. Val's words were drowned out by the rushing of the blood in Julia's head. All at once, her mind flashed back to the feeling of Samson's lips on hers and forward to visions of the two of them cuddled up on her couch, watching movies on a rainy day and going for a walk around town when the storms cleared. The mental picture was so real she swore she could smell the salt and butter from the bowl of popcorn she envisioned was settled in her lap. And she could practically feel the warmth of his arm around her shoulders, nestling her close.

Julia's heart lodged in her throat. Was this what love felt like?

The question disturbed her daydreams and stopped her runaway mind in its tracks. She'd never felt this way about anyone. She missed Samson. It had only been one day since their drive around town, but she missed him.

Samson was dressed in worn jeans and work boots, saturated from the rain. Water droplets scattered off the brim of his baseball cap. He looked behind the counter before his gaze roved around the dining room. When he spotted her, his face softened, and his lips turned upward before he broke eye contact and cautiously gave the room another once over.

This was the first time the two of them were in the coffee shop together since their initial meeting when she and her patrons had been less than welcoming. That seemed like a lifetime ago.

Now?

Now, she wanted to go all in with Samson.

It hit her as strongly as a triple shot of espresso.

If that was going to happen, she needed him to like her town, and she needed her town to like him. Their drive the other night warmed him up to Mapleton and its history, but now she needed to win over the village residents. It was time for Julia to take charge. She had a man to defend.

"Samson!" she said his name a little louder than necessary. The heads of her customers swiveled to observe her before rotating to him. "I'm glad you came in." She meant those words more than anyone there knew. She was pleased when Samson smiled more certainly at her. "Let me introduce you to some of my friends.

"Val." Julia touched the woman's shoulder and implored her with a look to stand up and help her out. Val, who had been at the café when Samson came in his first day in town, frowned as she tried to figure out what Julia was up to. Thankfully, she took the hint and stood as Samson made it to their table.

"I want to introduce you to Samson. I don't think you two have met." Julia held her breath as Samson extended his hand

and gave Val a charismatic smile.

"Nice to meet you, ma'am." He dipped his chin respectfully.

Julia bit back a grin. He wouldn't have any problem winning over the town—not with her help. Val, for one, was practically falling all over herself after just his introduction.

After making small talk with Val, Julia introduced Samson to everyone else who was in the café. Though the day was dark and stormy outside, everything looked brighter to Julia as she walked with Samson to the counter. Sure, Charlie and several of the older, former mill workers weren't around at the moment, so she had work to do. But it was a start.

"Hi." Samson turned all his attention to her when they were out of earshot of the rest of her customers, a wide slash of a sincere smile on his face. "Thanks for that." He angled his head backward, motioning to the dining room.

"I had some making up to do after your last visit here." Julia's cheeks burned with a combination of embarrassment at her past action and complete and utter attraction toward the man standing in front of her. She dabbed at her brow with the back of her hand, willing her pulse to settle itself the heck down. "What can I get for you? I didn't expect you to be in. Aren't you working?"

"Was working." Samson took off his cap and ran his hand through his hair.

Julia told herself not to stare, but she was fighting a losing battle. Her fingers twitched, wanting to have a turn.

"This rain forced us to stop. So, everyone went home, and here I am. I'll take a cup of your house roast, please. Best coffee in town." He winked, and Julia couldn't have stopped the over-the-moon smile from shining on her face if she wanted to.

Before she could say anything in response, a sudden rush of customers entered the café. Samson stepped off to the side to wait for his drink as Seth and Julia worked together to take and make orders.

When Julia handed Samson his coffee, their fingers brushed, and it was like the lightning from outside struck her. She met

Samson's eye, and they shared the sort of look that had Julia believing it was the two of them against the world. Like they were both in on the best kind of secret. He smiled at her and found a seat at Daniel's table, and the two of them launched into conversation.

Julia happily settled into her work until, twenty-five minutes later, Samson stopped by the counter before taking his leave.

"Any chance I can convince you to have dinner with me tonight?" he asked for her ears only.

Julia smiled. "You don't have to convince me. I'd like that very much."

"Seven o'clock? I'll pick you up this time."

"I'll be ready. Bye, Samson."

"Have a good afternoon, Julia."

Julia gazed after him as he left the café. She could get used to this—Samson dropping in on his breaks from work. Sharing mutual friends like Daniel. The promise of dinner dates and more kisses under the stars. Movie nights during thunderstorms.

Seth nudged her arm, jolting Julia out of her own thoughts.

"Uh, boss. Everyone's looking at you."

Julia's head shot around. Her patrons pretended to be interested in their coffee or their conversations, but their acts were unconvincing. She'd been made.

Julia cleared her throat. "Right. Back to work."

Chapter 24

JULIA

THAT NIGHT, JULIA LAID out her favorite floral dress. It fit her perfectly, and the bright colors popped against her shimmery summer skin. She took her hair out of her usual working ponytail and stood in front of her small bathroom mirror, taking extra time to curl it.

She hadn't asked where Samson planned to take her for dinner, so she wanted to dress up a little. She really hoped they'd go someplace other than Hal's. She loved Hal's, but she wanted to fly under the radar tonight. Not because she was embarrassed to be seen with Samson. Quite the contrary. She wanted Samson all to herself so she could sort some things out.

Were they friends? Friends who kissed? Friends whose touches shocked each other silly? Okay, so more than friends? Julia set down the curling wand. The two of them needed to talk. A dinner date was more than hanging out at the festival. It was more than a late-night drive around town—as wonderful as that was. But she was falling in love with Samson, and that made this date feel significant. She needed to hear it from him that he felt the same.

Julia finished touching up her makeup and left the bathroom for her bedroom where she stepped into her dress, adding a pair of funky clay earrings to complete the outfit. She turned and stared at herself in front of the mirror that leaned against the wall. Her cheeks were pinker than usual, and her eyes sparkled. Something about Samson agreed with her.

"Do I look okay?"

Mr. Waffles gave her an affirmative woof from where he dutifully sat next to her full-length mirror.

She patted her dog's head. "You're the best, buddy."

At the sound of a knock on her door, her stomach tipped like she'd just gone over the edge of a rollercoaster drop. She smoothed down her dress and gave herself one last look in the mirror before walking into the living room with Mr. Waffles on her heels. She draped her denim jacket over her arm in case the restaurant was chilly. Hank sat perched in the corner of her couch—pink fuzz clashing with the rest of her more patriotic décor. The sight of him made Julia relax.

She threw her shoulders back and opened the front door.

Samson drank her in with eyes so full of admiration she was thankful she'd taken the extra time to get ready.

He spoke, and the awe in his deep, low voice bowled her over. "You look amazing."

Julia's heart skipped. "Thank you. You clean up pretty well yourself."

He did. He was dressed in dark jeans and a white button-up shirt, rolled to his elbows. It accentuated his skin, tanned from the time spent outside the past few days.

"I didn't know where we were going." She forced herself to look away from his toned forearms and reached for her purse from the couch. "So I wasn't sure what to wear."

"You're perfect. I thought we'd check out a restaurant in Apple Creek."

Julia wanted to cheer. "Sounds good to me. Behave, Mr. Waffles."

Her dog jumped up on the sofa in front of the window to watch them leave.

Julia locked the door and let Samson lead her down the steps of her bungalow. He opened the truck door and held her hand to help her up before taking his seat behind the wheel.

"Ready?" Samson asked as he buckled up.

"I am."

In her mind, Julia wondered if they were talking about something bigger than the drive.

⋯♥⋅♥⋅♥⋅♥⋅♥⋯

Two hours later, after laughing and talking their way through appetizers and the main course at The Copper Club, a swanky, upscale restaurant in Apple Creek, Julia sat enjoying their shared piece of chocolate cheesecake as she told Samson about her plans for her house.

"So, you want to add on to the back of it?" Samson asked.

"Eventually. I mean I'm in no hurry, but the backyard extends pretty deep, and I always thought an extra great room would go a long way in terms of entertaining. And it would be nice for when I have a family someday."

"You want a lot of kids?"

Julia nodded. She'd always longed to be a mom. "I do. Obviously my husband will have some say, but yeah, I'd like a whole gaggle of them."

Samson's eyes sparkled in the dim restaurant light. "You'll be a great mom."

"Thanks." Julia lowered her gaze to her plate and took a bite of cheesecake, suddenly very aware of the intimacy of the subject they'd just covered. Her cheeks had taken on a pleasant warmth.

Samson dabbed his mouth with his napkin before speaking into the charged silence. "And adding on to your house makes sense. I do love old homes like the ones you showed me on our drive. There's something about the character they each have that gets me every time. Do you know the story behind yours?"

Julia placed her fork on the table and leaned back, grateful to take the conversation in a slightly less personal direction. "No. Not really. I haven't researched it much. Growing up, it seemed like it went through a lot of different owners, unlike many of the houses in town that stayed in one family for years —the building my café is in, for example."

"Really? What's the story there?"

"It was the Henderson house for the longest time. Bernard Henderson was a fixture in these parts. He was the toughest umpire Mapleton ever saw, but he also had a soft side. He'd come and cheer the kids on when he wasn't umping. He lived in that house alone for many years. Never married, and he didn't have any children of his own. So, when he died, he'd written into his will that he wanted his property to go to the village. They didn't do anything with it, and eventually, it fell into disrepair."

"Until you swooped in," Samson said.

She reveled in more of his subtle praise. "I guess so. It sparked an idea in me, and I've run with it. All day, I thought about how to take the coffee shop to the next level."

He was the first person she admitted that to.

Samson repositioned himself in his seat across from her. "Oh yeah?"

"I want to keep the same architectural footprint. Like you said, the house's original charm and character is what makes it so special. But if we add a drive-thru and upgrade the space a little, it could be really special." Under the table, Julia jiggled her knees with excitement. "And the building is a story and a half. I haven't touched the upstairs, but the potential is there."

Julia launched into a whole discussion, detailing the ways she wanted to add on and improve the café yet make it all blend in with the current look and feel of the space. Once she started saying her ideas out loud, she couldn't hide how eager she was about putting them in motion. She hadn't let herself go there in her head. She'd been worried about the whole thing falling apart. But now? Now it felt good to get her thoughts out in the open.

When she paused, Samson just stared at her, then shook his head, as if clearing out a bad memory. "Sorry." He smiled, but it didn't reach his eyes. "Those are impressive concepts."

Though he said the words, Julia was suddenly self-conscious, and a waterfall of doubt cascaded down her back. She expected Samson to be enthusiastic about her plans. This was his wheelhouse, wasn't it? Maybe she should have kept her mouth shut. Maybe her plans didn't have any legs and would be impossible, given the constraints of the space. Maybe she had no idea what she was talking about.

Samson must've sensed her internal backtracking. He covered her hand with his from across the table.

She looked him in the eyes, trying to read his mind. As the warmth of his touch shot to her heart, she relaxed.

"I mean it, Julia. I think you could take On Deck Café to new heights with these plans. Have you moved on any of them yet?"

"No. I need to purchase the actual building from the village before I can make any real changes." Julia picked up her fork and took another nibble of dessert. "The café is doing well. I guess I can finally believe that. I'm saving up. I should be able to get a loan soon and make the village an offer."

"That's great. Have you talked to anyone at the village?"

"No. I know I should, but I'd like to have things in order before I do so, especially given the history between Milo and me. Typically, everything around here is done with handshakes and verbal agreements, but I want to have my ducks in a row. When I go to make the village an offer, I'd like to come across as impressive."

"You are impressive." Samson looked at her with admiration, and Julia's heart almost burst at the force in his declaration. "I'm not just saying that, Julia. What you've built with your shop—what it adds to the community—there's a certain magic there that doesn't come along every day. It's a special place. Because of you."

Julia's confidence inflated under his kind words. Any worry she'd had about Samson thinking her ideas weren't good enough was erased with that comment. Her face burned under his appreciative gaze, and she broke eye contact. When she peered up at him through her lashes, he was still staring at her, like he couldn't get enough.

And when he paid for their dinner and led her out into the warm, night air, the stars shined a little brighter, and the streetlights in downtown Apple Creek seemed to twinkle just for her, reflecting off puddles from the morning's rainstorm.

Julia was falling hard, and she knew it. She spun around on the romantically lit street. When she faced Samson, she gathered her courage. "So, are we dating now?"

The corners of Samson's mouth curved up, and not for the first time, his good looks startled her. His face radiated kindness and a hint of humor. His eyes glowed, never leaving her face. "This was a date, yes."

She raised an eyebrow, waiting for him to continue and forcing herself not to shy away from his gaze.

"But I was hoping to make things official. Julia, would you like to be my girlfriend?"

Julia's limbs felt light and tingly, as if with her next step she'd be able to fly. She reached out and grabbed for Samson's hands to anchor herself, pressing them to her lips for a quick kiss. "Yes, I would. I'd like that very much."

Samson opened the door of his truck for her, and she climbed in. By the time he made it around to the driver's side, she'd scooted to the middle seat.

"I hope you don't mind." She batted her eyes at him.

Samson laughed and slipped his arm around her shoulder, pulling her close. "No. I definitely don't mind."

They made the drive to Mapleton in silence. No words were necessary. Julia rested her head on his shoulder and savored being in Samson's strong, steady presence.

"I have to work a double shift tomorrow," she informed him as they walked to her door. "I'm covering for Seth since he put in overtime during the festival. But maybe we could do something on Sunday."

"That would be great." Samson hugged her to him.

"Do you have a suit here?"

In response to her question, Samson leaned back and looked at her funny. "Come again?"

Julia giggled. "A swimming suit. I want to take you to the swim lake—you know, during regular operating hours."

"So we won't have to hop the fence this time?"

Julia swatted Samson's arm before leaning back into him. "Nope, this time everything will be by the book." She reached up and draped her arms around his neck.

"Sounds good. I'll find some swimming trunks by Sunday. Do you want me to pick you up?"

"Let's walk." Julia ran her hands through his hair and massaged the back of his neck. "It's supposed to be a nice day."

"Whatever you want."

Julia arched her brows before leaning forward and kissing him quickly. "There. That's what I want."

Samson's eyes smoldered, and he held her gaze as he brought his head slowly toward hers, stopping so close that when he spoke again, his lips brushed hers with each word. "Is that all?" he whispered.

Julia couldn't look away. She shook her head slightly, her breath coming in shallow gasps. She thought she might hyperventilate if he didn't kiss again. "No," she breathed against his mouth. "More please."

Samson swept his lips back and forth across hers before sinking into a lingering kiss. Julia sighed, melting into his arms.

He took his time, moving his mouth slowly. They took their cues from each other, and the kiss ramped up before they dialed it back down, creating a perfect balance of heat and tenderness. The whole thing somehow left Julia completely satisfied and dying for more.

Samson leaned back and kissed the outside corner of her lips, the soft spot of her cheek, her nose, and then her lips one last time before resting his forehead against hers. "I can't wait to see you again."

Julia sighed. "I can't wait to see you again, either." She closed her eyes and rested in his arms, enjoying the feeling of his breath against her skin.

She'd had all her questions about Samson answered tonight...and then some.

They were in this together, and it was the very best place to be.

Chapter 25

SAMSON

SAMSON TOOK JULIA'S HAND as they strolled down the tree-lined sidewalk along Mapleton Avenue to the swim lake. The air smelled like freshly laundered sheets and coconut sunscreen.

"You were right," he said. "The weather's perfect."

Julia tipped her head toward the sun, swinging their arms a little quicker as she skipped ahead. "It's going to be a good day. I can't wait for you to see the lake in action. Hope you brought your quarters."

"Uhh," Samson stuttered. "Was I supposed to?"

Julia laughed. "Only if you want to get a snack. I'm partial to the huge licorice ropes for seventy-five cents. Just have to be careful not to drag them in the sand."

By the gagging face she made, Samson imagined she spoke from experience, and he chuckled. When he spent time with Julia, he couldn't help but appreciate her zest for life. She lived each moment, not looking ahead like he found himself doing, but focusing on what—and who—was right in front of her.

The café came into view. The honey-colored wood-shingle siding glowed in the early afternoon sun, and the building's crisp trim gave it an air of dignity. It looked straight out of a storybook with its overflowing flower boxes and the white picket fence along the lot line. Samson wasn't surprised the parking lot was full. "Tell me about how you started your business. Why did you choose to sell coffee, anyway?"

Julia stared across the street at her café before looking at him. "Because coffee is always a good idea." She smirked before turning thoughtful. "But seriously, coffee was a logical choice. Everyone drinks coffee, and Mapleton doesn't have a lot of chain restaurants and shops."

"So I've noticed."

Her light laugh was so pure. Samson was surprised forest animals didn't trot out of the woods to dance circles around her every time she strolled by. He told himself to stop thinking in Disney and listened as Julia went on.

"It was about this time of year, five years ago, I started researching who owned the parcel of land. It seemed like a perfect spot for a business. Anyway, I worked out a rental agreement with Milo, who was the new Village Administrator at the time, and I got to work cleaning the place up. I power-washed the siding, rebuilt the deck, and gutted the compartmentalized inside to make way for the dining room space. The local credit union gave me a small business loan to pay for the coffee makers and other necessary equipment and to pour the slab for the parking lot." Julia paused and shot him a look out of the corner of her eye. "Want to know a secret, though?"

"Yes," Samson said without hesitation.

"I had no idea what I was doing." Julia burst out laughing and slapped her palm over her mouth.

Samson quirked his brow. He hadn't expected her to say that. Since the moment he met her, she was so sure of herself.

"See, I majored in business, but I didn't know the first thing about owning one of my own. I took evening hotel and restaurant management classes while working part-time at Hal's to pay the bills. That helped me learn a lot."

Samson nodded. He knew the importance and benefits of on-the-job experience.

Julia explained the roots of her business as they wandered past the café and around the bend. "When Amanda showed interest in the prospect of a coffee shop, I offered her a job. She's an accounting major and has been with me from the beginning. We went from being open four days per week to being a full-time establishment in two years. And now, I'm thinking I might have to hire more staff—especially if I expand."

"Wow." Samson was at a loss for words. From the breezy way Julia told the story, he'd have guessed everything with the business was smooth sailing, but he could only imagine the amount of sweat equity she put into the place and its patrons. His respect and admiration for her grew, and he once again tried to ignore the idea of the village taking her land to sell it off. There was no way. It would be a blight on the community and a terrible business decision.

Feeling somewhat at peace about it, Samson decided he would stop thinking about business for today. He wanted to enjoy his time with Julia in one of the unique, small-town spots that made Mapleton what it was.

"I don't think I could have done it anywhere but Mapleton, though," Julia said off-handedly. "The village has supported me for my whole life. The people here are good and kind, and I love being a part of the community and doing what I can to take care of the villagers." She shrugged as if it was all no big deal.

Samson looked at her in awe. If someone were going to write a story and try to capture Julia's heart in words, he doubted it would be possible. Every fairy-tale comparison he tried to come up with, every descriptor his head generated for her paled in comparison to the actual beautiful, wonderful human in front of him. He wondered if she knew her loyalty to Mapleton was one of her most endearing qualities.

"Come on." Julia broke into his thoughts. "We're almost there." She tugged on his hand, and they jogged across the street to the swim lake.

After they paid their admission fee, Julia led Samson across the sandy beach.

"Grab the chair there, will you?" She directed him across the beach as she started dragging one of the nearby lounge chairs his way. When they had two seats together, they laid out their towels. Julia shimmied out of her cut-off shorts and slipped off her tank top.

Samson gulped and looked out over the water. The sight of Julia in a bathing suit was not something he'd forget anytime soon. He pulled one arm across his body and stretched it before switching arms, if for no other reason than to give himself something to do. "You want to swim right away?"

"No."

She kicked up her feet onto the lounger and reclined. "First, I've got to get warm enough. Then, I'll swim."

"Good idea." Samson followed her lead and sank into the chair next to hers.

A local eighties and nineties radio station was blaring hits over the loudspeaker, and the shrieks of kids and families swirled around them on the wind. Samson peered at Julia out of the corner of his eye. She donned sunglasses, and a soft smile spread across her lips as she sighed. She was breathtaking.

She turned her head to face him. "What?"

Caught staring red-handed.

"Nothing." He blinked and turned his face up to the sky.

"Mmm," Julia murmured, and from her coy smile, he didn't think she believed him.

Good. She should know that he was looking and that he liked what he saw. Julia Derks was a catch in more ways than one. He'd make it his mission to make her believe that.

"Tell me something fun about you," she said.

"Something fun?"

"Sure. What do you like to do when you're not working?"

Samson thought for a minute. He spent so much of his time working he didn't know what to say. He finally settled on his favorite form of exercise. "I like to run."

"Is that so?"

"Yeah, me and Mr. Waffles have that in common."

Julia snorted. "I swear he usually doesn't run away. He just had to do that when you happened to be outside."

"Yes, getting back from my own run. See, I told you. I have lots in common with your dog."

"Oh yeah? What else?"

"We both really like you." Samson flashed a shameless grin, giving himself a mental pat on the back for not missing a beat.

Julia's musical laugh swept over him. "A little cheesy," she said, "but I'll take it. So, have you gotten out for some more runs since you've been here? Mapleton's a good running town."

Samson nodded. He'd gone exploring on his runs every morning. "Yep, and since your tour of town, I feel like I know what I'm looking at. Though, the other day, I freaked out these two women walking through the park. They couldn't hear me coming up behind them over the swishing of their track suits."

Julia laughed. "And over the sound of their own gossip."

It was Samson's turn to laugh. "I hadn't thought of that, but you're probably right. Anyway, I cut out into the grass to run around them, and one of them let out a shriek."

"Careful, or you'll be labeled as the boogeyman."

"As if I'm not already."

Julia leaned up on her elbows and pinned him with a steely gleam. "You're not." Her voice was firm. "I promise."

Samson nodded. He would have to take her word for it.

"Come on. Let's swim." She edged herself up and off her chair before tossing her sunglasses down behind her. "Ready?"

"Lead the way." Samson shed his tank top, and when he pulled it over his head, he caught Julia staring at his abs. "Are you checking me out?" he teased.

She dragged her eyes up and pressed her lips together. "So what if I am?" She tipped her chin in the air.

Samson chuckled, glad their attraction was mutual. He grabbed for her hand, and they walked toward the lake. It was full of people—families with young kids going down the yellow and orange slides in the shallow water and teenagers circled up and splashing each other out a little deeper.

At the water's edge, Julia dipped her toe in first but yanked it out as if she'd been stung by a bee. "It's never as warm as I want it to be. You'd think by July it would have warmed up more than this."

Samson walked in up to his ankles. "Oh, come on. It's not so bad. Weren't you a lifeguard?" He tugged her hand, and she squealed.

"Yes, but it's cold!"

Samson laughed. "Julia Derks. Don't tell me a little cold water is going to scare you away."

"Why do you think I hated the dunk tank so much?" Julia glared at him playfully. "When I was a lifeguard, I *had* to go into the cold water. I'm scarred from the memory of frostbite." She shivered.

Samson laughed again, deciding on his course of action. "Alright then. I see what I'm going to have to do." In one quick motion, he scooped her up into his arms.

"Samson!" Julia yelped as he strode out a little deeper. "Don't you dare dunk me." She squeezed his neck and pinched her eyes closed, as if waiting to be submerged.

"I'm not going to dunk you." Samson repositioned her in his arms so when she cracked her eyes open, she was looking directly at him. "Julia, I'm not Milo."

Julia exhaled and he felt her body relax. She pressed a kiss to his cheek bone. "I know you're not."

Samson felt at once like a hero and a hypocrite. Was he any better than Milo if he knew of the man's intentions and did nothing about it?

He vowed to get to the bottom of the Village Administrator's plans first thing tomorrow...no matter how uncomfortable the conversation and outcome would be.

But for now, he wasn't going to give Milo a second thought. He was going to enjoy the gorgeous weather, easy conversation, and the woman who had made a place for herself in his heart.

He waded out into deeper water, allowing Julia to get acclimated as he went. And when she said she was ready, he sunk down onto his knees, keeping her in his arms and letting her body rest against his under the water, never wanting to let her go.

Chapter 26

SAMSON

THE NEXT MORNING, SAMSON arrived at the village offices shortly after opening.

Melly greeted him with a familiar smile. "Samson, how's it going? I hope you enjoyed the swim lake with Julia yesterday. Isn't it a great little spot?"

Samson's jaw tightened. A naïve sliver of his brain had held out hope that maybe Milo hadn't heard of his developing relationship with Julia. But he knew better. This was Mapleton, Wisconsin, after all, and news traveled fast. If Melly knew how he had spent his Sunday, then surely Milo did, too, and that wasn't going to help his cause.

He made small talk with Melly for several minutes, further prolonging the inevitable. It wasn't like him to shy away from unpleasant conversations. In the past, he had no problem making the tough ask or delivering the difficult news. But this was personal. And he was afraid of what he might find out.

Finally, when he'd asked after Melly's kids and her husband and about any upcoming summer plans, and Melly was looking at him expectantly, he put in his request to see Milo.

"I can check if he's free. Hold on a minute." Melly picked up the phone and waited for Milo to answer. Samson turned away from the desk and wandered over to the black-and-white pictures that lined the walls, taking time to read the captions.

The town had a history of hosting baseball and softball tournaments. Some of the photos were close to one hundred years old. He tried to imagine a new, upscale restaurant and a hotel surrounding the fields. Based on these old photos, and after spending time in Mapleton, he couldn't picture it. That sort of development was so opposite of everything Sunrise Park stood for.

"Milo will see you in five minutes, Samson. You're welcome to take a seat," Melly said from behind the desk.

"Thanks." Samson finished studying the old photos as fresh tension rolled across his shoulders. He had a sneaking suspicion the Village Administrator was making him wait in an indirect display of power. Samson closed his eyes and reminded himself why he was there.

This was for Julia. He would figure this out for her. If it was bad news, he would do what he could do to fix it, and if it was no news and he'd made a mountain out of a molehill, all the better, but he needed to know. He opened his eyes and saw the village's quarterly magazine on the side table. He sat down on the bench opposite of Melly's desk and began flipping through the pages while he waited on Milo.

Samson couldn't help but smile as he saw several familiar faces. There was a feature on Sally's Salon, news about the garbage pickup route being adjusted for Memorial Day, the Fourth of July, and Labor Day, and a list of villagers with summer birthdays.

"Samson," Milo's voice echoed across the small reception area, and the short-lived cheer and solace Samson had found in the village magazine evaporated.

Melly glanced up from her computer and gave him an encouraging nod.

He rose and followed Milo through the door and down the hallway to his office.

There was no small talk. No useless filler conversation this time around. Milo looked the part of the man in control. He strode behind his desk and took a seat before addressing Samson.

"Please, sit. What can I do for you?"

Samson decided beating around the bush wasn't worth it. Milo may have been into playing games, but that wasn't

Samson's style. "Look, Milo. I don't want to waste your time here. I had a couple questions regarding your plans for further expansion throughout the village. I wanted to know exactly what you were thinking and where—"

"Oh, yes, yes. Good. You must have talked to Jerry. I've been in touch with him since the Fourth, and I think we're about to work through a deal that'll be in the best interest of both the village and your company. Has Jerry told you much about it?"

Samson tensed. It wouldn't do any good to reveal to Milo that he didn't know what his boss was planning. Doing so would only put him at more of a disadvantage. He needed to appear calm and in control, so he fell back on his years of experience playing that part and lied through his teeth.

"Yes. Jerry mentioned it."

Milo nodded. "I figured he would. It's no secret. And after all, since you're already in town, I know Jerry has you pegged to carry out much of the work when it's all said and done. Now, as for breaking the news to Julia."

Samson's pulse thrummed in his temples as Milo continued.

"Julia is...well, she's a little...how can I say this?"

Samson ground his jaw to try to keep his temper under control. "She's magnificent." The gritted words came out with seething force. His passion surprised him. He was falling for Julia, yes, but he prided himself on always being in command of his emotions. Apparently, when it came to someone disrespecting Julia, all bets were off.

"Yeah, yeah. Of course she is. Don't forget I dated her for a year." Milo's voice turned hard, and he let the meaning behind his comment hang in the air for a second longer than necessary.

Samson breathed through his nose like a bull, compressing his lips and stopping himself from saying anything he would regret. There was no use making Milo even more of an enemy than he already was.

"All I'm saying is Julia is going to have to come to terms with things changing around here. The rent she's paying us is measly. It's chump change. And the offer your company is prepared to make for the land with the promise of turning it into something truly one-of-a-kind is a deal I don't think the village can pass up. I certainly couldn't advise the village board to pass it up in good conscious—personal relationships aside," he said pointedly.

This was Samson's worst nightmare. Every fiber in his body was screaming for him to defend Julia, to tell Milo about her plans, about her desire to buy the building. But it wasn't his place, and it would be a huge conflict of interest for Gabler, Burns, and Associates if he spoke for her while working for them. Really, what good would that do at this point? Whether Milo and the village would consider selling the Henderson house directly to Julia would be a moot point if his company would offer them more money for it, not to mention the purchase price of the land that surrounded it. As for the mood Milo was in, Samson bet he wouldn't be up for a discussion of the good Julia's café did for the town or the benefits of a local establishment versus a large, impersonal development. He needed to bide his time.

Samson schooled his features. He'd gotten all the information he needed from Milo. It was time to work this out from another angle. "I appreciate your time, Milo. I'm sure we'll be in touch in the near future."

"I'll let you know when Jerry and I come to an agreement. He suggested maybe he'd send you in to pitch the proposal. You know, since you know the town and all."

Milo sat behind the desk with smugness in his eyes and his fingers pressed together in front of his face, but Samson refused to shrink, no matter how badly he'd been bludgeoned. He gave Milo a curt nod and barely made eye contact before turning to leave.

The second he got out to the parking lot, he dialed his home office's number. He climbed into his truck, fuming, and slammed the door.

Victoria picked up on the third ring.

"I need to talk to Jerry now." Samson checked himself. "Please," he added. He shouldn't be a jerk to Victoria. She wasn't involved in any of this.

"Sorry, Samson. He's out of the office for a meeting. I can leave a message and have him give you a call. Or you can try his cell phone."

Samson hung up the phone and scrubbed his hands across his face. He stared straight ahead at the brick building. How had he gotten here? A week ago, he was content to give the girl next door a hard time—to tease her about her dog. Now, he was falling in love with her and personally invested in her life and business.

Julia was in the dark about Milo's plans at this point, but Samson sensed his time was running out. Sooner or later, everything was going to come to a head.

He pulled out of his parking space and used the voice command system in his truck to dial Jerry's cell phone. It went straight to voicemail. Not helpful.

Stopped at the stop sign at the intersection of Mapleton Avenue, he texted Julia and gave her a heads up that he'd be busy for the rest of the day. Thank goodness she couldn't gauge his stress level through a text message, because he was a mess, but he knew what he needed to do.

Turning out of the parking lot, he drove through town and merged onto the interstate.

·♥·♥·♥·♥·♥·

Samson parked in front of the sleek office building that was home to Gabler, Burns, and Associates. He only had a loose plan in place. The lengthy drive wasn't long enough for him to sort out his feelings.

He rode the elevator to the eleventh floor, and when the doors opened, he spotted Victoria behind the front desk.

The secretary's head popped up from her computer, and her eyes went wide. "Samson! What are you doing here?"

"I really need to speak with Jerry."

"That's what a telephone is for, silly." Victoria laughed.

"This is important. Is he in?"

Something in his voice must've tipped her off to the fact that he wasn't in the mood to joke around. She grabbed the phone and dialed.

A minute later, Samson was walking the long corridor to Jerry's office. Stopping before the sturdy oak door, he paused and dragged in a rough breath. Was he ready to do this? He'd only known Julia for a couple of weeks, and yet he was going to stick his neck out for her. This could cost him his job, everything he'd worked for. He should have been apprehensive about his boss's reaction, but he wasn't. That knowledge steadied him. He knocked.

"Come in."

Samson opened the door to find Jerry shuffling papers around on his massive desk. The floor-to-ceiling windows behind him offered a full view of the city's skyline.

"Sir, thanks for seeing me on such short notice."

"I figured when Victoria said you were here in the flesh it was important. Sit. Tell me what's going on."

"I need to talk to you about Mapleton and Milo Moore's plans to develop the area around Sunrise Park. I understand you two have spoken."

"After you tipped me off to the prospect of another investment opportunity, I reached out to him, yes."

Samson's chest clenched with guilt. This was all his fault. He wished he wouldn't have said anything about Milo's plans. At least, maybe then, this all wouldn't be happening so fast.

"And are you going to make an offer to buy the land?"

"I've been researching the area. I had a surveyor scope out the park last week, and I am about ready to draft a proposal."

Samson's spirits sank. "With all due respect, sir, I don't think that's a good idea."

Jerry laughed. "Samson, what on earth do you mean? We have a town looking to sell land, where we've already established a working relationship. This is a no-brainer."

"It's not that simple, Jerry. I've gotten to know these people. And this town. They don't want a development there. I wouldn't put it past them to boycott any new businesses that go up. And having new construction in that spot wouldn't work with the flow of the area. It's not good business. A coffee shop already exists on the grounds Milo wants the village to sell to us. It's owned by one of the town's daughters. Everyone loves her, and if we buy the land and develop it, the business she worked hard to build will suffer or cease to exist entirely."

"If I didn't know you better, I'd think you'd grown soft, Samson." Jerry eyed him closely over his spectacles. "All business is good business. Isn't that what we always say? You've never had a problem with it in the past. You're my go-to guy for pushing jobs through."

Samson stopped breathing. He hated that what Jerry said was true. While he'd always considered his charm, for lack of a better word, to be innocent, he'd been using it to his advantage —to his company's advantage—on a regular basis. He was sent in to smooth everything over. Then, he got out of dodge the second the deal was done or the project was underway. It was what he thought he'd be doing in Mapleton.

And the company played to his pride. How many times did Jerry compliment him on a job or tell him no one else did it quite like he did? Too many to count. And Samson ate it up without thinking twice. But at what cost? He knew one thing. If Julia's café was going to be affected by his company's doings, that would be a serious cost.

Samson blinked, a wave of nausea pummeling him. He'd turned a blind eye to the fallout of his company's development efforts on past jobs, but now, it was all he could think about.

"Sir, this time, it's different. Julia's café is thriving. It's not like the mill site." His voice held a hint of desperation he couldn't mask. "I'm asking you to let this project go. I don't believe it's good business."

His boss studied him for a minute. "I'll consider what you've said, but I can't make any promises."

Samson exhaled. That was about all he could ask for at this point. "Thank you." He stood to shake Jerry's hand. "Keep me posted. I'm headed back to Mapleton tonight to check in on the job site tomorrow."

"Let me know if there are any hiccups with the mill project."
"Yes, sir."

Chapter 27

SAMSON

THREE HOURS LATER, SAMSON exited the highway and turned his truck in the direction of Mapleton. He drove over the hill, and in the distance, the woods of Sunrise Park came into view. The sky was illuminated beyond the trees with the field lights of the baseball diamond. There must be a late game.

He slowed down to obey the speed limit as he passed the *Welcome to Mapleton!* sign on the side of the road. He couldn't help but think about the last time he had driven into the village. He had been laser-focused on work and making a good impression, the latter of which blew up in his face the second he stepped foot into Julia's café. But now, he had more important things to worry about.

Like Julia herself.

As he approached downtown Mapleton, his heart yearned to be on its small-town sidewalks, walking the flag-lined streets with Julia at his side. Mapleton already felt more like home to him than any of the previous places he had lived. That might be a problem since he was, technically, a visitor.

He needed to come clean with Julia about Jerry and Milo's plans. It was the only way to move forward. If something happened to her business because of him, he would never forgive himself.

Samson rolled down his window and inhaled the summer night air. He passed the turn that would take him to the swim lake and the wooded grounds of Sunrise Park, and the ballfields came into view. He heard cheering and the faint echo of the announcer calling out the score at the bottom of the eighth. Tie game. They'd be playing for a while longer. He slowed down in front of On Deck Café. A few cars dotted the parking lot. The clock on his dash read 9:07 pm, so Samson figured the night crew was finishing up. Julia worked earlier in the day, and he wasn't ready to face her yet, but he wondered if Seth was working. On a whim, he pulled in and parked his truck. He stepped out and jogged to the front door. The bell jingled.

"Sorry, we're closed for the night," Seth called from somewhere in the back of the shop.

"I know. I don't need anything."

"Samson?" Seth appeared a moment later. "I thought that was you." He stepped from behind the counter and shook Samson's hand. "What's up?"

"Just getting back into town. I figured you'd be here. I'm amped up from my drive, and thought I'd stop by."

The door to the deck slammed.

"Hey, Seth, can you help me move some of these tables back?" a deep voice sounded from the hallway. "Oh, hi." A guy a couple of inches taller than Seth appeared.

"Nick, this is Samson...Julia's new *boyfriend*," Seth emphasized the word, and Samson's lips twitched. "Samson, this is Nick. He works here with me."

"Nice to meet you, man." Nick reached out his hand.

Samson shook it. "Likewise. I didn't mean to interrupt you guys. I was killing time before heading home."

"No plans with Julia tonight?"

Samson raised an eyebrow.

"What? Amanda and I are dating now. I know things."

Samson chuckled. "No. No plans with Julia. But I'm glad to hear that about you and Amanda—not that you two did a very good job of hiding your feelings for each other."

"Hey, I could say the same to you about Julia."

"Touché." Samson laughed in spite of himself, already feeling some of the stress of the day dissipating in the company of his new friends. "Want me to help with those tables, Nick, so you can stay in here and do whatever you were doing, Seth?"

"That would be great, actually."

Samson went with Nick outside and helped him rearrange the seating.

The crack of a bat and cheering from the ballfield drifted over on the evening breeze as they put tables in order.

"This is quite a place, isn't it?" Nick followed Samson's gaze to the diamonds.

He nodded. It certainly was. What Julia built was genius. The sky was the limit if she had a chance to enact her plans. He only hoped Jerry took their meeting—and what he said—to heart.

"I'm done here." Seth met them in the dining room when they reentered the café. "Either of you interested in getting a late bite at Hal's? I'm hungry."

Samson gladly agreed. He could use the diversion.

The trio drove across town, and less than five minutes later, Samson sat at a bar-height table with Seth and Nick, who he learned had lived in Mapleton since the second grade. Daniel Smith, whom he had met at Julia's café, joined them at their table along with a guy named Ford Marshall, who was a local real estate agent. Hal came out and plopped a giant platter of loaded nachos in front of them, and they dug in.

Samson allowed the conversation to flow over him. He appreciated the discussion between friends. The carefree joking almost made him forget the mess he'd gotten himself into.

Almost.

Every so often, over the course of their time at the diner, Samson caught Hal staring at him from behind the bar, and an ominous feeling scurried up his spine.

As Nick was scraping the last of the cheese from the bottom of the platter, Hal approached from the kitchen. "Anything else I can get for you gentlemen tonight?"

"Nah," Seth answered for the group. "It was delicious, though. Have you met Samson?" Seth tipped his head in

Samson's direction.

Samson held out his hand, relieved when Hal shook it.

"Glad to see you've made some friends." The older man pulled up a chair and sat down at their table.

Samson raised his eyebrows and waited for Hal to go on, but Nick spoke up first. "What do you mean?"

"Well, there was a group in here earlier, and they didn't have the kindest things to say about you." He bobbed his head at Samson. "Mostly just those who are still bitter about the mill closing and the way it was handled. I know you didn't have anything to do with the way everything went down, but that doesn't change that you're now associated with the mill, and people here take that personally."

Seth grimaced at Samson before questioning Hal. "Who was talking about Samson and the mill?"

"Charlie and several of his old buddies. Julia's dad was here, too, though he didn't say much." Hal brushed some chip crumbs from their table. "Anyway, I told them the crew who had been in here to eat had been nothing but friendly. Most of them didn't seem to want to hear me, but I tried to put in a good word."

"Thanks for that, I guess." Samson's voice sounded defeated in his own ears.

Hal nodded. "Don't you forget there are plenty of people around who've made their peace with the mill situation and don't have a bone to pick with you or your company—as you've found." He gestured to Seth, Nick, Daniel, and Ford. "And with Julia in your corner, you can't really lose...even if the old guard doesn't make it easy on you." With that, Hal bid them goodbye and made his way around to the bar, leaving the men to their own thoughts.

Seth took a sip of his drink.

Nick looked sideways at Samson.

Daniel stared down at the table.

Ford fixed his gaze on a spot over the bar.

Samson's head spun. He deserved this. Julia tried to win over the town to his side the other day when he came into the café.

But to what end? Thanks to the mill, Julia's own father was likely against him. What would he say when he found out about Samson's role in Milo's new plans? Not that it would matter. Julia wouldn't want anything to do with him at that point, either.

Daniel's low voice stopped Samson's thoughts before they ran completely away from him. "I wouldn't read too much into that, man."

Samson looked at the writer, praying Daniel had some fix for the predicament Samson found himself in.

"I know those guys. I've been around them and this town my whole life. It's been tough for a lot of them since the mill closed, but they're nothing if not fair. They'll give you a shot once they realize you're not a bad guy."

Samson nodded as they all stood to leave. He tossed a couple of extra dollars down on the table for Hal. "Thanks, Daniel. I hope so."

And he did. There was a chance Jerry would abort the proposal. He'd done what he could to convince his boss, and maybe that would give Julia enough time to organize her plans and put an offer together to purchase the café herself.

He'd tell her what was going on—apologize for his role in it and pray she'd forgive him. Then, if she'd have him, he'd help her save the Café.

Chapter 28

JULIA

JULIA HUNG UP THE phone and walked into the café. Her plan was coming together. "Alright," she said to Amanda. "My parents will be here, and so will Melly and her family. Do you think Seth minds manning the counter?"

"He said he was all for it," Amanda assured her. "And he spoke to Daniel and Ford, who are planning on coming, too."

Julia nodded. It wasn't much, but as part of her mission to get the town to warm up to Samson, she was throwing together a last-minute surprise birthday party for him. It would be a timely chance for people to come out and get to know Samson. She frowned and stared at her phone.

"What is it?" Amanda asked.

"I'm trying to decide whether or not to call Lorraine. If anyone can get Charlie here, it's her, but I don't know if it's too soon. My mom said he was pretty up in arms about Samson at the festival. I'd hate for him to bring the whole mood of the group down."

Amanda shrugged. "What's the worst that can happen? Samson won't leave feeling any more ostracized than he did the first day he came in here, and at least this time around, you have his back."

There was a fluttering in Julia's chest. She *did* have Samson's back. In fact, they had each other. When she thought of Samson, she thought of a future. Of a life together. Of a family. She wanted to do everything in her power to make her man feel welcome in her town. Because she hoped, someday, they'd consider it *their* town.

"You know what? You're right. I'm going to call her."

Amanda shot her a thumbs up before turning as the bell over the door jingled. "Hello, Sylvie!"

Julia waved to the teenage waitress from Hal's before dialing Lorraine and putting her phone to her ear. She ducked into the kitchen, and three rings later, Lorraine picked up.

"Lorraine, hello, this is Julia Derks."

"Julia. What a treat. How are you, dear?" Lorraine was like a grandmother figure to the whole town. Her voice came over the phone like a harp.

"I'm doing well, thanks." Julia smiled. "Listen, I don't want to take too much of your time, but I wanted to invite you and Charlie to the café tonight. I'm throwing a little surprise party for Samson. It's his birthday later this week."

"Is this the same gentleman who is in town to work on the construction at the mill site?" Lorraine's skepticism dripped over the line.

"Yes." Julia straightened a stack of napkins, her confidence fading.

"I see, I see." Lorraine mumbled more to herself than to Julia, but then she spoke louder. "And you like him, I presume?"

Julia willed her voice to remain level as she pled her case. "I do, Lorraine. And I think you and Charlie will, too, if you give him a chance. It would mean a lot to me if both of you showed up."

Lorraine didn't respond right away, and Julia held her breath, worried she was about to get taken to task by the older woman.

The silence seemed to stretch on forever before Lorraine broke it. "Well, now. You know I trust you, Julia. I've known you since the day you were born, so if you think bringing this man into town is a good thing, then I'm sure we can all get on board. I'll go to work convincing Charlie, and we'll see you tonight. What time should we arrive?"

Julia exhaled and did a quick happy dance. She rattled off the details of the party and explained to Lorraine where they should park so as not to draw attention to the café.

"Thank you, Lorraine. I'm looking forward to seeing you."

"You as well, my dear. And you'll have to introduce me to your new beau. I'm sure he's great if he's won over your heart."

Julia was about to protest and downplay their relationship, but she stopped herself. Samson was great. The greatest, actually. So she owned it. "He's the best. You'll see."

·♥·♥·♥·♥·♥·

A few hours later, Julia actively told herself not to bounce her knees in nervous anticipation as she sat in the front of Samson's truck. "Thanks for coming with me. I feel like such a space cadet."

"It's no problem at all." He threw her a small smile. "I'm sorry I wasn't able to see you yesterday. I got tied up with some work stuff."

"Everything okay on the site?" Julia tried to make conversation to keep Samson from realizing it was nonsensical to keep a spare house key at the café versus in her yard. Her excuse of needing to go back to work because she locked herself out of her house was as weak as watered-down lemonade, but it was the best she could come up with.

"Yeah, everything is fine with that project."

"That project? Are you working on something else?"

Samson shifted in his seat, readjusting his grip on the steering wheel. "Not at the moment. There might be something in the works, though, so I'm trying to cover my bases."

"Gotcha. You always have to be on your toes, don't you? That would stress me out. I appreciate how the café is a finite beast. It's a lot of work, sure, but at least it's a sure thing. It's not going anywhere. I can't imagine having to scope out and buy new land all the time, not to mention recruiting new businesses to lease the properties." Julia shook her head.

Samson's work was enough to make her eyes cross.

Chapter 29

SAMSON

SAMSON GRIMACED BUT TRIED to hide it with a laugh. Julia had no idea. He had to tell her what was going on.

He was neck deep in phone calls and discussions with every contact he had in the property development world to try to find a legal loophole in Milo and Jerry Gabler's potential plans. He was sure he was in breach of contract in about a million different ways, but it would all be worth it if he saved Julia some heartache in the end.

"It's not a cake walk," he said after reflecting on his day.

"But you're good at it." She nudged his shoulder with hers.

"That's what the boss says." *Though probably not anymore,* Samson thought, readying himself to break the news. "Speaking of work, there's something I should talk to you about."

He pulled into the parking lot in front of the café.

"Oh yeah? What's up?" Julia reached to open her door. She glanced toward the café before pausing and looking back at him.

Samson clenched his jaw. This wasn't a good time. "It's no big deal." *Lies.* "It can wait."

"Okay. Well, Seth's working," Julia informed him. "Do you want to come in and say, 'Hey'?"

"Sure. Let me grab your door." He hopped out and hurried around to help her out of the truck.

She linked their hands together, and Samson glanced down at her small fingers. They fit like puzzle pieces between his larger ones. It was almost impossible to believe that a week ago at the festival she was afraid to be seen with him. Now, he felt like they were a team—like he could conquer just about anything with her by his side.

They strolled across the parking lot, and Samson reached forward with his other hand and opened the door of the café for her. The familiar bell rang overhead, and Seth looked up from the drink he was preparing.

"Julia. Samson. Good to see you both."

Samson took in the crowd. Only a few people sat in the dining room. That was odd. Usually, the place was packed until closing time.

"I've got to grab my spare key. I swear, I can't remember anything lately." Julia cut behind the counter, and Seth's eyebrows twitched in Samson's direction.

"I don't suppose that could be the result of, I don't know, living on cloud nine thanks to the affections of a particular someone?"

Julia's cheeks turned pink, but she threw Seth's teasing right back at him. "You've been spending so much time with Amanda you're starting to sound like her."

Samson laughed at the two friends.

"Hey, while you're both here"—Seth's voice took on a serious edge as he turned to Julia—"did you want Samson to check out that loose board on the deck? I don't want it to become a liability."

The smile fell from Julia's face. "Ugh. You're right. Thanks for reminding me. Samson, do you want to lend your construction expertise? Seth texted me earlier, and he thinks we might need a new foundation on at least part of the deck."

"Of course. Lead the way." Samson let her go first down the hallway to the deck where he'd helped Nick move tables last night. He hadn't noticed anything sagging or amiss, but he hadn't been looking for it, either.

Julia pushed open the screen door, and he followed her outside.

"SURPRISE!!!!"

Samson froze.

Grinning back at him—cheering and clapping—was a crowd of people. His jaw hung suspended as he slowly turned to Julia.

She was jumping up and down on the balls of her feet with an irresistible twinkle in her eyes.

He wanted to kiss her right there, but he checked himself. From the looks of it, half the town was on the deck in front of them.

"This is for me?"

"Happy early birthday!" She grinned and threw herself into his arms.

Samson was speechless. He took a deep pull of the heady, floral scent of her shampoo, and when she leaned out of the hug, he kept his arm around her shoulder, enjoying the natural feel of her pressed to his side with her arm looped around his back.

"Let me introduce you to some people." She led him forward to the group of well-wishers.

"You've already met my mom, Gloria." Julia smiled as her mother walked toward them. A tall man with salt-and-pepper hair and a slight pot belly followed her. "And this is my dad, Joe."

Samson took his arm down from around Julia and bent to kiss Gloria's cheek. "It's nice to see you again, ma'am. Thank you for coming."

"Of course. We wouldn't miss this. Happy birthday, Samson."

Joe Derks cleared his throat.

Samson stood to his full height and met Joe's stare. The man had a wary look in his eyes, but then he glanced at Julia, and Joe's face softened. He held out his hand, and Samson readily shook it. After Hal's comment last night, he wasn't sure what to expect.

"Nice to meet you, sir."

"You as well. I hope you've been taking care of our Jules."

Samson nodded. "I'm doing my best."

"He's doing a very good job, Dad." Julia reached for Samson's hand and squeezed.

Joe grunted but appeared to be placated—for now. "Good. I'm sure we'll be seeing you around then. It would be nice to get to know you since you haven't been in town too long. We'll have you both over for dinner sometime soon. Now, I'm sure Julia wants to show you off. You two kids have fun."

"See you guys later." Julia tugged gently on Samson's hand. "Come on. I've got some more people I want you to meet."

She hauled him across the deck, and Samson stuck a smile on his face. Julia was trying to welcome him into the fold, but he didn't feel like he deserved that at the moment.

Then again, what could he do? Pull her aside and tell her the truth about Milo's plans and his own inadvertent role as a catalyst for them? In front of the majority of the town? No. He needed time alone with her to do that. So, he decided to play his role and act the part of the happy-go-lucky boyfriend even though all he wanted to do was go home and figure out what his next steps should be.

"Alright. Brace yourself." Julia led him toward an older couple. The gentleman was currently shooting daggers at him. "Charlie was the president of the mill's labor union," Julia explained.

Samson's stomach sunk. He wasn't sure if he could handle this right now.

But Julia wasn't to be deterred. She spoke quickly under her breath. "He took my dad under his wing when he was green and starting on the floor. The two worked together for twenty-five years until the decision was made to shut down the mill. Charlie was devastated. He was older, so he was able to retire early and start collecting his veteran's pension from his time in Vietnam, but he lost a part of himself when the mill shut its doors. Less than a year later, his wife Jeanne was diagnosed with stage-4 ovarian cancer. She died within three months." Julia's whispered voice caught, and she swallowed to compose herself.

"That's awful." His heart was heavy as he considered Charlie's loss.

Julia took a deep breath. "I want you to understand where he's coming from and why he might seem a little cold. He's definitely regained some of his spirit as time passed. He struck up a friendship with Lorraine, the town's retired librarian." Julia tipped her chin in the direction of a matronly woman standing with Charlie. "They're so sweet to each other."

Before Samson could respond or collect his thoughts, Julia positioned him directly in front of the couple. "Charlie, Lorraine. I'm so glad you came tonight." Julia stood, arm in arm, with him.

Samson looked down into the elderly faces of the man and woman he'd seen at the festival. The older man's reaction to Samson made a whole lot of sense now that Julia had filled him in on the back story, but what could he do to go about setting things right?

Julia was either going to make him a whole lot of new friends tonight or further entrench battle lines. She spoke with much more confidence than he felt. "This is Samson. I don't think you've been properly introduced."

Lorraine held out her hand, and Samson raised it to his lips and gave her a kiss on the knuckles. "Lovely to meet you, Lorraine."

The older woman blushed, but Charlie scowled. Samson held out his hand and prayed he would shake it, an idea brewing.

"Charlie, I'm wondering if you can tell me some of the history of the town, particularly as it pertains to the old gazebo that stands off of Mapleton Avenue."

"I'll tell you one thing, young man," Charlie spat. "That gazebo is a historic landmark, so don't get any ideas about messing with it."

Samson wagged his head back and forth. "Of course not. I wasn't thinking about changing it. I was hoping you could tell me what it was like once upon a time. I want to restore it to its former glory."

Julia let out a surprised gasp. He hadn't shared this plan with her.

Lorraine clasped her knobby hands in front of her chest. "How wonderful!"

Charlie studied him for what felt like an eternity before extending his hand. "Well, then. I'm sure I have some old pictures at my house. I can show them to you sometime."

Samson gave him a strong handshake. "I'd like that. Maybe we can meet at the café for coffee this weekend and you can bring them along."

Charlie grunted. "It'll be a good deal of work to get that old heap of wood back into prime shape."

Charlie launched into a discussion of the gazebo, and Samson was happy to stand back and listen.

"You see, it was a beauty in its day. That shingled roof made it look all fancy—before it started falling apart. And the wood was so smooth the white paint on it shone like glass as the sun set over the river. But time passes, and things change." Charlie got a faraway look in his eyes.

Samson frowned, afraid he had lost the older man to thoughts about the mill closing.

"I remember the gazebo from when I was a little girl, Charlie." Julia inched forward a half step, drawing Charlie's attention. "You and Jeanne would come and watch my shows."

Samson looked down at Julia, wondering what she was getting at. She had a gentle smile on her face.

"You were quite the entertainer." Charlie scratched his chin as if to jog his memory. "Ballet, tap, and cheerleading—sometimes all three at once, if I recall!"

Julia laughed. "And to think, I never had an hour of lessons. You guys were good sports for putting up with me. You always made me feel so proud."

"That was mostly Jeanne. She would recruit as many villagers as possible whenever your dad would tell me you were getting antsy to put on another performance. That was why you always had such an audience."

"And I loved every minute of it."

The distant look vanished from Charlie's face as he reminisced with Julia. In its place, the older man's features were set with pure determination. He nodded at Samson, his mind evidently made up. "Well, if you think you can fix up the old gazebo, I'd be right proud to help in any way I can. It's about time for another generation of performers to be able to take the stage."

Samson listened as Lorraine started talking to Julia about some community theater production scheduled for the fall. His thoughts drifted to a young Julia, dancing her heart out in front of the town. He could picture the scene with startling clarity, not only because he'd come to know Julia and her effervescent personality, but also because he'd come to understand the village. The people here loved and supported their own.

Julia scooched closer to him and gently rubbed her hand up and down his back.

He relaxed under her touch and soaked in the love and joy of the villagers surrounding him. He pushed all thoughts of the future and his work out of his head. Tonight, he wanted to enjoy Julia's presence and the people of Mapleton—even if their good opinion of him may be short-lived.

Chapter 30

JULIA

"WHAT DO YOU MEAN he seemed off?" Amanda asked. "He seemed pretty happy to me. It was a great party."

Julia couldn't argue with that. But there was something she couldn't put her finger on about Samson's behavior. He seemed a bit detached. Like he was trying a little too hard. When he'd said goodbye to her last night, she got the feeling he wanted to say more but didn't, or couldn't, or wouldn't for some reason. She shook her head. She was over-thinking this. "You know what. You're right. I'm making this out to be more than it is. It was a surprise party, after all, so naturally, he'd be thrown off."

"He wasn't thrown off too much. Charlie is his new biggest fan. Not sure how that happened."

"I know." Julia sighed with contentment at the thought of Samson making the older man feel valued and important. Samson, too, had relaxed the further he got into conversation with Charlie. Her heart swelled at the memory. "It was brilliant of Samson to include him in the discussion of the gazebo restoration," Julia marveled.

"Did you know he was taking that on, by the way?" Amanda asked as she stocked the fridge.

"No. I'm a little shocked he didn't tell me."

"He probably wanted it to be a surprise but figured winning Charlie over was more important."

Julia shrugged. "Either way, it makes me happy. I'm afraid one more harsh winter and the gazebo's roof is just going to cave in."

Amanda shuddered. "We're not going to talk about winter. Look at this beautiful day!" She pointed out the window to the rising sun and the bright-blue sky. "I refuse to focus on the cold when we have more summer and fall to look forward to."

Julia laughed. "Fair enough."

They settled into their rhythm, getting everything ready for the day ahead. The sound of percolating coffee was punctuated with the clank of the coffee mugs Amanda stacked on the counter.

"Hey," Julia spoke up after a few minutes. "What are you up to tonight?"

"No plans." Amanda retrieved a box of paper straws that was wedged in the drawer. "Seth's working here, so I was going to head home and go to bed early. Why?"

"Want to come over and talk business?"

"Not as exciting as talking about our love lives, but sure, I'm in. What are you thinking?"

"I want to come up with a plan to build On Deck Café into something even more special." Julia had turned it over in her head since her dinner with Samson on Friday. She was ready to move forward with plans to renovate and expand the café. Samson's encouragement coupled with Amanda's continual hints and her own growing belief that she had what it took got her over the hump of her hesitation. Since Amanda was a whiz with finances and idea generation, Julia wanted to bring her in on her plans.

Amanda stared blankly at her while the words sunk in. Then she squealed and hugged Julia before swinging her around in a glee-filled dance. "Yes! Finally! I was hoping you'd say that. I think that's so, so smart, Julia. What you've built here is a gold mine, but we could be doing even more. Yes!"

Julia squeezed her arms around herself when Amanda finally released her. Her friend's enthusiasm filled her with the same warmth and energy as a cup of On Deck Café's perfected house blend, and she wanted to capture it and store it up. The business venture wouldn't be without its ups and downs—Julia had enough experience with the café to know that. But

Amanda was in her corner, and that meant everything to her. "I'm so glad you're excited about this."

"Um, yeah. I'm pumped! You're a bit more conservative in your business ways." Amanda held up her hands, palms out, when Julia opened her mouth to protest. "Not that there's anything wrong with that. But I believe there are ways to make this place even better. Thank you for asking me to be a part of it. Ah!" Amanda gave Julia another fierce hug.

"Are you kidding? You've been in this with me from the beginning. Obviously, I need your vision on it moving forward."

"Let's do it."

Julia floated around the café, despite the early hour. She was a ball of energy, itching to share her new ideas with Amanda and get her friend's input. She also wanted to propose a split business venture. If she was going to grow, Julia needed to bring a partner on board, and she wanted Amanda to be that partner. But for now, she needed to focus on her customers and making the coffee they ordered.

She and Amanda tag-teamed their efforts through the morning rush. Then, from eight until about ten, they had what she considered their mid-morning lull. Most everyone was at work by that point, and no one was coming in for lunch yet. Julia poured a coffee for Marge and listened to the next months' worth of community news.

"Sounds like a great line-up of events, Marge." Julia snapped the lid on Marge's to-go cup.

"Never a dull moment, that's for sure. I trust you'll be around to help out?"

Julia smiled. "I'm always happy to do my part."

Marge gave a brisk nod, but her expression remained sour when she bid them goodbye.

As she stalked out of the café, Julia frowned. "I feel like Marge is Santa Claus, and I'm on the naughty list."

Amanda giggled.

Julia looked around, finding everyone else was taken care of. "I'm going to go take inventory in the kitchen," she told

Amanda. "Then, I'll run out and shop for what we need before Jimmy gets here. Holler if you need me for anything."

"You got it."

Julia walked into the small, U-shaped space and saw it with new eyes. Revamping and upgrading the kitchen was one of the major parts of her plan for the new-and-improved On Deck Café.

As it stood now, the kitchen was fine. But *fine* no longer felt good enough. The counter space was minimal, and when she'd first remodeled, she hadn't had enough money to carry the stone surface from the café's front counter and service bar into the kitchen, so the old laminate counters were what they worked with back here. Jimmy deserved more.

She could use some of the space from the storage closet and incorporate it to make a more functional kitchen. She wanted to reconfigure the layout to make room for a full-scale cooking island. Julia hummed with excitement as she imagined it all coming together.

As she took inventory of the items on one of the open shelves, the bell above the front door jingled. Amanda was at the register, so Julia kept at her work, smiling to herself at their current set-up and all she dreamed it could become.

Chapter 31

SAMSON

AFTER CHECKING IN AT the work site, Samson decided to swing over to On Deck Café to see Julia. He'd called his boss earlier, hoping to find out if Jerry had scrapped his plans to buy the land around Sunrise Park so he could breathe easier, but he hadn't gotten an answer.

Samson rolled his shoulders, trying to relax, as he drove down Mapleton Avenue. The flower baskets hanging from each of the light poles lining the terrace swayed gently in the morning breeze. It was going to be another scorcher of a day, but right now, it was a pleasant sixty-five degrees. He passed Hal's, where the owner was sweeping his front walk. Samson waved out the open truck window.

Hal raised his hand to block the sun before greeting Samson as he passed by. A young woman jogged down the sidewalk, pushing a double stroller. A man in a neon-yellow vest zipped around on a riding lawnmower, cutting the strip of grass along the street. The village hummed with an addictive vitality.

Samson never considered himself a small-town guy before now. Then again, he wasn't a big-city guy, either. He hadn't settled anywhere long enough to become attached or associated with a place. In Mapleton, though, he could. He liked the pace. He liked the patterns. He liked the people. He liked Julia—a lot. Seeing her, listening to her talk, and soaking up the warmth of her hospitality would make his day.

As he approached the On Deck Café parking lot, he saw Milo and—

"You have got to be kidding me," Samson said aloud to his dashboard.

Jerry Gabler was walking into Julia's café with Milo.

"No, no, no," Samson chanted as he pulled into the nearest parking spot he could find. He leapt from his crookedly parked truck and sprinted to the front door. He offered up a silent prayer in desperation.

Please, God, don't let Julia be here.

Samson had no idea what he would find when he walked through the front door, but he ripped it open like he was ripping off a Band-Aid. The bell on the door clattered above him as he burst into the café. His eyes shot behind the counter, and he saw Amanda.

Only Amanda.

Samson took a deep breath.

Amanda glanced up and gave him a half smile. Jerry turned around, and a flash of guilt crossed his face. Milo just looked pretentious.

"Samson!" Jerry recovered his composure and masked his surprise. "Good to see you." He walked to the door and shook Samson's hand.

"I've been trying to get a hold of you." Samson's voice came out sounding strained. "I wish I knew about your plans to visit."

Amanda eyed the three of them with curiosity etched all over her face. If only he could move this conversation outside. The only other person in the dining room at the moment was Daniel. If Samson could save face for a little longer, he might be able to buy himself some time to at least tell Julia what was going on before news got to her some other way.

"Yes, well"—Jerry cleared his throat—"I've been talking to Milo here quite a bit, and we decided it would be best if I came and saw things in person. I had some other work to do, so I drove up first thing this morning."

Milo smirked, and Samson realized he'd been kept in the dark on purpose. Samson hated that, but he wasn't going to make a scene in the café.

"Can I get y'all anything?" Amanda piped up from behind the counter. Her face twisted in confusion as she stared at Samson. Samson shook his head slightly and hoped she took the hint not to ask any questions. He would explain everything —if he could just do it on his terms.

"Yes, that would be nice." Jerry bellied up to the counter. "I'll take a medium caffè mocha, please."

"You got it. Samson, anything for you?"

"No thanks, Amanda."

"Ah, I see you've met the locals." His boss's closed-lip smile made him look like a cunning wolf.

Samson winced as Amanda's eyes widened to the size of saucers.

"Like I told you before, I've gotten to know the people in Mapleton." He tried to cover for Jerry's predatory implications. The last thing he wanted was for Amanda to think he'd been faking his way into friendship with her and the others—or worse, thinking he wasn't sincere in his feelings for Julia.

"This is why I send him." Jerry turned to explain to Milo. "He's very good with people. He usually gets his way." Jerry laughed, and Samson cringed. Jerry was making him sound like a scoundrel. Before he had a chance to collect himself, Milo spoke up.

"I can see that, Jerry. From what I can tell, your man Samson here has sweet-talked most of the town. Not an easy task, considering people around here are pretty stuck in their ways. But he's made nice with the right folks."

Amanda pressed her lips together so hard they turned as white as frothed milk.

"Milo." Samson bit out his name like a warning.

"Well, now. That'll only serve all of us well, won't it, Milo?" Jerry smiled at him. "Samson, when we buy this land, you'll have to stick around to oversee the establishments we have planned for it."

The world came to a full stop.

Samson closed his eyes as the room tilted.

There it was. Out in the open. Everything he feared was true, and both Amanda and Daniel heard it.

"You're planning to buy *this* land? Like the land we're standing on?" Amanda spoke into the silence of the dining room. Although she directed her question at Jerry and Milo, she was staring right at Samson.

"Amanda, I can explain—"

"The village board has to have a hearing about it, of course," Milo interjected, cutting him off. "It's not like I can run around selling off parts of the village's land, willy-nilly." He cackled, and Samson fought a strong desire to punch him in the mouth.

"They'll weigh the options and decide whether to keep ownership or to sell. I really like the plans Jerry has come up with and plan to give the board my two cents. At this point, I'd say it's basically a done deal. It really comes down to whether or not the village wants to retain ownership with Gabler, Burns, and Associates coming in to do the work, or if we sell to them for an outright profit."

Amanda's jaw went slack even as her eyes blazed. Samson opened his mouth, but she shot up her pointer finger in his direction to silence him. "And what about Julia and the café?"

"Of course, we'll give Julia a chance to speak at the village hearing," Milo said to Amanda. "But she pays almost nothing for rent here, so it isn't in the village's best interest to keep things the way they are, especially if another offer is on the table."

Jerry nodded. "If I may be frank with you both, as long as interest is high from potential businesses who'd want to lease this space—and I don't doubt it will be—we plan to make the Village of Mapleton a cash offer they can't refuse." He shrugged in Amanda's direction. "It's nothing personal; it's just business."

Milo nodded.

Amanda's hands jerked with what Samson understood as suppressed rage as she set Jerry's order down on the high counter. "Your drink."

"Thank you." Jerry offered her a carefree smile, either oblivious or indifferent to the bombshell he had dropped. Turning to leave, he addressed Samson. "I'm headed to the village offices to go over some particulars with Milo. Let's meet at the mill job site in an hour so you can catch me up, and we can talk about future plans."

Samson didn't say anything, but he gave Jerry a terse nod. Milo strode after Jerry with a self-satisfied look on his face.

Samson flinched as the door slammed shut. The café was eerily quiet. He turned to Amanda, ready to beg. "Amanda, please. Don't tell Julia. I—"

Movement caught his eye, and Julia emerged from the open kitchen door behind the counter, her face ashen.

Chapter 32

JULIA

"JULIA."

Her name on Samson's lips sounded like a prayer, and his voice snapped Julia out of the trance she was in. The café walls closed in on her, and Julia couldn't breathe. She needed to get out of there. She turned on her heel, knocking her shoulder into the wall, and strode down the hallway.

"Julia, wait," Samson called for her as she rushed to the deck.

She wrenched open the screen door and fled down the stairs on the side of the building, ignoring the startled gasps of her customers.

"Julia, please," Samson yelled.

But Julia didn't turn back. She couldn't. A hand clamped down on her arm, and she whirled around as she shook herself free. "Don't touch me. Don't talk to me. Just don't." Julia recoiled, not bothering to hide the hurt and anger from her voice.

"Julia, I can explain."

"No. I don't think you can. And quite honestly, I don't want to hear it." Julia covered her face with her hands. Her whole body trembled, and her mind wouldn't compute. She stood there for a long time, in silence, breathing in and out, trying to make sense of what was going on. This couldn't be happening. And yet, it was happening. She'd heard it all with her own two ears.

When she finally looked up, Samson was standing in front of her, arms hanging at his sides and his face lined with desperation. He opened his mouth to say something, but she shook her head, using the sheer force of her own willpower to keep the tears that were balancing on her lower eyelids from sliding down her face.

"No. Don't, Samson." Julia held up her hand, trying to keep a physical wall up between them, even though she was about to fall to pieces. "You know what? You waltzed into this town, and I knew you were bad news. I *knew* it. And yet, against my better judgment, I let you in. I let myself fall for you. I guess that was —what was it that man said?—your ability to win people over? Is that what you were doing with me? Trying to win me over so you and your company could score another deal?"

"Of course not! You have to know that is not the truth."

Julia ignored the agony in his voice, thinking only of the pain he brought into her life. Right now, the hurt hit her so badly she swore she was splitting in two, right down the middle—spine cracking, skin peeling...a total body torture.

"How am I supposed to know that, Samson? When I was pouring out my hopes and dreams for this place to you the other night, and you sat there telling me my ideas were great and what I had here was magic, were you just biding your time? Or were you planning to steal my ideas to use for your company's ends?"

"I would never do that to you." Samson's eyes flashed, desperation turning to outrage.

"You should have told me," Julia's voice cracked, and she took a deep, shuddering breath, trying to steady herself. "You knew about your company's plans, didn't you? Did you know about Milo's plans? It sure sounded like it."

"I can explain everything, Julia."

"Tell me the truth, Samson. You owe me that, at least."

Samson bowed his head. "Yes, I knew. But—"

"That's all I need to hear. I trusted you, Samson. I did. And I thought I knew you. The real you. But this is too much. You need to leave. I don't want you back here. For as long as this is my property, I don't want you on it. And I don't want to be your girlfriend anymore, either. We're done. I'm done."

"Julia, please." Samson reached for her hand and implored her with his eyes.

"Go, Samson." Julia pulled her arm away and didn't wait to see what he would do. She couldn't be this close to him anymore. She cut through the parking lot to the front door of the café, not daring to turn around and face the man who had trampled her heart and tore up her dreams for the future.

Julia yanked open the café's door as the first tear splashed from her eye. One look at Amanda's face—all concerned and full of righteous indignation—and the flood gates opened. Julia dissolved into a puddle, letting Amanda and Daniel steer her to the couch in front of the latent fireplace. Amanda left her side as Daniel rubbed a soothing hand across her back. He didn't say anything, but it meant a lot to her that he was there.

When Amanda returned moments later, she thrust a cup of coffee into Julia's quaking hands. "He's gone."

She didn't have to elaborate. Julia understood Amanda was referring to Samson. Thankfully, he hadn't followed her back inside. She didn't want to break down in front of him, and she couldn't have held her composure any longer.

She leaned her elbow on the arm of the couch and propped her head up against the tips of her fingers as the shock from being blindsided wore off. "I don't believe this." Julia felt like someone had cut her heart out of her chest and started using it as a tennis ball. The pain came at her from two directions, and she reeled from the whiplash.

Her café—her pride and joy and the place she'd poured her blood, sweat, and tears into—was in jeopardy. She was so stupid for not considering the village could do with this land what it wanted. It had not even crossed her mind as a possibility.

Until now.

Now, it was made clear that if the financial incentive was great enough, she'd be evicted and her café done away with to make room for development. The thought made her stomach plummet, so she thrust it aside. But when she did that, she was faced with the second part of the blow.

Samson betrayed her. There was no way around it. The man she allowed herself to trust turned out to be who she initially feared he was: some big-shot businessman who was all charm and no substance. She let him in, and he trampled all over her heart. And her town.

She'd shared things with him that she hadn't shared with anyone—stories from her past, parts of her family history she treasured. He made her feel safe. Yet, now she was left exposed, vulnerable, and just plain sad. And he was responsible.

Amanda glanced over Julia's shoulder to the parking lot as the sound of slamming car doors reached their ears. "Looks like we have customers coming in. You should go home, Julia. Let me handle the rest of the morning here."

"No." Julia smudged the leftover moisture away from under her eyes. "I'm not going to leave the café." She couldn't. Not while its future hung in the balance. If one thing had crystalized in clarity this morning, it was how much she loved this café. This was where she wanted to be.

Julia downed the rest of her coffee, and it fortified her. She hoisted herself off the couch, and as the bell over the door jingled, Julia turned to greet her patrons with a smile on her face—albeit, a watery one—and got to work.

Chapter 33

SAMSON

SAMSON DROVE DOWN MAPLETON Avenue, but what had looked charming and bright less than an hour earlier now looked dark and bleak. Already he was haunted by the closed-up expression on Julia's face when she had told him to leave. It was as if he was a stranger to her, like she didn't know him at all. For a split second, he had toyed with the idea of following her into the café and pleading to be heard, but he didn't think that would accomplish anything—at least not anything productive. He would respect her wishes, and as much as it killed him, he'd leave her alone.

Parking by the mill grounds, he slammed his truck door with enough force to rattle the tailgate. Several of the workers on site turned to look in his direction. He shoved the hard hat on his head and waited for his boss to show up. He wanted an explanation, pronto.

Twenty minutes later, Jerry pulled up in his sleek, black Lexus sedan. He stepped out, wearing his shiny loafers and black suit. Samson balled his hands into fists and released them. He was thankful Milo wasn't with Jerry. There were some things he needed to hash out with his boss, and the prying ears and eyes of enemy number one in this town would not be welcome.

Samson strode over to the road. He snatched a spare hard hat from one of the trailers they'd set up on the property and met Jerry by his vehicle. He held out the hard hat. "Company policy," he said evenly. "*Your* company."

Samson took a snippet of satisfaction from seeing his boss in a hard hat. There was nothing like an unflattering piece of hard plastic to even the playing field a little.

Once Jerry got himself situated in his personal protective equipment, he surveyed the grounds.

Samson tracked his line of sight as it swung over the beeping machinery, across the turned-over dirt and grounds, and to the rushing Squirrel River beyond. The morning sun glinted off both the metal equipment and the water, sending sparkles into the sky.

Jerry finally spoke after taking it all in. "This is quite the place."

The levy holding Samson's emotions in check started leaking. "Cut the crap, Jerry. What's going on? You screen my calls. You keep me in the dark. Then, you show up in town unannounced. I thought you were considering throwing out your proposal. A heads-up would have been nice."

"Samson." Jerry pointed to Samson's chest and leveled him with a patronizing glare. "You're taking this too personally. And maybe that's the problem. Maybe it has gotten personal for you."

Samson raised an eyebrow, challenging his boss to clarify his point.

"I spoke to Milo after your little visit to my office. He informed me you took an interest in the woman who owns the café you spoke of. Once I found that out, it wasn't hard to see your only objection to our project was a personal one."

Samson's blood began to boil. "You're taking Milo's word over mine, Jerry? You didn't even ask me about it!"

Jerry held up his hands defensively. "It's water under the bridge. Like I said before, this is business. There's money to be made here. Now, what I need to know is whether or not you are going to be able to do this, Samson. We're going to offer the village a fair sum for that property. I want it, and I plan to get it. You've been my man on the ground here, and you're obviously doing a good job. But if you can't handle this—if you can't reconcile your work with your personal life—I won't make you facilitate the new deal. You can go back to Madison, leave this current job, and never come back to Mapleton. No hard feelings. If you can handle this, then I'll put you in charge of securing the businesses that'll fill the new development and eventually overseeing the construction. I need to know I can count on you."

Samson was quiet for a minute as he tried to get his blood pressure under control. He hated this. He hated it so much. But he knew what he had to do. He didn't have another option at this point, so he resigned himself to the situation. "I can handle it, Jerry. My relationship with Julia is over."

"I see. Okay, then. I'm trusting you, Samson. If you pull this off, it'll mean big things for your future. I want you to stay in contact, though. Get in touch with our pool of restaurant and hotel prospects. See who's interested in moving on this with us. This is a big deal, and if we land it, it'll go a long way toward cementing our position as the premiere developer in the state and maybe even in the region. I've hammered out most of the details with Milo and given him enough information about our offer to whet his appetite. I can't imagine we'll have much competition, but if you hear anything, you need to let me know ASAP. I'll be back in town for the hearing."

"Right. Has a date been set for the village board's decision?" Samson needed an idea of what sort of time constraints he'd be working under.

"The village board meets the last Monday of each month, so Milo is shooting for July 31st."

Samson did the math in his head. That meant, in less than three weeks, this chapter would all be over. He could handle that. He'd done business before in less time. He would do it again. "Alright. I'm going to get back to work. I'll see you at the end of the month."

"And you'll talk to me before then if anything comes up." Jerry's tone left no room for argument as he shook Samson's hand.

"Understood." Samson trekked with his boss to the entrance of the job site and said goodbye.

The second his taillights were out of sight, Samson set his jaw, dug out his cell phone, and started making calls.

Chapter 34

JULIA

JULIA SAT STIFFLY ON her parents' patio with Mr. Waffles lying on her feet. Her mother had transformed their backyard into a bonus living space, complete with comfy, cushioned furniture and an outdoor TV suspended from the house. The flowers were in full bloom, and the twinkle lights Gloria hung from the pergola cast a warm glow overhead while a fire crackled in the freestanding fireplace.

The idyllic locale sat in stark contrast to the gloomy weight pressing down on Julia's shoulders. Her head throbbed from the events of the day, but she forced herself to focus through the ache. She could do this. She *had* to do this.

She wasn't going to go down without a fight.

News of Milo's plans and Samson's deceit had spread through the town, and a group of friends and fellow villagers had gathered at the Derks' residence in solidarity. Now, people were hurling suggestions left and right.

"The village board won't hear of this." Gloria shot a look around the circle. "Will they?" Her mom's question undercut her guarantee.

Amanda crossed her arms and frowned. "If they knew what was good for them and this town, they wouldn't."

Marge clicked her tongue, drawing everyone's attention to where she sat in one of the wicker chairs on the opposite side of the patio. "Technically, your rental agreement has to be honored unless you've violated the terms. So, the village can't kick you out before that's up."

Julia's heart swelled. She had been surprised to see Marge at her parents' house after the less-than-ideal treatment she'd received from the woman as of late. Yet here she was, proving her allegiance and trying to help.

Julia shot her a sad smile. "Unfortunately, I renew my lease every year at the end of August, so it'll come up in less than two months." She'd need to prove her worth to the village board fair and square.

"Who's on the village board these days?" Sally piped up. Her pixie-cut hair was dyed a light grayish-blue color that reminded Julia of thunderstorm clouds. It fit Julia's mood perfectly.

Her father ticked off a list of seven people, including Neil Schaumburg, the village president. They all knew Julia, but none of them were particularly close to her or her family.

"I say we start calling the board members at home," Seth said. "The more people who call and share their feelings about the land around Sunrise Park, the better."

Amanda nodded. "You're right. They are supposed to represent the people, and if the people are unhappy, the board members should act in accordance. We should start there."

"I can reach out to the folks at *The Village Tattler*." Daniel's voice was steady. He'd witnessed the entire debacle, and if anyone had to, she was thankful it was him. "I could even write a feature article. I'm sure my editor would run it, no questions asked. I can highlight your café and what it means to the community. After all, I'd say I am your most devoted customer." The corner of one side of his mouth rose ever so slightly at his quip as everyone started arguing in jest over who was more loyal to the café.

Julia let loose an exhausted smile. She had a long road ahead, but she wasn't going it alone. Most of the village had her back, and Daniel was right. Getting the local paper involved was a smart idea.

"Thank you, Daniel. I'd appreciate that. Thank you, all." Julia looked out over the group assembled on the patio. Her parents and all their friends from around town. Kristy and her husband, Ashton. Amanda, Seth, and Nick. Even Chef Jimmy called in sick at his other job to be there to support her. These were her people, and she appreciated every one of them.

Since her initial breakdown at the café, Julia had held in the tears, but now the throbbing behind her eyes was making it difficult to see straight. Amanda came over and plopped down on the outdoor couch. Mr. Waffles sat up and laid his head in Amanda's lap, begging for attention.

Julia rested her head on Amanda's shoulder, leaning into her friend. "We were going to get together tonight to develop a business plan for going forward."

It was painfully ironic. The day she decided to take the plunge and get some ideas on paper for moving her business to the next level was the same day she found out it would likely cease to exist as she knew it.

Julia shook her head. Self-doubt kept trying to weasel its ugly way into her thoughts, but she wanted to shut it down. She could do this. She would save her business because she couldn't imagine her life without it.

She sat upright. "I think we should postpone our meeting until tomorrow night."

"That's what I like to hear. What are you thinking?" Amanda leaned forward in her seat, turning to face Julia.

"I have built a business in Mapleton, in the Henderson house. A profitable business and an asset to this community. That doesn't go away because somebody decides a bigger development would be better. No way. We're going to get together and plan for the future like we were going to do before—before the fallout of today." She shuddered, the memory of this morning still raw.

"Milo said they'd give me a chance to speak. If all of the people here, and anyone else around town who's willing to help out, can start petitioning board members, and we get a plan together, we can pitch it to the board at the end of the month. What they do with it is up to them, but I have to give them another option—an alternative to Milo's plan."

"Now we're talking!" Amanda cracked a grin, and her eyes ignited with determination. She held up her hand for a high five.

The exchange between the two of them drew the attention of the rest of those gathered.

"We're in business, ladies and gentlemen." Amanda rubbed her hands together, and everyone else cheered. The clink of glasses being tapped filled the early evening air.

Julia's mom wove her way through the guests, and Julia stood to hug her.

"It'll work out, dear. I know it."

"Thanks, Mom."

Gloria let go and turned to talk to some others, but Julia grabbed for her arm.

"Is it okay if I sleep here tonight? Mr. Waffles, too?" The truth was, she didn't want to be alone, and the thought of driving home and knowing Samson was less than a block away was something her heart wasn't ready to handle—at least not tonight. Because though she was going to fight for her business, thinking about doing it without Samson by her side—and worse, against him—made her nauseated.

"Sure you can, honey. Your room is always here for you."

Julia sighed and squeezed her arms around herself to ward off the night chill. "I know." She gave her mom a weak smile. "I'm tired."

"Not surprising after the day you've had. You should head inside. I'll make your goodbyes for you."

Julia took in the crowd of people—people who loved her and who were willing to go to bat for her. She appreciated them more than she could say right now, so she nodded in agreement, her eyes filling with another round of tears.

Gloria scooted away, and Amanda pulled Julia into a tight hug.

"It's going to be okay."

Over Amanda's shoulder, Julia saw her family and friends.

Her village.

She dug her chin into Amanda's shoulder, the back of her throat burning with tears. "I know."

Chapter 35

SAMSON

"YES, SIR." SAMSON SPOKE confidently into the phone, the excitement of a new deal coursing through his veins. He looked beyond the worksite and out over the river. "I look forward to meeting with you as well. I'll see you at the park on Wednesday. Mmhmm. Goodbye."

Hanging up, Samson pulled up a new text message and sent off the address to the investor's assistant so he'd come to the right place the following week.

This one held promise. Abe Nichols was interested in the land, and if Samson gave him the right pitch when he was here to see it in person, he might get on board.

Samson entered a list of talking points into his phone before stowing his device. It was his birthday, and he was spending it wheeling and dealing on the job...like always. Less than a week ago, he thought this birthday would be different, but he'd cooked his own goose—charred it to a crisp, actually—and now he had to live with the ashes.

He turned his attention to survey the activity on the mill site. It was a massive project, but the site had been excavated, and the footings were being formed for the large multi-use facility that was going up in the middle of the space. Next up, they'd pour the concrete. He made a mental note to check in with the concrete company to be sure they were on tap to show up Monday morning. After the footings cured, they'd move on to walls. Then, they'd waterproof the whole foundation structure and work out the drainage before backfilling and laying the ground floor. He was exhausted, and his head ached, thinking about all the moving parts. He'd spent the past two days working two jobs: his day job at the mill site and securing investors for the new park development.

Some robust coffee sounded good.

At the thought, both his head and his heart pounded. He couldn't go to On Deck Café. Julia told him to stay away, and though he figured nothing he did would make her think any less of him at this point, he was going to respect her wishes.

But Samson would give anything to be able to stroll through the café's door and see Julia's smiling face behind the counter. It had only been two days since Milo and Jerry turned his world upside down, but it felt like a lifetime. He couldn't stop picturing every one of Julia's laugh lines, the precise way her nose crinkled when she was happy—and when she was unhappy—and the soul-searching blue of her eyes. It was as if her very essence was on a loop in his brain.

But dwelling on Julia did him no good. She had made herself clear when she dismissed him that morning in the parking lot. Of course, he deserved it. He deserved every word she said, every assumption she made, and if he could do things differently, he would. This fiasco was entirely his fault. He should have been honest with her. Now, he'd ruined the best thing that had ever happened to him. He ran a weary hand across the back of his neck, massaging his stiff muscles. He really needed the weekend to lick his wounds.

The diggers were quieting down, so Samson jogged over to check in with Larry, his foreman, and the crew.

Reassured everything was in place, he turned to leave the site for the night.

"Hey, man, we're going to Hal's," Larry said. "Want to join?"

Samson hesitated. He'd been avoiding the local establishment since news broke of his betrayal. But he figured it was early enough in the evening that not many people would be around. And it was his birthday. He deserved some decent food. "Sure. I'm starving."

Ten minutes later, as he brought up the rear of the group that arrived at Hal's, Samson realized going with them was a major mistake. Hal greeted Larry cheerfully and made small talk with several of the guys on the crew, but the noise level in the restaurant dropped to a furious hush when Samson stepped inside. There were only a few people at a smattering of tables, and all eyes were on him. When Hal spotted Samson, his eyes turned to slits, and he spun around and walked away without a word.

In the past, Samson would have plastered on an indifferent poker face. But he wasn't indifferent. He was torn up. He grimaced and let the melancholy he felt cloud his features.

Charlie sat with Lorraine at a table in the corner of the open room. The older man glared in Samson's direction with contempt before a different expression washed over his face. If Samson wasn't mistaken, it was sadness, and that was worse. He had let the man down.

Brice, one of the machine operators, leaned toward him as he took his seat. "Yo, man. What's up? Hal looked ticked at you."

"It's a long story."

When Brice's forehead puckered, Samson explained himself. "I made a mistake, and now most of the town thinks I'm a jerk."

"What'd you do?" Larry asked from across the table.

"I was dating Julia, the owner of the café. Now my company wants to buy the land she rents for the coffee shop, and I didn't tell her."

"Dude." Brice tipped his head to the side. "Bad move. I don't know much about women, but I've learned withholding information never ends well. They always find out in the end." The young man was only in his early twenties, so his life experience was questionable, but in this case, he was right.

"What are you going to do about it?" Larry asked him quietly.

Before Samson could formulate an answer, someone shuffled behind him, and he turned in his seat to see Charlie, who was leaving with Lorraine. She walked past him and stood waiting by the door, but Charlie stopped at his table.

Samson stood and held out his hand. "Charlie. Nice to see you again."

"I don't have a habit of shaking hands with snakes." Charlie raised his chin into the air and looked up at Samson, eyes flashing. "Shame," Charlie went on. "I liked your ideas for the gazebo, but I won't be talking to you about it anymore. And you should know you won't find many other women with as much of a heart as Julia. In some of my lowest moments, she's been there to pick an old man up, dust him off, and tell him it's going to be okay. What you did to her? It's inexcusable." Charlie's eyes watered, and he was starting to shake.

Samson bowed his head and clasped his hands behind his back. Charlie was right. There was nothing he could say.

"Come on, Charlie. It'll do no good now." Lorraine retraced her steps and put her hand in the crook of Charlie's elbow. The woman who was so friendly to him earlier in the week steered Charlie to the door without giving Samson so much as a second look.

"Yikes," Brice broke the silence in the restaurant as the older pair took their leave. "Seems like you've really stepped in it."

That was the understatement of the month. And Samson was no longer hungry.

Lost in thought, he made the quick drive to his rental. He sat parked in front of the house for a long time, his mind full of lessons learned and a backlog of regret. He felt too weighted down to move.

Eventually, when he started to sweat in the late day heat, he reached for the door handle. His ears perked up as the rumble of a familiar vehicle grew louder, approaching from down the road. He froze with his hand on the lever and didn't blink as he stared in the rearview mirror. A couple seconds later, Julia appeared in her truck.

Samson gripped the slick metal of the handle and struggled to fill his lungs. He hadn't been this close to her since their confrontation in the café's parking lot. He prayed she would look in his direction, if only so he could drink in her face, but she drove right by, staring straight ahead. She turned into her driveway, parked the truck, and hopped out. She opened the tailgate for Mr. Waffles who bounded down and ran off to sniff the grass before stopping to chase his tail. Samson's heart lurched further at the sight of her dog.

Julia didn't pay his house any attention. And why would she? She cut in front of her truck and walked straight to her side door. Mr. Waffles followed her, and when they disappeared, Samson let his forehead fall against the steering wheel.

Finally, he climbed out of his truck and cast a last look at Julia's bungalow before unlocking his front door. Walking inside, he dropped his bag on the floor and took a step toward the kitchen when a knock sounded. Samson jumped.

Julia?

He spun around and flung open the door.

Samson's shoulders slumped. "Hi, Melly."

She stood with her arms crossed in front of her chest, her mouth set in a hard line. "Hello, Samson."

Before Samson could invite her in, she walked past him and took a seat on his living room couch. When he raised an eyebrow at her, she lifted a shoulder and patted the seat next to her. "I figured you could use a friend. Now sit. Tell me what's going on."

Samson sunk down beside Melly. He told her the whole story. When he finished, he stared at her, praying she understood where he was coming from.

"I messed up, Melly. But deep down, I'm not the bad guy everyone is painting me to be."

Melly nodded as if it was decided. "What can I do to help?"

Chapter 36

JULIA

JULIA PLAYED WITH THE tassel on her purse while she waited for assistance at Community Credit Union.

After several days of planning and tweaking, she and Amanda had shown their plans for the café to Seth the night before, and with his encouragement, Julia vowed to try to secure funding to buy the Henderson house ahead of the board meeting. Without proof of funds, she didn't think the village board would give her the time of day.

Fortunately, when the member services representative called her into her office, she gave Julia one look and said, "Okay, hun. We're all rooting for you. Tell me what you need."

It turned out, there was a lot Julia could do with the evidence of the successful business she built and the threat of the village taking it away. She had no problem getting pre-approved for a loan to purchase the building and the land it sat on outright. She couldn't wait to tell Amanda and Seth the good news.

When she walked out of the credit union, she felt lighter than she had in a week, optimistic about her chances and excited for what might lay ahead. Everyone was rallying around her. They'd all stepped up and were there for her when the going got tough. With their belief in her and her café, she dared to hope maybe everything would work out.

The drive to On Deck Café was a quick one. Julia parked in her usual spot along the side of the building nearest the ballfields. She tossed her keys in her purse before giving the park a quick scan.

Her lungs seized at the sight in front of her. Samson stood, angled away from her, with a man she didn't recognize. Julia sucked in a painful breath as she realized the stranger was likely someone in town to see the park for themselves before deciding they wanted in on the development.

Samson pointed and gestured to different features of the grounds, looking confident, capable, and—Julia hated herself for still thinking it—crazy handsome. Her heart knotted, longing for what might have been, even as her gaze flitted a stone's throw away to the exact spot in the parking lot where everything had blown up.

Julia couldn't help but replay their last exchange in her head. She hadn't let Samson explain himself, and maybe she should have. But what good would have come of it? What was done was done, and he wasn't wasting any time getting on with the job at hand.

The pair of men turned away from her, and Julia decided that was enough torture for one day. She exited her truck and hurried to the café's back entrance. As she pulled the door open, she cast a quick glance over her shoulder.

Samson was staring directly at her.

Time stopped, and his gaze bore into hers, locking them together with the strength of a magnetic field. Julia wanted to run to him. She wanted him to run to her. But they both stood rooted in place.

Eventually, the man standing with Samson said something and tapped Samson on the shoulder. Samson turned to his companion before shooting her one more look, but the force field was severed.

Julia flung open the door of her café and rushed inside. She stopped in the hallway and did some deep breathing. She pressed her hands against her cheeks. The sight of Samson made her skin feel warm and tight.

It would only get easier as time passed, she told herself, and he would leave soon. At that thought, fresh queasiness crawled up the walls of her stomach. She took in a couple gulps of coffee-scented air, willing herself to focus on the café. She had enough to worry about with her business.

Steadied, she marched into the dining room. A group of her regulars was milling about. She walked up behind Amanda who was intent on pouring the perfect heart cappuccino. When she stood to admire her work, Julia wrapped her arms around her waist in a hug.

"Jules!" Amanda yelped, setting down her pitcher of steamed milk. "I didn't expect you back already."

"I got good news." Julia released Amanda who turned and waited for Julia to continue. "The credit union pre-approved us to buy this building."

Cheers went up from their customers as Amanda wrapped her in a bear hug. Seth piled on, and Julia stumbled as she tried to keep her balance under the weight of her friends' embrace. A laugh bubbled up, and before she knew it, she was laughing so hard she was crying. It was a relief to be among friends.

Packing thoughts of Samson up into a neat little box and shelving it in the very back corner of her brain (and covering it with a ratty, old tarp for good measure), Julia threw herself into her work. She blended ice for a frozen cappuccino, made a perfect pour-over, and chatted with her customers. She lost track of time until Marge came through the front door of the café.

"Marge, good to see you."

The older woman nodded as she approached the counter, the usual urgency of her gait noticeably absent. "I'm glad you're here, Julia. Can I have a word? Privately."

Amanda stepped away. "I can cover the counter. Why don't you two go out to the deck? I think it's pretty empty out there right now."

Marge nodded, and Julia led the way outside. Reflexively, Julia's gaze shot to where she last saw Samson, but thankfully, he and the man he was with were no longer around. She turned her attention to Marge, who appeared to be fiddling with the hem of her blouse.

Marge *never* fiddled. This couldn't be good. Julia braced for whatever Marge was about to say. She didn't think she could take any more bad news.

"What's up, Marge?"

The older woman squared her shoulders, a resolute expression on her face. "I've come to apologize."

Julia's mouth dropped open. "Pardon me?"

Marge took a deep breath. "That's right. I owe you an apology."

"For what?" Julia was dumbstruck.

"Well, for the festival and how everything shook out. I was thinking back on it, and I realized I was especially uncharitable to you. I told myself I wasn't doing it on purpose—scheduling you back to back at the dunk tank and food tent and then forcing you into dealing with the money at the end of the day. But the truth is, I was. You see, I was...well, I am...feeling a little intimidated."

"Intimidated?" Julia asked, sure the confusion was clear on her face. Then it dawned on her, and she felt her eyes double in size. "Wait. You're intimidated...by me?" That couldn't be right either.

"Yes." Marge squirmed and looked like she'd been forced to kiss her cousin. She raised her arms and shoulders in an enormous shrug. "You are this beacon of light and energy. You breathe life into everything you do. I thought maybe you were gunning for my position. The people around town would be only too happy to see you take over for me, so I got defensive and catty, and I'm sorry."

Julia plunked down onto the bench of one of her picnic tables. She needed a minute to take in everything Marge had said.

Marge sat down across from her.

"Wow. I mean, wow, Marge. I had no idea. I would *never* try to steal your position from you. You chair the festival better than anyone else. I'm just happy to help."

Marge shifted her gaze, looking unconvinced.

"I'm serious, Marge. I don't want the responsibility of running things. I appreciate you seeing me as a valuable member of the community. And I'm glad I wasn't crazy when I thought I kept drawing the short straw when it came to festival assignments."

Marge let out a wry laugh. "No. That's on me. I won't take advantage of you again."

Julia studied the older woman sitting across from her. Marge prided herself on being right, so to have to admit to anything less than perfection was a tough pill for her to swallow. When the older woman went to stand, Julia instinctively rose and hugged her. "I'm really glad you stopped by, Marge."

"Yes, well, my conscience wouldn't let me sleep. And listen, I know this is a tough time for the café with everything going on with the village, but you have a lot of people who believe in you. Whatever happens, you'll have our support."

These words of encouragement touched Julia's heart more than her apology. Marge wasn't the sentimental type. For her to say anything was meaningful. Julia's eyes misted, and she swallowed around a lump in her throat. "Thank you, Marge."

Marge waved her hand. "Don't mention it. You keep me posted, and let me know if there's anything I can help with. I have you signed up to work the concession stand at a couple of games yet this month, so I'm sure I'll see you there, if not before."

There was the Marge Julia knew and loved—back to business.

She grinned. "I'll see you then, Marge."

They walked into the dining room together.

"Wait, one second." Julia went behind the counter and poured a travel mug full of their signature coffee. "This one's on the house."

Marge glanced at her and at the cup of coffee before taking it into her hands. She raised it in salute and took a sip. She nodded at Julia, turned, and walked out the door.

Julia swung around to find Amanda standing with her hands on her hips, eyebrows lifted to her hairline. "What was that all about?"

Julia laughed. "Let's just say she's Santa Claus, and I'm back on the nice list."

Chapter 37

SAMSON

"THIS ALL LOOKS VERY promising, Mr. Baker." Abe Nichols crossed his arms and scoped out the park in front of them.

They'd walked to the far side of the amphitheater, so Samson no longer had a clear view of On Deck Café, which was a good thing.

Because otherwise, he thought he might lose his mind.

Julia was inside the café, and having that knowledge and not being able to do anything about it was as unbearable as being one number away from having the winning lottery ticket. Worse, actually. Because in this case, he felt like he'd *had* the winning lottery ticket...and he'd thrown it away.

Samson followed Abe's gaze. He had to stay focused on the task at hand. He was pulling out all the stops to appeal to this potential investor.

"I'm glad you think so, sir. I've only been in Mapleton for a short time, but I can already tell you it's a one-of-a-kind place. Why don't you let me drive you around and show you the rest of town so you can get a feel for it for yourself?"

Abe nodded, and they walked across the grass to where Samson's truck was parked.

Taking a page out of Julia's book, Samson gave Abe a tour of the village. He drove down Mapleton Avenue, pointing out Hal's, the village offices and library, and finally making his way past the mill site. A twinge of guilt crept in when he saw the crew at work. He should have been out there with them, not wining and dining potential buyers for the land on the opposite side of town.

But no, this had to be done. And he had to do it.

"This is what Gabler, Burns, and Associates is currently working on. It's the project that landed me in town," Samson explained, pointing toward the construction.

Abe observed the work going on at the mill site with an investor's eye. "Looks like a decent-sized project. And your thoughts on the land we saw this morning? Are you picturing the same sort of large-scale development?"

Samson spent five minutes explaining what he had in mind.

Abe flexed his mouth down and back up again. "That makes good sense to me, too."

Samson nodded and glanced out the open window of his truck as the warm morning air blew into his face. He studied the houses he passed by. He spotted the Vander Kempen's house easily—the wraparound porch was a dead giveaway. On either side of it, though, were smaller houses in disrepair. Samson frowned. Julia wanted to see these homes revived. He wanted that, too.

"Tell me about these houses," Abe requested, as if reading Samson's mind.

Samson used what he learned from Julia to describe the homes that were stately and in pristine condition. He went on to describe the neglected properties. "Several of the old houses that were once inhabited and well-kept were foreclosed upon and got lost in the shuffle as people moved away when the mill shut down. After a while, no one wanted to buy them because they looked like too much work."

"Looks like a good project to me," Abe said offhandedly.

Samson stilled and shot his guest a look, an idea that sat dormant in his head springing to life.

"Me too." He considered the other man with renewed interest. When Abe turned from studying a particularly dilapidated home and faced Samson, Samson took a deep breath. "In fact, I have another proposition for you."

Chapter 38

JULIA

JULIA HUMMED TO HERSELF as she put away equipment and utensils in the café's small kitchen. Seth and Nick were manning the counter, Jimmy left for work at his other restaurant, and she was taking some much-needed quiet time to get organized.

Noise from the ballfields drifted in through the open window. There was a doubleheader tonight for the local team. Amanda was working at the concession stand at the fields for Marge, and if Julia got her work done, she wanted to go and catch some of the game. A relaxing evening at the ballpark sounded like just what the doctor ordered after a stressful week.

Amanda also promised to listen to Julia's pitch—again.

Since Julia got financing from the credit union a week ago, Amanda had listened to her proposal, in full, five times. Julia was sure Amanda could *give* the proposal at this point. Yet, she hadn't complained once. She'd been nothing but supportive. Her advice was always spot on, and not for the first time, Julia said a prayer of thanksgiving for her friend.

Glancing around the kitchen, Julia pictured what an expansion and some cosmetic improvements would do for this space. If things worked out, she might be able to afford a full-time chef. An expanded menu was sure to both please the town and bring in more revenue. It made so much sense, and she didn't know why she had waited so long to take a leap forward with the café. Now, she hoped she wasn't too late.

The village board hearing was only a few days away. If she let herself dwell on it, she felt like she might pass out, so she busied herself with work. If this was going to be her last week in business—at least her last week in business as she knew it—she wanted to make the most of it.

She smacked her closed fist on her forehead. "No, Julia! You will think positively." She tapped her head three more times.

"Interesting strategy you have there, Jules."

Julia wielded the chopping knife to defend herself and whirled around.

Milo lifted a brow, giving a pointed look at her hand.

Following his gaze, Julia placed the knife on the counter. "Milo, you scared the sugar out of me." Julia wiped her hands against her apron and steadied her voice. "What can I do for you?"

"I wanted to talk to you. It's been a crazy couple of weeks."

"Tell me about it." Julia scoffed.

The day after Julia overheard his plans to sell her property, Milo stopped by to officially put Julia on notice. Since then, she hadn't seen much of him. Not that she expected to. But still. Most of the rest of the town came to offer their opinions—welcome or not—and assure her of their support.

Now, Milo stood in front of her and had the audacity to smile. "That's what I wanted to talk to you about."

Seth poked his head into the kitchen, displeasure registering on his face at the sight of Milo. "Hey, Jules, are you good?"

She nodded. "Yeah, it's fine. Thanks, Seth."

He turned to go, his brow furrowed as he stared down Milo before walking in the direction of the dining room.

"What is it, Milo?" Julia asked. She rested her hip against the counter, waiting for him to make his point.

"I wanted to apologize."

Julia stood up straight and folded her arms in front of her chest. "Really? For what?"

"For how this all came about. I realize it was out of the blue. I should have let you know what I—err, the village was thinking before you found out through the town grapevine. Not like I could have beaten that thing. The communication network in Mapleton rivals our nation's CIA."

Julia cracked a smile at his comparison. Her mother and her friends shared news over the phone lines and through text trees 24/7. Milo wasn't wrong, and she appreciated his apology. He wasn't a bad guy. Overly opportunistic, sure. But not a bad guy. "Thank you, Milo."

"You're welcome. Hey listen." He moved closer to her. "I know this café has been like your baby for the past five years. I don't know what's going to happen on Monday. Obviously, I have to share my opinion of what's in the best interest of the village with the board. It's not personal—"

"It is personal, Milo. This is my livelihood we're talking about. What I've spent years building could all be gone in a matter of a one-hour meeting. It's extremely personal to me."

"Maybe so." Milo nodded, undeterred. "But I wanted to talk to you about us."

Julia stiffened. Where was Milo going with this?

"I know the uncertainty of your prospects is scary, and I wanted you to know I'm here. You said, when you broke up with me, we didn't have a future together, but maybe present circumstances have changed your mind. We made a good team, Julia. We fit well together, and we fit well into this town. I'm sure if we got back together, we could work something out."

Wait. What? Was Milo trying to bribe her to date him with the incentive of saving her business?

"I-I don't think I understand." Julia didn't dare believe her ears. "Are you saying you'd spare the café if I agreed to be your girlfriend?"

"I can't make any promises. But I'd take our relationship into consideration when giving my recommendation to the board." He paused. "What do you say, Jules? Be my girlfriend, and I'm sure we could make it even more official soon."

Movement in the hallway caught Julia's eye, but before she could figure out what it was, Milo grabbed for her hand. Julia dropped her gaze to their intertwined fingers, trying to process what he said before she snatched her hand away.

She stepped back, bumping into the counter and sending the chopping knife to the floor with a clatter.

"Are you proposing to me?" Julia pressed her fingers to her temples and her thumbs against her cheek bones. "Please don't be ridiculous, Milo. Look, I'm sure you have noble intentions here, but this is not the right solution to my problems, nor is it going to make either of us happy in the long run. You know we are *not* a good fit."

Milo frowned. "But your business—"

Julia flung her head back and forth. "No way am I bartering my business with the promise of being in a relationship with you. I'm pretty sure that's illegal. And if it's not, it's still wrong on so many levels."

She needed a nap. Or a vacation. Harnessing the last of her emotional resolve, she lowered her voice. "Milo, you're a good guy. I believe that. I do. But like I told you before, you're not the right guy for me. I am fine without you, and I will be fine no matter what happens with this land and my café. I'm sure of it." She held up her chin, proud of herself for actually meaning those words. It had taken a lot for her to get to this point, but she had people who believed in her, and more importantly, she believed in herself.

Julia searched Milo's face for some trace of understanding. She half expected him to burst out laughing and yell, "Gotcha!"

He remained wholly composed, though, looking into her eyes but not seeing her. Finally, he shrugged his shoulders. "Suit yourself. I thought I'd offer. I guess I'll see you at the hearing on Monday. Good luck with your proposal."

With that, Milo turned and left her kitchen.

Julia slumped against the counter and buried her head in her hands. Laughter rose up in her chest. She clamped her hand over her mouth to contain it until the tinkle of the bell over the door signaled Milo's departure. No use further offending the man whose opinion held substantial weight in the decision to keep her business open or to shut it down. Still, this was comical, and if she didn't laugh about it, she'd cry.

Chapter 39

JULIA

ON THE DAY OF the board meeting, Julia walked into the village offices and was greeted by a mob of villagers positioned in a line that extended down the hall. Charlie stood with Lorraine. Ted and Linda Koke were there, too. Marge's face was set, and she gave Julia a strong nod of encouragement. Sally and her fellow festival committee members waved and shouted their support. Susan Tillersand toasted her with a to-go cup from the café. Kristy was hand-in-hand with Ashton.

She reached out and squeezed Julia's arm with her free hand before settling it back on top of her baby bump. "We're here for you."

"I know." Julia tried to swallow the wobble in her voice. She wouldn't ever be able to thank all these people for showing up for her.

"You've got this, Miss Julia!" One of Melly's sons waved as she stopped in front of the door that led to the village chambers.

Julia gave him a thumbs up, afraid if she spoke, her voice would betray her nerves.

Milo appeared and addressed the crowd behind her. "Unfortunately, we're at capacity, folks. I'm sorry we cannot let anyone else in."

"We'll wait here, then," Sally said staunchly. Her hair was colored bright red today, and she looked fired up and ready to do battle.

Julia shot her a grateful look. She entered the boardroom and took a seat in the front row next to her mom and dad.

Amanda, Seth, Nick, and Jimmy squeezed in behind them.

There was a dull roar coming from behind the closed doors to the chamber, and Julia's lips tugged upward. The thought of the villagers sticking around—despite having to stay outside the conference room—gave her courage. And she needed it.

Village board members flitted about in front of her. The man who had broken this whole thing open three weeks ago in her café sauntered forward and shook Milo's hand. Jerry Gabler was his name, and she'd gathered he was Samson's boss.

She didn't see Samson. She hadn't been sure if he'd show up, but it was a relief he hadn't. It might have sent her over the edge. She was barely hanging on to her composure as it was.

Amanda scooted forward in her seat. "How are you doing?"

"I've been better." Julia clenched her folded hands together to try to stop them from shaking.

"Here, I brought you this." Amanda held up a thermos. "Iced strawberry americano. Coffee is a cure-all, am I right?"

Julia grabbed for the drink like a lifeline and took a revitalizing sip. "Thank you."

"Anytime, girlfriend. Have I told you how proud I am of you?"

Julia smiled at her as Neil Schaumburg took his seat in the chair at the center of the long conference room table behind the name placard reading *Village President*. The other board members followed suit. Milo was last to be seated, farthest from her.

Neil rapped the gavel and called the meeting to order. After a moment of silence, they all recited the Pledge of Allegiance. The board worked efficiently through its agenda. The usual items were addressed. Julia half listened as liquor licenses were approved for the upcoming calendar year and board members discussed the effectiveness of village yard waste plans. Finally, Milo gave his monthly report.

"In conclusion," he said, "as many of you have heard, I propose the village board votes tonight on a proposal put forth by Gabler, Burns, and Associates to buy or lease the land surrounding Sunrise Park. It's in the best interest of our community to act now and turn a profit that we can reinvest in our community. This action will take Mapleton to the forefront of economic and civic development in the state. As you know"—he turned his attention from the board and motioned to Julia—"Julia Derks has been renting the property on the corner of Mapleton Avenue and the entrance of Sunrise Park. These plans would disrupt her business. Her lease is up at the end of August, so technically, the village doesn't owe her anything at that point."

Julia sat rigid in her seat.

"However, I thought it only right to give her a chance to speak with you tonight and share her belief as to why we shouldn't take Mr. Gabler and his company up on their proposal. Julia." Milo turned and made a sweeping gesture, indicating the mic was hers.

Julia stood and tried to clear her throat. She approached the podium and lowered the microphone before peering at the board members. They all sat looking at her with varying degrees of interest.

Here goes nothing.

As she opened her mouth to begin, the conference room door creaked open behind her. She cast a quick look over her shoulder.

Samson walked in with an older man trailing in his wake. Samson's eyes found hers in an instant. A look of agony dotted his expression before he bowed his head and took a seat behind his boss.

Julia willed herself to relax and release the tension in her face. *So much for getting through this without Samson here.* She glanced at her parents who held tightly to each other's hands. Behind them, Amanda smiled encouragingly, and Seth nodded at her.

Julia exhaled as she turned to face the board. She could do this.

"Thank you, Milo. Ladies and gentlemen of the board, I appreciate the opportunity to speak to you today. A little over five years ago, you took a chance on a new college graduate. I was fresh out of business school with no experience and nothing but a dream. When you rented the Henderson house to me, you played a huge part in making my dream a reality. Since then, On Deck Café has become a fixture in this community. People know On Deck Café for our friendly, home-grown service. They know us for the golden retriever who is often outside and the warm welcome they'll get as soon as they walk inside. And they know us for our delicious coffee. We service our town's visitors who come to the park to enjoy baseball or soccer games or different river activities. And as you can tell by the crowd of people outside here tonight, our main area of service is to our own village residents. I can safely say I've seen each of you in the café more than a time or two."

She looked at each board member directly. When she got to Milo, she shrugged. She couldn't resist a little jab in his direction. "Well, at least those of you who haven't given up sugar."

Milo's mouth evened into a straight line.

Amanda must've tried to stifle a giggle behind her, and her muffled snort gave Julia another shot of confidence. Standing straighter, she went on. "I know you are going to be presented with a monetary offer to buy the land where my café sits as well as the acreage surrounding Sunrise Park. Financially speaking, it may sound like a no-brainer. I'd argue otherwise. The people of Mapleton and our visitors have come to expect a small-town experience. Sunrise Park and the baseball fields there have survived and thrived for nearly one hundred years without big-business development encroaching on the land or breathing 'new life' into the space." She made air quotes and made sure to keep eye contact.

"I think it's the old blood and the way of life we've established here that keeps people coming back. What we have at Sunrise Park is unique. It can't be replicated. It can't be mass-produced, and it certainly wouldn't be enhanced by some swanky new structures that would cast shadows on the field and ruin the view of the river that everyone enjoys. Don't get me started on the trees surrounding the park. If you mess with the landscape, the park as we know it ceases to exist, and the tourism we rely on would follow the same course. On Deck Café is part of the special charm Sunrise Park has to offer."

That was Amanda's cue. Her friend stood up and passed out folders to each of the board members. As they eyed them with curiosity, hope fluttered in Julia's chest.

"I have a solution to give the village some of the immediate capital Milo has argued we so desperately need. What you see in front of you is proof from Community Credit Union of my approval for a loan. I would like to buy the building where I've spent the last five years running On Deck Café. If you allow me to do so, I promise to work hard every day to continue to serve the people of this community and all those who visit here. You have my word, and my history backs me up." Julia took a deep breath.

"I also want to draw your attention to pages two and three in your folder. I have worked up a business plan to grow On Deck Café. While this doesn't have anything to do with you... nor will it have anything to do with anything if you don't sell to me..." She trailed off before shaking her head and continuing. "I wanted to prove to you I've poured time and effort into planning how to take On Deck Café to the next level. You'll see I hope to remodel the upstairs of the building and add a second-story deck. We'd like to revamp our kitchen and hire a full-time chef to serve those who want lunch and dinner while they're at the ballfields. And we'll put in a drive-thru window. If you sell to me, I assure you I will do things to keep my business moving forward, but I'll do so in a way that respects the history of the land and the magic of small-town living." She stuttered, remembering when Samson used the word 'magic' to compliment *her*, but she recovered herself just enough to squeak out the final words of her prepared speech. "Thank you for your time."

She nodded at the board members, half of whom were looking at her and half of whom were studying the paperwork.

Milo was frowning into his cup of whatever it was he drank since giving up sugar.

She'd done all she could. It was in their hands now. Julia turned to make her way to her seat.

Don't look at him. Don't look at him, she repeated to herself.

But as if they were detached from her brain, her eyes gravitated to Samson in the back row. He was laser focused on her. Julia ripped her gaze away before she could overthink the look of pride and longing in his eyes.

Her mom squeezed her knee when she sat down. "You nailed that."

Julia nodded. She was all out of words. She just hoped she'd done enough.

Milo introduced Jerry Gabler, who stood to make his pitch. Julia zoned out halfway through. All that discussion of money, and land gradients, and blah, blah, blah. Julia didn't try to keep it all straight. She wondered why Samson wasn't the one who spoke to the board. Hidden in the kitchen of her café, she heard Jerry talk about Samson like he was the company's Casanova. The guy who they sent in when they needed to win people over.

It didn't matter. It was a small shred of mercy that she didn't have to listen to him try to sway the board over and explain all the businesses he found to replace hers. Jerry finished his speech and walked past her row to sit down.

She stared straight ahead and didn't meet his eye.

Milo stood. "Okay, then. We'll let the board convene into closed session for deliberation."

Chapter 40

SAMSON

IT WAS NOW OR never.

Samson raised his voice. "Mr. Moore, there's one other thing."

In the front row, Julia's spine snapped straighter, as if someone had yanked her from behind when he spoke.

Jerry turned around in his seat. "What is the meaning of this?" he hissed.

Samson ignored him, stood up, and walked to the front of the conference room. Milo gave him a quizzical look as he made his way forward. He didn't dare look at Julia, her family, or her friends. He approached the board's table with Abe hustling behind him.

Milo was shaking his head. "Sorry, Samson. If you're not on the agenda or signed in before the meeting begins, you're not allowed to speak."

"Oops. Silly me! Did I not give you guys the updated agenda?" Melly leapt up from taking notes. She winked at Samson and proceeded to hand out fresh agendas to all of the board members. "Samson asked to be added yesterday, with plenty of time to spare. We must've printed the old version of the agenda. Sorry about that!"

Melly's cheerful voice stood in stark contrast to Milo's livid expression. His face was beet red, and his nostrils flared as he read the new document in front of him. Somebody was not a fan of surprises.

Samson nodded to Melly as she retook her seat, crossing her leg and bopping her toe up and down as if she didn't have a care in the world.

"Abe Nichols of Nichols Investments? Who's he?" Milo shot Samson a dirty look.

"Mr. Moore, board members, and village residents, I'd like to introduce you to Mr. Abe Nichols. I brought him to Mapleton after learning of my company's planned proposal to buy the land around Sunrise Park. I couldn't, in good conscience, support Gabler, Burns, and Associates' plans to demolish On Deck Café and much of the surrounding grounds to make room for an upscale hotel and chain restaurants. So, I sought out another buyer for the land so that if the village decides it wants to sell, it'll have the option of selling to someone who wouldn't develop it commercially, but who would keep it for the small-business feel that Ms. Derks' coffee shop provides. Mr. Nichols can share his resume and experience with you. He's also prepared to discuss it as an investment opportunity rather than buying the land outright. So there's that to consider. I hope you'll hear him."

When Samson finished talking, a whispered buzz rose from the board members and all those packed into the chamber. He'd surprised them.

Samson risked looking in Julia's direction, though he knew it would break him. Her eyes were shiny with unshed tears. He'd give anything to wrap her in a hug and tell her everything would be okay, but it wasn't his place. He ducked his chin and walked to the back of the room.

Jerry met him in the aisle, his face contorted with anger. "Samson, what do you think you're doing?"

"I'm quitting, sir." He said it loud enough for the entire room to hear. He heard a gasp from somewhere near the front, but he didn't stick around. He fished an envelope out of the interior pocket of his suit and handed it to his boss—well, his former boss. "Here's my notice. Goodbye, Jerry."

And with that, Samson walked out of the room.

Chapter 49

JULIA

JULIA'S MOUTH FELL OPEN, and she gasped. She couldn't help it.

Samson was quitting?

Back up.

He worked to *save* her business—not replace it?

Neil rapped his gavel, encouraging everyone to quiet down.

Julia's heart strained in her chest as if it wanted to break free from her rib cage and flop down the aisle after Samson. But she couldn't leave this stuffy board room until the meeting was over. She had to wait and see the fate of her business before she tried to figure out what this meant for her and Samson.

So, she sat there and listened to Abe Nichols. While he appeared a little rumpled on the outside, he had an eye for business and investment. He complimented her and her proposal several times, and by the end of his speech, Julia wanted to hug him.

"Alright, alright," Milo said by way of silencing the chatty crowd. "Now the board will convene in closed session."

The board members shuffled to the meeting room attached to the chamber, and Abe approached.

Julia stood as he held out his hand to her.

"I appreciated hearing your proposal, Ms. Derks. I respect what you've built here. I hope we get the chance to work together."

Julia nodded. "Me too, sir."

He moved on to talk to Melly before she could say more.

"How about that?" her dad asked.

"Tell me about it, Mr. D." Amanda's eyes were wide with shock. "Leave it to Samson to barge in here like a modern-day knight in shining armor. I had no idea, did you?" She turned to look at Julia's mom.

"None at all. Though, I'm not surprised. I could tell there was something good in that man's soul the second I met him." Her mom stared Julia down. "But I don't think Julia needed a knight in shining armor today. I think she saved herself! You were fabulous up there."

"Absolutely right, my dear." Her dad hugged her.

"I hope so. We'll see." Julia couldn't stand still. She shoved her hair behind her ears and kneaded her hands together as she shifted her weight from leg to leg.

Finally, after what felt like a decade, the doors to the meeting room reopened.

Milo stood as the board members filed out.

Neil waited for those in attendance to get to their seats before he spoke. "We've come to a conclusion regarding the issue of buying or leasing the land surrounding Sunrise Park."

Julia's eyes were locked on Neil, and she held her breath, waiting to hear her fate.

"It's a unanimous decision. We'd like to thank Mr. Gabler and his company for their offer, but we're going to keep things local...and special. Ms. Derks and Mr. Nichols, we look forward to working with you on a plan that will be best for all of us. This meeting is adjourned." He winked at Julia.

Julia punched out a breath. She'd done it. She'd actually done it.

Amanda whooped and jumped up behind her, pressing her hands against Julia's shoulders with exuberance. Her mom and dad stood and embraced before turning to her. Julia was enveloped by her family and friends, and when the doors to the chamber were opened, the rest of the town poured in. People were screaming and cheering.

Daniel cut his way through the crowd. "We were listening to the whole meeting through the door. Congratulations, Julia. I'm so happy for you."

"Thanks, Daniel. See you tomorrow, then?"

"You got it. Thank goodness I don't have to find another office!" Daniel shot her a grin before his face turned serious. "Look Julia, I know it's not my place, and maybe I'm way off base here, but if you have feelings for Samson, don't let him get away. Believe me when I say I speak from experience."

Julia's jaw went slack, and she blinked at her friend, conjuring up an image of him and his long-time girlfriend... before she left town and left him behind.

"Just think about it, okay?" He waited for her to nod before he gave her a quick hug and went to mingle.

Julia turned and hugged Marge and the Kokes.

Melly approached and gave Julia an extra squeeze before pulling back to study her face. "Congratulations, Julia. I'm so happy for you."

"Thank you, Melly. Something tells me I should be thanking you for more than just your well wishes."

Melly lifted a nonchalant shoulder. "It was nothing I did." The look she pinned on Julia told her it was all Samson. "I must say I've gotten to know Samson, and he's a good man. Yes, he should have been more honest with you about all of this, but he never intended for you to get hurt. He tried to protect you. I think if you search your heart, you'll realize that. I hope you two can make things right."

Julia's heart thudded. She hoped so, too.

Daniel's advice and Melly's opinion only confirmed the conclusion Julia had come to. She wanted to see Samson. She needed to see him.

Desperation slapped her across the face.

He quit, and he didn't stay around for the board to reach its verdict. What if he left town before she could find him?

"Thanks, Melly," Julia croaked. "For everything."

Melly nodded and gave Julia a final hug before leaving her alone.

Julia caught Amanda's eye and waved her friend over.

"I've got to go see him."

Amanda understood exactly who she was referring to. "Um, yeah, you do. What are you still doing here?"

"I don't know," Julia wailed. "I don't even know where to look."

"Well, try his house. Try his work. Try Hal's. Though, from what I've heard, he's been run out of there. Then again, that was before he basically saved the day, so..." Amanda cocked her head and shrugged.

"Huge help. Thanks," Julia said dryly.

Amanda laughed as she shoved her toward the door. "You'll find him. Just go. I'll let everyone know."

In other words, it would be a matter of minutes and the entire village would know Julia went after Samson in hopes of reconciling. In this case, Julia didn't care. She was more grateful than anything. This was the same village that showed up to support her. If they had a weird fixation on her love life—or what remained of it—so be it.

"Alright. I'm going. Thanks, Amanda. I can't believe we did it!"

Amanda pulled her back into a tight hug. "*You* did it. Now go get your man. And text me everything."

Julia laughed and hurried out of the room.

While Amanda's advice about where to find Samson may have been tongue-in-cheek, Julia decided to check his house first. She made it to his rental in record time, even by small-town standards, and knew immediately he wasn't there. His truck was gone, and her heart sank.

She left her truck idling on the road with the keys in the ignition and leapt out. She ran up to the front door and peered in through the sidelight.

"He's not here, Julia."

Julia's head snapped around. There stood Nancy Hollace who lived two doors down.

"I saw him drive off not five minutes ago. He drove toward Mapleton Avenue and turned right."

Julia was off the porch in a flash. "Thank you, Mrs. Hollace!" she yelled over her shoulder.

For once, the neighborhood watch was working in her favor. She banged a Y-turn in her truck and sped toward the mill site. As she got closer, she saw Samson's truck parked on the road. A wave of relief washed over her, sending a tremor from her toes to the tips of her earlobes.

She found him.

Chapter 42

SAMSON

SAMSON ROLLED UP THE sleeves of his shirt and folded his arms over his chest, leaning against one of the pillars on the side of the gazebo. The languid evening sun rested in the sky, veiled in thin clouds. The dimming light it cast over the river was hazy and romantic.

He stared out across the construction site. The crew had made a lot of progress. In his resignation letter, he agreed to stay on as overseer until a replacement could be found, but he wouldn't be surprised if Jerry told him to pack his bags tonight. Bringing Abe Nichols into the business transaction was a monumental violation of trust, and Samson would be replaced soon.

It would be weird not working with the crews on the mill project. He'd really come to like the guys. He had no regrets, though. He'd do it again in a heartbeat. He hoped the village board members weren't so brainwashed by Milo that they didn't consider a good alternative when presented. As it turned out, they might have been swayed by Julia alone.

She was something else. He should have known she wouldn't go down without a fight. Hopefully Abe's proposal helped her cause. Samson looked out over the water and was consoled knowing he'd done all he could do.

At the creak of the wooden step behind him, Samson spun around.

"Julia." Her name came out of his lips in a whisper. Her cheeks were tear stained, and his heart lodged in his throat, cutting off any other words.

She stopped on the top step of the gazebo across from where he was standing. "Hi."

They stood staring at each other in silence until she spoke again.

"The village denied Gabler's proposal."

Samson flexed his fingers at his sides before relaxing his fists. She'd come to tell him the news. Of course. That was all this was.

"I'm so glad to hear they made the smart decision. They'd be fools to destroy what you've built, Julia." Glancing over her shoulder, he tried to remain cool. "So, where's Milo?"

"Milo?" Julia's forehead creased. "I have no idea. Why?"

Samson dropped his head and scuffed his shoe against the warped wood of the gazebo's base. "I overheard the two of you talking in your kitchen at the café the other day." He put up his hands defensively, raising his gaze to meet hers. "I know you told me you didn't want me there, but I wanted to try to give you a heads-up about Nichols. Anyway, I left to give you your privacy, but I heard Milo ask you to date him again."

Julia blinked and held her eyes closed for an extended second, chuckling to herself. "That was you?"

"Uh, yeah. Like I said, I'm sorry for invading your space. I just thought—"

"Samson." Julia cut him off, and his name never sounded better.

He looked at her even though the sight of her made his whole body hurt with a deep, unmet need.

There was an amused glimmer lighting her eyes. "I told Milo no. Surely you know that, right? He is very much not the man for me. And I could never be the one to make him happy."

As her words sunk in, hope filled Samson's heart like bubbles spreading into bathwater. "I am so sorry, Julia. I should have come clean with you the second I caught wind of Milo's plans. You deserve honesty, and I failed to give that to you. Please believe me when I say I never meant to hurt you, and everything I told you about your business plans and ideas was the truth. I never lied to you about how smart your ideas are. I meant every word." He stopped to drag in a gulp of air.

Julia chewed her bottom lip. "Thank you for apologizing. Thank you for owning your mistakes." She ducked her chin. "And I'm sorry, too, for not giving you a chance to explain earlier and for the things I said about you. I was angry and I lashed out. It was unfair of me."

Samson shook his head. "You had every right to be upset."

"Yeah, but if I'd let you talk to me, we could have saved ourselves days of angst." She held his gaze as if to make sure he understood exactly what she was saying.

Samson took a tentative step in her direction, his eyes fixed on her. "Could we have?"

"Yeah. You see, I've been sort of miserable without you these past few weeks."

Samson didn't need to hear anything else. He closed the gap between them.

Chapter 43

JULIA

JULIA THOUGHT SHE MIGHT die if Samson didn't take her into his arms right then and there.

She opened her mouth to tell him as much, but he reached out and place his finger delicately against her lips. All her senses surged forward and piled up on that one point of connection between them. She shivered in the best kind of way.

"Julia, before you say anything else, you should know I didn't seek out Abe Nichols just because of our relationship. I sought out an alternative to Milo and Gabler's plan because it was the right thing to do. I wanted to do the right thing, regardless of what was in it for me. That's how I intend to act from now on."

Julia's breath caught in her throat as Samson let his finger drop, dusting her chin with a butterfly-light caress on its way down.

"I believe you. And you know, I'm not here talking to you because you helped save my business. I'm here because I missed you. The real you. The man who I've come to know who'll dance to bad eighties music with me. The man who likes to go for drives around town and have lazy days by the lake, and who's being converted into a dog person."

Samson laughed a low, rumbly laugh that vibrated from his chest and seeped its joy into hers.

"I missed the man who makes guys like Charlie feel like they matter." Julia paused. "I missed the man who'll stand up for what is right—who respects me and listens to me and makes me believe in who I am and who I can be."

Samson bent and rested his forehead on hers. He reached for her hands and gently brushed his thumbs along her knuckles.

"Can I be your man, Julia?"

"I'd like that."

"Good. Because there's something else you need to know."

Julia swept her gaze across his face. "Oh yeah? What's that?"

"I'm in love with you. I know we haven't known each other very long, and this might sound crazy, but I'm vowing right now to be honest with you about anything and everything going forward. So I'm not keeping something like this from you. I love you, and I'm going to keep loving you—if you'll let me."

Julia's heart burst into tiny little pieces of confetti at the sight of the man in front of her, his face chiseled with passion, determination, and—yes—love.

She ran her hands up and down his arms, never taking her eyes off of him. "Promise?"

He nodded, slowly blinking and taking a deep breath. "I promise."

"Well, then." Julia angled toward him as Samson wrapped his arms fully around her.

Their lips met, and Julia poured her whole heart into that kiss, letting Samson fill her back up in return. Their embrace was both tender and urgent. It was as if they were both trying to make up for lost time while also giddy with the knowledge that they had their whole lives to look forward to *this*—the two of them together.

Samson leaned back, stealing a series of kisses along her neck, and Julia's mouth curved into a full-blown, bases-loaded, walk-off-grand-slam smile.

Samson pulled her in close again, and Julia rested her head against his chest. They just had their own gazebo moment.

Someday, maybe their kids would tell their story.

Epilogue

JULIA ~ 11 MONTHS LATER

JULIA DRUMMED HER FINGERS on the steering wheel of her truck as she cruised down Mapleton Avenue toward On Deck Café. She smiled as she passed several houses under construction along the way. It was difficult to believe it had been a year since her business was in jeopardy. So much had happened.

Samson was officially fired from Gabler, Burns, and Associates. Fortunately, Abe Nichols was more than happy to work with him. The two arranged a deal with Samson serving as Abe's primary general contractor. Their goal? To restore the abandoned homes throughout Mapleton. The dream was to bring new families to town with a varied real estate offering. Overwhelming pride hit her every time a house was restored. That was her guy helping to rebuild their town.

And it was *their* town now. Julia couldn't wipe the smile off her face as she drove past Hal's Diner. Samson extended his contract at his rental indefinitely, so they'd officially been neighbors for going on a year. Milo resigned a month ago, after taking a job in a bigger city, and Samson was considering applying for the Village Administrator position. Julia knew he'd do a great job.

July would be a busy month. Julia had a ton to do to prepare for the Fourth of July Festival. Marge had her in charge of all sorts of odd jobs this year, and she had the café to tend to. Samson was also helping her there. They'd spent time renovating the upstairs, and the new second-story balcony would have a soft opening the week of the Fourth. She loved the way the space had come together.

She couldn't believe she'd been away from it for two whole days, but it wasn't every day her best friend shopped for a wedding dress. When Seth proposed to Amanda, three months ago, she had immediately asked Julia to be her maid of honor and then insisted Julia and Gloria come with her to meet her mother for a weekend shopping spree in Chicago. They'd laughed and drank champagne, and Amanda found the perfect dress to walk down the aisle in. Happy tears formed at the corners of Julia's eyes every time she thought about it.

But now, she was back in town and itching to get to work. Samson was at the café, putting some finishing touches on the second-story deck. She was excited to see it. And him.

Julia parked her truck in the lot, and Mr. Waffles greeted her with a happy yip.

"Hi, buddy!" She stroked his face. "Did you miss me? Aww, that's a good boy." Mr. Waffles licked her face before trotting around in a circle and plopping down on the grass outside the front door as Julia walked inside.

"Hey, guys!" Julia beamed at Seth and Nick, who were behind the counter.

"Welcome back, Jules. I hear my bride found her dress?"

Julia pretended to turn a key in front of her mouth. "My lips are sealed, but it's safe to say she's going to blow you away." Julia's smile widened as Seth tucked his head shyly. "Is Samson here?"

"He's out back," Nick directed, pointing to the hallway.

"Thanks!" Julia skipped toward the door. Pushing through it, she came to an abrupt stop. The deck was empty. Beyond it, in the backyard of the café, was Samson. He stood in front of a brand-new gazebo with crisp white paint and a black shingled roof—a mirror image of the one that stood across town.

"What is this?" Julia whispered.

Samson gave her a lopsided grin and met her at the bottom of the steps. He grabbed her hand and guided her to the gazebo.

"This...is for you. Do you like it?"

"Do I like it? I love it." Julia couldn't find the words. "But how did you...I haven't been gone...it's only been two days."

Samson grinned. "I built it off site, and then we laid footings yesterday and transferred it here today. Come on in."

Julia followed Samson up the two wooden steps and into the gazebo.

There was a small picnic table in the center, and flowers that matched the ones in the boxes on the deck railings hung from baskets along the outer lip of the gazebo's ceiling.

Julia spun around, taking it all in.

Samson stood watching her.

"Thank you for this." She stood up on her tiptoes and kissed his lips, relishing the feel of his mouth on hers as she melted into him. It was good to be home. In Mapleton. And with Samson.

When he started pulling back, she protested. "Not yet! I missed you!" Julia buried her head into his shoulder, pressing herself closer.

Samson placed his hands on her upper arms and gently eased her away from him.

"What's wrong?" She felt a twinge of panic as she tried to read his face.

Samson grinned. "Nothing. Except I didn't do this...yet."

Julia's mind flashed back to the night he had first kissed her, when he uttered those same words. A warm glow ignited in her chest at the memory.

Samson dropped to his knee, and all other thoughts fled. Julia clapped her hands over her mouth before Samson reached up and took them into his. His hands trembled, and tears began to cascade down her face.

"Julia, I fell in love with you a year ago. It was the day you showed me around your town and told me all its stories. The old gazebo where your dad proposed to your mom is filled with memories of the village and its history. I want to spend all of my days making our own memories and building a life here together."

Julia gasped when she saw the stunning, circle-cut diamond ring he retrieved from his pocket. Her gaze locked on his. Eyes as bright as the sun-soaked green grass in the fields of Sunrise Park shone back at her, radiating certainty and love.

"I promise I will love you forever. Julia Derks, will you marry me?"

"Yes. Oh, yes, yes, yes! I love you, Samson." Julia dropped to her knees, pressed her hands to his face, and kissed him through her tears.

Samson wrapped his arms around her and stood, twirling her in a circle. When he set her down and slid the gold-banded ring onto her finger, cheers erupted from both stories of the deck. Samson anchored her to his side and turned her to face the café. "I invited some of our friends," he whispered into her ear, nuzzling his nose into her hair before placing a kiss on her temple.

Amanda. Seth. Melly. Her parents. Marge. Charlie and Lorraine. Daniel. The whole village was there.

And Julia wouldn't have it any other way.

·♥·♥·♥·♥·♥·

Acknowledgments

All glory to God, now and forever.

First, thank YOU, dear reader. Thank you for picking up this book and giving it a try. I hope you enjoyed it!

To my publishing dream team. Jenn Lockwood, my fearless editor. You are the very best. Thanks for your careful eye and your kindness. Ana Voicu, I have long stood in awe of your cover designs, and to see one on my own book is pretty spectacular. Thank you. Thanks to Claire Cain for lending your expertise in the world of indie publishing. I'm so grateful. Thanks also to C. D'Angelo for your countless hours of encouragement and friendship along the journey to publication. A big thank you to my wonderful ARC readers for your honesty and support.

To my teachers. You all are true heroes. Special thanks to Mr. Scholz, for making me believe I could write; to Ms. VanderPas, for reminding me that if someone critiques my work it means they think it's worthwhile; and to Ms. Moyer, for teaching me to write well.

To my friends. You know who you are, and I love you. Thanks for making me way cooler than I'd be without you. I'm so grateful to my CRHP/Welcome crew who heard my dream of publishing a book years ago and have been along for the ride. You guys sure know how to make a girl feel loved.

To my sweet Well Read Mom book club ladies. I can't tell you how much I value your insights on life, love, and literature. You all are proof of the good in the world. Thank you for challenging me and making me see things from new perspectives. You fill my cup.

To Molly and Bailey. Your Tuesday prayers and check-ins have gotten me through some of the longest days and weeks. I don't have the words to say how much you inspire me with your faith and generosity, but please know I am eternally grateful to be walking through this life with you.

To my extended family. Thanks for making me laugh and giving me all sorts of story ideas. Aunt Anne and Sam, thank you for reading my books and telling me you love them. Rachael, Clare, and Ashley, thanks for being my biggest "fans." I love you guys.

To my in laws. I don't take it for granted that I married into such a great family. Thanks for loving me like one of your own. Marcy, thanks for screaming and jumping with me in the kitchen over publishing news.

To my siblings. Luke, I want to be just like you. Ben, ditto. (I'm glad we got you and not a dog.) You're the best brothers a girl could ask for, and I'm so proud to call you mine. Thanks for reading my stuff, texting me play-by-play feedback, and making me smile. Bailey, you need a shout-out here, too. Love you, sis!

To my parents. Thank you for your endless support and guidance. I'm so grateful for your example of selfless love. Dad, thanks for working so hard for our family. Thank you for teaching me the importance of integrity, the rules of football, and how to navigate an airport. You've never let me down. Mom, thanks for being the writer and the person I strive to be. I've always looked up to you and your way with words. Thank you for being my first reader—for editing my stuff when it's down-right awful and for taking time and care to make it better (...quirked *is* a word, but you're right, I probably don't need to use it *that* much!). Thanks for knowing when I need a good cry and for talking me down from countless worry-filled ledges. You always know just what to say. I love you.

To Miriam, Lyla, Ellen, and Francis. I write for you. I pray you come to know and believe in the power of your own words and your own stories. Being your mom is my all-time favorite job. Thank you for group hugs and for forgiving me when I fall short. You inspire me every single day with your resiliency, thoughtfulness, humor, and kindness. The world needs who you are. I love you so very much.

Finally, to Nick. Ours will forever be my favorite love story. Just thank you. I love you always.

About the Author

Leah Dobrinska earned her degree in English Literature from UW-Madison and has since worked as a freelance writer, editor, and content marketer. As an author, she writes small town romance novels and cozy mysteries. She's a sucker for a good sentence, a happy ending, and the smell of books—both old and new. *Love at On Deck Café* is her debut novel.

Leah lives out her very own happily ever after in a small Wisconsin town with her husband and their gaggle of kids. When she's not handing out snacks, visiting local parks, and doing projects around the house, Leah enjoys reading and running. Find out more about Leah and connect with her through her website, leahdobrinska.com.

Book Club Discussion Guide

1. Who was your favorite character in *Love at On Deck Café*? Who would you most like to meet?

2. Did you relate to a particular character? How so? Did a character remind you of someone you know?

3. Which character underwent the most growth throughout the story?

4. Was there a specific place within the Village of Mapleton you could especially visualize? If you could visit Mapleton, where would you go first?

5. Do you have experience living in a small town? In your opinion, what are the pros and cons?

6. Early in the book, Julia argues you can't have a business without it being personal. Do you agree with her? Why or why not?

7. The theme of integrity plays a key role in the novel. In the end, Samson does what he does not to win Julia back but because he believes it is the right thing to do. Talk about a moment when you acted with integrity. How did you feel? Have you been inspired by someone else's integrity?

8. What other major themes are explored throughout the story?

9. Is there anything in the book you wish had gone differently?

10. Share your favorite quote or scene from *Love at On Deck Café*. Why did it stand out to you?

CPSIA information can be obtained
at www.ICGtesting.com
Printed in the USA
LVHW041920111022
730461LV00002B/305